# PRAISE FOR LISA GRAY

T0405598

"*The Final Act* is a riveting page-turner that exposes Hollywood's dark underbelly. This book is a fast-paced, nonstop thrill ride filled with scandal, intrigue, and endless twists and turns you won't see coming. If you pick this up, make sure you clear your schedule first because you won't be able to put it down!"

—Lisa Regan, *USA Today* and *Wall Street Journal* bestselling author

"A gripping, compelling, pacy tale that explores the MeToo movement and the seedy side of Hollywood, showcasing how young women have historically been exploited in their ambition to become famous. Glamour, greed, and gaslighting abound, this one's a knockout!"

—Christina McDonald, *USA Today* bestselling author of the Jess Lambert series

"So much more than a mystery, *The Final Act* exposes the wealthy and powerful who prey on the desperation of dreamers. With an emotionally bruised detective on a mission to find a missing actress, this gritty suspense explores the darkness lurking below the bright lights in the City of Angels. And just when you think you've solved the case, Lisa Gray flips the script, proving her expert talent. A beguiling thriller that will make your head spin."

—Samantha M. Bailey, *USA Today* bestselling author of *A Friend in the Dark*

"Glamorous, twisty, and utterly deadly! This stylish thriller digs beneath the Hollywood gloss and exposes the seediness lurking beneath the surface. An absolute must-read for summer."

—Steph Broadribb, author of *Death in the Sunshine*

"The dark underbelly of Hollywood unravels when a former scream queen goes missing. Totally gripping from start to finish—I loved it!"

—Susi Holliday, author of *The Hike*

# DEAD
# OF
# NIGHT

# DEAD OF NIGHT

## LISA GRAY

THOMAS & MERCER

Published by Thomas & Mercer, Seattle

www.apub.com

Amazon, the Amazon logo, and Thomas & Mercer are trademarks of Amazon.com, Inc., or its affiliates.

EU Product Safety contact:
Amazon Publishing, Amazon Media EU S.à r.l.
38, avenue John F. Kennedy, L-1855 Luxembourg
amazonpublishing-gpsr@amazon.com

ISBN-13: 9781662519178
eISBN: 9781662519161

Cover design by Will Speed
Cover image: © Nic Skerten / Arcangel; © Aimee Marie Lewis / Arcangel

Printed in the United States of America

# DEAD
# OF
# NIGHT

# PROLOGUE

## THE CLIFF HOUSE

## SEPTEMBER 1994

Dani Duprie tried to focus on the mundane task of preparing dinner instead of thinking about the fifty thousand dollars stuffed inside a duffel bag on the kitchen table. But even the simple chore of chopping carrots wasn't easy when the hand holding the knife was shaking so much.

Even though her husband, Bill, always arrived home from work at the same time every evening, Dani still jumped at the sound of the front door shutting. She heard Bill toss his keys into the ceramic dish on the console table in the foyer and make his way down the hallway, the heels of his dress shoes clicking on the parquet flooring.

The footsteps stopped abruptly when he entered the kitchen. Usually, he'd greet her with a "Hi, honey, how was your day?" and a kiss on the cheek. Tonight, there was a beat of silence. Then, "What's going on, Dani? Why is there a bag full of cash on the table?"

Dani didn't turn around from where she stood at the countertop. She used the blade to scrape the carrot slices from the chopping board into a pan, along with some diced onion.

"I emptied our checking and savings accounts," she said.

"Okay." Bill spoke in that reasonable way of his that could be infuriating or reassuring depending on the circumstances. "Can I ask why?"

The clothes dryer hit a fast spin just then and the vibration of the machine echoed the nerves that thrummed through her body. The hand still holding the knife was white-knuckled.

"We need to leave," she said tightly. "Tonight."

Bill walked over to her and took the knife from her hand and placed it on the chopping board. He gripped her gently by the shoulders and turned her to face him.

"Tell me what happened," he said.

"I went into town earlier, to pick up some groceries."

"Uh-huh."

"There was a woman. Not from around here. She was watching me from across the street. Just standing there, not moving, staring straight at me. It was like I could feel the weight of her eyes on me. It was . . . unnerving."

Bill frowned. "It doesn't sound like a whole lot to get upset about, honey."

His reasonable tone was bordering on infuriating now. Dani pressed her lips together. "I'm not so sure."

"Did this woman approach you? Try to speak to you?"

"No."

"There you go then. Maybe she was admiring your outfit. Or thought you were someone she knew and then realized you weren't." He nodded toward the bag on the table and attempted a smile. "No need for all the drama."

"I'm not being dramatic, Bill. Something was definitely off about—"

Her husband cut her off, his tone firmer now. "You know we can't keep running every time you get spooked or think someone is getting too close or asking too many questions, right? Or because someone *looked* at you outside the grocery store. You're being ridiculous, honey."

Dani glared at him, pissed now. "This is all down to you, remember? The way we live our lives? It's because of what *you* did."

"I did it for us," he snapped. "Are you seriously saying you'd want things any different? That you'd give up everything that we have?"

Dani felt her anger deflate like air escaping from a pricked balloon. She sighed. "No, of course not. But I'm scared, Bill. It's not the first time I've seen her."

"What do you mean?"

"I saw her yesterday too. Down by the marina, near where the restaurants are. Kind of hanging around, people-watching. Or that's what I thought." She met Bill's eye. "Maybe she was looking for someone."

The muscles in his jaw worked now. "Why didn't you tell me this before?"

"It's like you said, I thought it was nothing. After all these years, I thought we were safe here."

"Was it her?"

"I don't know. It's been a long time. Maybe. I guess the age would be about right."

"Did she follow you home?"

"I don't think so. I took a longer route. Kept an eye on the rearview mirror the whole way."

"Where's Charlotte?" Bill asked.

Dani's eyes went to the ceiling. "Upstairs in her room, doing her homework. She doesn't know anything's wrong."

Bill glanced at the money on the table and rubbed his face. "Shit."

"I mean it, Bill, we need to leave tonight. Once it's fully dark out. We eat, we pack, and then we go. Get as far away from Seaton Point as we can."

"What do we tell Charlotte?"

"Same as last time—that we need to move to a new town because of your job. We'll tell her you got a big promotion."

Bill stared at her. "So, what? We just pack up all our stuff and leave in the middle of the night, and you don't think she's going to find that even a little bit odd?"

"She's ten years old. We're her parents. She'll believe whatever we tell her."

"She's not a baby anymore. She'll ask questions."

"So, we'll leave at first light then."

Bill shook his head sadly. "Charlotte will be heartbroken. She loves it here."

"I know. I love it here too." Dani stared out of the window. The sun was sinking into an inky blue ocean, the sky painted fiery shades of orange. Now that the clothes dryer had stopped, she could hear the waves crashing off the rocks down below. Her heart clenched. "We don't have a choice. You know we don't. This might be nothing, but it might be something. We can't take any chances."

Bill nodded slowly, resigned. "Okay. We'll leave at dawn. That way, we can get some sleep ahead of the drive." He pulled Dani into an embrace. "Everything's going to be okay, honey. It always is."

"You promise?"

"I promise." He kissed the top of her head, then chuckled. "I still think the cash was a little OTT, though. Like something from a movie."

Dani gave a little laugh. "I know, right? I got it into my head that we should change our names this time. Get some fake IDs for the three of us. Go completely off-grid. I wasn't thinking straight. I guess I panicked."

They held each other for a long moment, then Dani felt him stiffen in her arms. She pulled away. "What is it? What's wrong?"

Bill's face was pale under the fluorescent striplight. "I thought I heard a car outside. Tires on gravel."

Dani listened hard. Heard the unmistakable *thunk* of a car door closing. There was a long moment of silence, followed by a knock at the front door.

Dani stared at Bill with wide eyes. She didn't need to ask if he was expecting a visitor because they never had visitors. Not once in the whole time that they'd lived here had they ever entertained guests. No dinner parties or barbecues or even sleepovers for Charlotte's school friends.

Now there was someone outside their house. Someone uninvited. Someone who shouldn't be here.

*Someone who knows what we did?*

There was another knock. Louder this time. More insistent.

Dani followed Bill down the hallway, feeling like a woman being taken to the gallows. He stopped at the door, called out, "Who's there?"

No answer.

The glass in the window by the door was pebbled and there was no spyhole. Bill shrugged at Dani and opened the door.

A woman was standing on the doorstep.

The same woman from the marina yesterday and the grocery store today.

She was pointing a gun at them.

# 1

## SERENA

## NOW

"Tell me about the murder."

The restaurant was on the top floor of the Museum of Arts and Design and boasted impressive views of Manhattan, which were even better if you were lucky enough—or connected enough—to snag a coveted window table. Serena Winters had been gazing distractedly at the people down below on Columbus Circle, but now her attention snapped back to the woman sitting opposite her.

"Murder?" she said sharply. "Who said anything about a murder?"

Her literary agent, Margot Hoffman, arched an eyebrow above her red plastic glasses, which was no mean feat seeing as they were oversized. Everything she wore was loud and expensive and designed to make an impact. In a city full of stylish women who didn't fade into the crowd, Margot was determined to stand out from everyone else.

"I'm not sure how to break this to you," she said slowly, as though talking to a child. "But a murder mystery usually has, you know, a murder in it."

Serena realized Margot was talking about the novel she was supposed to be writing. Of course she was. It was why they were here, after all. The lunch date had been pitched as a "little catch-up," but Serena had known it was more likely to be an interrogation.

"Right," she said. "The new book."

"Yes, the new book. So, tell me all about it."

Serena stalled by taking a sip of champagne. The bottle of Ruinart was not because they were celebrating, it was because Margot only ever drank champagne when dining out.

The celebrations had actually taken place six months ago, when Serena had scored another instant *New York Times* bestseller. Number three on the list. Serena hadn't topped the chart since *Murder After Midnight* two years ago, but three was still good. Better than good. Her publisher had been thrilled. Eleven books in and the Layne Farraday mystery series was still as popular as ever. Then the celebrations had turned quickly—and unexpectedly—to condolences, smack dab in the middle of her book tour.

Her partner, Michael, was dead.

Gone.

His life snuffed out like one of Serena's characters.

Now that the main courses had arrived, Margot was done with the small talk and eager to get down to business. She was going to be disappointed. Before Serena could answer, Margot groaned.

"Oh jeez."

"What's wrong?"

Margot tilted her head. "Superfan incoming, three o'clock."

A woman in her mid-fifties was making a beeline for their table, a cell phone clutched to her bosom. She was approaching with a mixture of excitement and hesitancy, like she wasn't sure whether she should intrude on their lunch but was going to anyway. The result was a kind of tippy-toe dance across the restaurant floor.

"Is it really you?" she said breathlessly when she reached them, her accent unmistakably Southern.

Serena smiled. "It's really me."

"Lenora Jackson." She pumped Serena's hand enthusiastically. "I'm such a huge fan. I have all your books and I've read each of them at least twice. Layne Farraday is my all-time favorite literary character. I absolutely adore her."

"That's so wonderful to hear."

Lenora held up her phone. "Could I trouble you for a photo together?"

"Of course."

Margot did the honors and, to her credit, didn't even tut or roll her eyes when asked to snap a couple more shots to ensure she got a good one.

"The girls in my book group back home aren't going to believe it," Lenora said. "We always check out your tour dates in the hope that you'll do an event in Lafayette one day. That's in Louisiana, by the way. And now, here you are, in the very restaurant my husband booked for our special anniversary lunch. What are the chances!"

"Yeah, what are the chances?" Margot muttered.

"I'll be sure to mention Louisiana to my publisher as a possible stop on a future book tour," Serena said. "Oh, and happy anniversary!"

Her jaw was starting to ache from all the smiling. Then the woman hit a nerve without even realizing it.

"Please tell me there's going to be another Layne Farraday mystery soon? I literally can't wait to find out what she does next."

The smile felt frozen in place now. "Oh, absolutely. I'm working super-hard on the next book right now. I'm sure you'll love it as much as the rest of the series."

Once the woman had finally returned to her own table, Margot said, "It's just as well you're a great writer because you're a terrible actress."

"What do you mean?"

"I mean all that bullshit about working hard on the next Layne Farraday mystery. You can fool Annie Wilkes over there, but you can't fool me. How many chapters have you written?"

Serena pushed her uneaten salmon around her plate and shrugged.

"Okay, pages then," Margot pressed. "How many pages?"

Serena sighed and put down her fork.

"Words?" Margot asked hopefully. "Please tell me there *are* some words."

Serena stared at her miserably. It was time to come clean. "No words. None. A big fat zero."

Margot winced, drank some expensive fizz, and then set the flute carefully on the table. She nodded. "So, we'll ask Emma for an extension on the deadline. It'll be fine."

Emma Rivera had been Serena's editor for more than a decade—almost as long as Margot had been her agent—and had worked on all of her books.

"She already gave me an extension," Serena pointed out.

"She'll give you another one. It's only been six months since the accident."

*The accident.*

An image of twisted limbs flashed unbidden into Serena's mind. Dead eyes staring at nothing. A neck bent at an unnatural angle. She pushed the intrusive thoughts away.

"No more extensions," she said firmly. She gestured toward Lenora, who was still stealing glances in her direction. "You heard what that woman said. She's desperate for the next Layne Farraday mystery. All my fans are. I can't let them down."

Serena knew she was something of a star in the literary world. She always attracted a packed-out crowd at bookstore signings and author panels at the big mystery conventions. She was pretty much guaranteed to make the bestseller lists, even if she was still waiting for a rave in the *New York Times Book Review*. A major studio had bought the film rights to her series. She'd sold millions of books and made a lot of money. And, sometimes, she was even recognized in restaurants.

But Serena wasn't Jennifer Aniston or Taylor Swift. She wasn't a Hollywood actress or a global popstar and that meant—thankfully— no one was particularly interested in her personal life. Her author biography used to conclude with the sentence "Serena Winters lives in New York City." A few years back, it had changed to "Serena Winters lives in New York City and New Jersey with her partner, Michael." No one had batted an eyelid. No one cared who she shared a bed and a life with. There was no cover story in *People* magazine. Michael hadn't been famous. He'd worked in finance and was independently wealthy and wasn't a big reader and that had made Serena happy because she knew he wasn't with her for her money or her fame.

Michael Robb had been five years her senior and kind and reliable and faithful to the point of being a little bit boring.

Or so she'd thought.

His death had been condensed into a few paragraphs on an inside page of the *New York Post*. The headline read: *Bestselling mystery author's partner dies in freak accident*.

The article had contained none of the more sordid details.

The cops knew who Michael was with that night—and why. Margot knew too. The team at Serena's publishing house didn't, but no doubt would have spent plenty of time gathered around the water cooler speculating about the identity of the mystery witness and wondering what the woman was doing at his house.

None of them knew the whole truth.

Not even the cops. Especially not the cops.

Margot was talking again. "Look, I know you said no before, but have you given any more thought to therapy? My shrink is great. She has a waitlist longer than the line at the Oscar de la Renta sample sale, but I can get you an in, no problem."

"No therapist," Serena said firmly. "I don't want to talk to anyone about Michael."

"Right. Got it. No therapist. But maybe . . ." Margot hesitated, which wasn't like her. Direct to the point of rude was more her style.

"Maybe what?"

"Maybe we should get you a little, uh, help with the writing."

Serena narrowed her eyes. "What do you mean by 'help' exactly?"

"A ghostwriter."

Serena was appalled. "Have someone else write my novel for me? Absolutely not."

"A cowriter, then. Someone who can jumpstart things, get the ball rolling. A collaborative project. We can put their name on the cover too, give them full credit. Whatever it takes."

Serena was shaking her head before Margot had even finished speaking. "No ghostwriter. No cowriter. I write the Layne Farraday mysteries. No one else."

Her agent sighed. "So, how do we fix this problem?"

Turn back the clock, Serena thought. Jump in a time machine and do things differently. Make sure the events of that night never happened.

Margot was her friend as well as her agent and was trying her best to be sympathetic and supportive, trying not to let her professional frustrations show. But she'd also be wondering why the grieving process was proving to be quite so difficult. She'd been aware of problems in their relationship, that Serena and Michael were likely on the outs. Maybe Margot thought Michael's death had made Serena realize just how much she loved him after all.

12

If only.

"You know, Michael and I ate here a few times," Serena said sadly. "In fact, I think we might've been seated at this very table. I remember the view."

"Ah shit. I didn't realize this was a regular spot of yours or I would have booked someplace else."

"That's the point, though. It doesn't matter where I go or what I do, I'm constantly reminded of him. His ghost is everywhere. I feel like I can't escape him."

Margot regarded Serena over the top of the big red glasses. "Well, in the absence of a priest with some holy water to perform an exorcism, there's really only one solution."

"What's that?"

"A change of scenery."

◆ ◆ ◆

After lunch, Serena returned to her apartment building on the Upper West Side.

She nodded a greeting to the doorman and rode the elevator to the fourteenth floor. Once inside, she kicked off the new Manolos that had been pinching her toes all afternoon and padded barefoot through to the bedroom. She slipped out of her Diane von Furstenberg dress and changed into sweats and a tee, and pulled her long dark hair into a ponytail.

Michael's belongings had been packed up and donated to Goodwill months ago, but his presence still lingered in the apartment. Sometimes, Serena would walk into a room and think she caught the faintest hint of his cologne. Other times, she'd wake in the dead of night, drenched in sweat, and wonder why the other side of the bed was cold and empty.

Then she'd remember.

Serena made some coffee and took a mug into her office and booted up the computer. She opened a new file and typed the words "Untitled Book 12" and then "Chapter 1." Then she stared at the blinking cursor for a while.

When she'd sat down to write her debut novel more than ten years ago, Serena had treated herself to a pink Leuchtturm1917 notebook, and it had become a tradition to purchase a new one for each novel since then. She wasn't a meticulous planner, but she needed a broad idea of where the story was going to go and how it would end before she started. The pages of her notebook would usually be filled with ideas, snatches of dialogue, character descriptions and major plot points by the time she wrote the first sentence of the manuscript.

The spine of the yellow notebook sitting next to the iMac now hadn't even been cracked yet. This time she had nothing. Lenora from Louisiana was desperate to know what Layne Farraday was going to do next. So was Serena.

She shut down the Word file and opened Google. Maybe Margot was right about a change of scenery; maybe escaping New York for a couple of months wasn't such a bad idea. Serena plugged some details into the search engine for summer rentals and scrolled past a bunch of photos until a property caught her eye.

The huge white and glass construction was perched on a rocky bluff with incredible views of the Pacific Ocean. It was located on the edge of a town called Seaton Point, in Southern California, which appeared to be postcard-perfect with white sandy beaches and a marina and designer boutiques and waterfront restaurants.

Serena checked the dates and discovered the Cliff House was available to rent all summer. It wasn't cheap but still well within what she could afford. She clicked through the gallery of photos. The rooms were bright and airy and sun-filled.

The house was perfect.

The kind of place where nothing bad ever happened.

# 2

---

## SERENA

---

## NOW

Three days later, Serena was on an early-morning flight from Newark to John Wayne Airport.

She had no pets or plants to take care of and didn't see any point in wasting time. Margot had a spare key to her apartment and would drop by once a week to pick up the mail and make sure that squatters hadn't moved in and the place hadn't spontaneously combusted.

The cab ride from Santa Ana to Seaton Point took forty minutes. The driver spent the first couple of minutes going through his repertoire of standard questions—*Was she here on vacation? Kind of. Was she staying with friends? Nope. Was it her first time visiting Seaton Point? Yep*—before giving up on small talk and turning up the radio for the remainder of the journey.

The town was just like the photos had suggested. Hazy blue skies and fat palm trees swaying in the breeze. Squat candy-colored buildings and the scent of seaweed and coconut oil in the air. Sports cars with the tops down and electric beach buggies cruising the narrow streets.

Serena had figured renting a car locally would be cheaper than an airport hire, and more convenient if she ran into any problems during her stay. The cab pulled up outside a two-story mixed retail building with gleaming white siding that could have been freshly painted that morning. A unit with the words "Dale's Rent-A-Car" stenciled on a turquoise-and-white striped awning was squeezed between a surf shop offering board hire and lessons and an interiors store offering fancy furnishings.

The cab driver unloaded her two Louis Vuitton suitcases and matching duffel onto the sidewalk outside Dale's open front door. Serena pushed her sunglasses up on top of her head and rolled the luggage into an AC-cooled office space, and blinked in the sudden striplight brightness.

The guy behind the counter was college age, with a deep surfer's tan and sun-bleached blond hair, and looked like he should be working next door. He was dressed in board shorts and a Hawaiian shirt with a plastic tag pinned on the chest that identified him as "Jody."

Jody greeted her with a smile so dazzlingly white that she was tempted to drop the shades back into place.

"Hey there!" he said. "How can I help you?"

"Hi. I'm looking for a long-term rental?"

"Cool. How long for?"

"Two months."

"Awesome. We have a fleet of ten vehicles, but the Nissan Kicks and Chevy Malibu are both out on hire right now." Jody tapped a laminated card on the counter that displayed photos of cars and prices. "The rest are available, though."

Serena studied the options. She should probably opt for a sensible SUV, but she didn't feel like being sensible.

"I'll take the Ford Mustang," she said.

The sleek black convertible was one of the premium selections. "Awesome!"

She fished in her purse for her driver's license and insurance documents and handed them over along with her credit card. Once the transaction was complete, Jody gave her the car keys and a map of Seaton Point and some flyers for local bars and restaurants.

"Let me grab your bags and I'll show you to the Mustang in the lot out back," he said.

He slung the duffel over his shoulder and picked up a case in each hand, despite the roller wheels, then kicked open a rear fire door. Serena followed him outside and used the key fob to unlock the car. She opened the trunk and Jody loaded the luggage inside.

"Anything else I can do for you?" he asked.

"Yes, actually. I'll need directions to my accommodation." She held up the map he'd given her and smiled. "I could use this, but I guess it'll be quicker if you just tell me where to go."

"Sure thing. Are you staying at the Harbor View Inn?"

"No, I'm renting a property for the summer. The imaginatively named Cliff House on the imaginatively named Cliffside Drive."

Serena laughed. Jody didn't.

A frown clouded his sunny expression. "Oh. That place."

Serena frowned now too. "Is there something wrong with it?"

She hoped she hadn't just splurged several grand on a dive that looked much better in the photos.

"No, it's just a little . . . isolated. You're on your own, right?"

The website had used the word "secluded." Serena preferred "secluded" to "isolated."

She said, "I'll be doing some work while I'm staying there, so the peace and quiet will suit me. So long as the house is in good shape?"

Jody pushed his hair off his face, his brow still furrowed. "Oh yeah. It's a great place. Awesome."

"You don't sound too sure."

"It's just that . . ." He laughed, shook his head. "Nah, you'll think it's stupid . . ."

"Try me."

"Before the place was an Airbnb, it was empty for years. When I was a kid, we all thought it was kind of spooky. There were rumors that the guy who built it died in a freak accident and then folks started disappearing. That if you went up there at night you'd hear the screams of the dead. But they were just stories kids told at sleepovers to scare each other." He showed her the white teeth again. "See, I told you—stupid, huh?"

*Freak accident.*

That phrase again.

Serena smiled tightly. "Those directions?"

Jody told her how to get from Dale's to Cliffside Drive. "Then, after half a mile or so you'll see George Evans's place," he said. "He's lived there, like, forever. Keep going for another mile and you'll come to the Cliff House. You can't miss it."

"Wait. It's a mile away from the nearest property?"

Jody nodded. "Yeah. Like I said, it's—"

"Isolated." Serena finished the sentence for him. "Got it."

◆ ◆ ◆

Cliffside Drive was a winding two-lane that hugged rugged rocky bluffs and overlooked ocean waves that sparkled like diamonds in the sun. Serena drove with the Mustang's top down, the breeze whipping her hair and the early-afternoon rays warming her skin.

She spotted a modest olive-green cottage-style bungalow up ahead that she assumed belonged to George Evans. There were two

18

white rocking chairs on the front porch next to a blue Dutch door with the top half open. An elderly man was sitting on one of the chairs. He got up as she drew closer and raised a pair of binoculars to his eyes, tracking her as she drove past as if the Mustang was a float in a small-town parade.

*What the hell?*

Around a mile later—Jody's directions were spot-on—the Cliff House came into view. The peeper with the binos was forgotten as Serena's breath caught in her throat. The house was every bit as spectacular in real life as the online photos had promised. She turned onto a gravel driveway and parked next to a little Fiat 500. As Serena climbed the steps up to a gleaming white concrete porch, the double-wide front door opened to reveal a slight woman with a silver Judi Dench pixie cut, wearing navy slacks and a cream blouse.

"Mrs. Winters?" the woman asked. "I'm Wanda Stockwell, the housekeeper."

The booking had been made under the name *Ms.* Serena Winters, but she figured Wanda Stockwell's generation assumed all women in their forties must have been married off years ago.

"It's actually 'Ms.,' not 'Mrs.,'" she corrected. "But please, just call me Serena."

The housekeeper nodded curtly and beckoned her inside.

Serena had never been one of those little girls who dreamed of a big white wedding. She didn't want to be a wife or a mom. Her aspirations had only ever involved storytelling. She thought now of Michael's proposal last year. Thankfully there had been no ring, no getting down on one knee, no grand gestures; just a casual suggestion over dinner one evening that they should think about getting married. Michael had an ex-wife and a grown-up daughter. He had been the marrying type. Serena was not. She wondered if her rejection had been the beginning of the end for them.

Serena followed Wanda down a hallway with exquisite parquet flooring and a vintage console table which led to a vast living area. The decor here was contemporary, the color palette muted tones of white, gray, and beige, but the money shot was undoubtedly the floor-to-ceiling windows overlooking the Pacific.

"Oh wow." Serena was impressed. "What an amazing view."

"Yes, it is rather lovely."

Wanda walked briskly into the adjoining kitchen. The units and countertops were a little dated, but everything was spotlessly clean. Serena knew from the listing that the kitchen door opened onto a patio at the side of the house with a barbecue and pizza oven and some outdoor furniture.

"The pantry and refrigerator have both been fully stocked with the groceries you requested," Wanda said.

For an additional fee, guests could make a grocery order for their arrival. Serena had requested coffee and cream and bread and cheeses and cooked meats and lots of wine.

She'd also paid extra for the weekly housekeeping service, and now felt guilty that this woman, who must be at least seventy, would be cleaning up after her. But—she reminded herself—she was here to work on her novel, not spend time dusting and vacuuming and doing laundry.

As though reading her thoughts, Wanda said, "I'll be here Mondays at ten a.m. to clean and provide fresh bedding and towels." Today was Thursday. "I have my own key so there's no need for you to be at home. If it's ever not convenient for me to be here at that time, please let me know in advance so I can reschedule."

Wanda continued the tour, showing Serena the downstairs powder room, before making her way toward the staircase. There were a couple of doors she didn't open, but Serena guessed those were closets where mops and brooms and other household items were kept. The upstairs floor comprised a family bathroom and three bedrooms.

The primary bedroom didn't have an en suite, but it did have French doors leading out to a balcony with a two-seater wrought-iron bistro set. Wanda opened the doors and Serena stepped outside. There was nothing but vast blue ocean and the taste of salt air on her lips and the sound of waves crashing off the rocks fifty feet below. She breathed it all in and felt herself relax for the first time in months. It was exactly what she needed after the stifling claustrophobia of New York. The plan had been to use one of the smaller bedrooms as an office, but Serena figured she'd do a lot of her writing out here.

She turned from the safety railing and realized Wanda was still standing in the doorway and hadn't joined her on the balcony. She was wringing her hands nervously and appeared relieved when Serena returned to the bedroom.

"Are you staying here alone?" Wanda asked.

Jody had asked the same question.

"Yes, it's just me. A kind of solo retreat. I'm hoping this place will provide some inspiration for my work. Get the creative juices flowing."

"You're an artist?"

Serena shook her head. "A writer."

Wanda's face darkened. "Are you a journalist?"

"No, not a journalist. I write books."

"What kinds of books?" Wanda demanded. "Crime books?"

"Well, yes, sort of. I write mysteries."

The older woman was shaking her head now. "You rented this house because of what happened to that poor family, didn't you? That's why you're here. So you can write about them. Dig up the past and pick at old wounds and upset people all over again for the sake of some stupid book."

Serena was shocked by the verbal volley, and also to see that Wanda Stockwell's eyes were wet with tears.

"What family?" she said. "Mrs. Stockwell, I have no idea what you're talking about . . ."

But Wanda wasn't listening. She turned on her heel and left the bedroom without another word. There was the sound of hurried footsteps descending the stairs. Then the front door slammed shut.

Serena was left standing in the middle of the room, stunned.

*What the hell just happened?*

# 3

## RUBY

### JUNE 1983

Ruby Bryant moved down the narrow aisle toward the rear of the Greyhound bus, away from the screaming toddler at the front, his face beet-red, eyes and nose streaming, fat fists lashing out at his harassed mom. The kid didn't seem to be hurt, just pissed off. Ruby knew the feeling.

The prospect of spending the summer at Grandma Pearl's house in Monroe didn't exactly fill her with joy. Eight whole weeks. She'd be bored to death—and she'd miss her friends. While she'd be helping to tidy the yard and hang washing on the line, Kim and Tammy would be hanging out at Lloyd Center, trying on clothes at Meier & Frank, and eating too much candy at Joe Brown's Carmel Corn.

Her mom had already started asking around local salons for any openings, insisting that Ruby earn her keep now that she was done with high school, even though she had zero interest in cutting hair and giving dye jobs to seniors. This would be her last summer of freedom before she had to get a job, and she'd be spending it helping to take care of Grandma Pearl. It wasn't fair. Then Ruby felt bad about the mean thought. She loved her grandma and the affection had always been reciprocated, unlike with her mother. She had never felt the warmth of Coral's love.

Ruby sat by the aisle and dumped her nylon tote bag on the seat next to the window as though she was saving it for a friend. She hoped it would deter anyone from sitting next to her—another stressed parent with noisy kids or a lonely traveler who wanted to chew her ear off for the next three hours. Or, worse, some creepazoid who'd spread his legs too wide, so they rubbed up against her own. Ruby had had enough of that kind of behavior recently.

Her mom's new boyfriend, Ray, was the real reason for the trip to Washington state. Ruby used to spend every summer in Monroe as a kid, climbing trees, exploring the woods, and swimming in Lake Tye. She hadn't been back since she was twelve, her mom having decided she was old enough then to be useful around the apartment, doing the laundry and dishes and dusting, while Coral was working at the salon or God knows where else.

Now Ruby was almost eighteen, on the cusp of womanhood, and it hadn't gone unnoticed by her mom's latest beau. The way his eyes crawled over her body like grabby fingers made her want to heave. Then there had been that incident last month, when Ruby hadn't fastened the bathroom lock properly and he burst in when she was in the shower. Claimed he didn't know she was in there despite the noise of the water and the steam. Her mom had noticed Ray's interest too. That's why she'd sent Ruby packing. Instead of kicking the douchebag into touch, Coral's instinct was to be jealous and resentful of her own daughter. Get her out of the picture for a while.

Ruby knew Coral blamed her for ruining her life, like it was her fault her mom got knocked up at seventeen. "If it wasn't for you, I'd be a stewardess," she'd say. Or, "If I hadn't sacrificed the best years of my life to have a baby, I'd be in Paris or Rome or Monaco right now." As if. Maybe a break from all the shit at home wouldn't be such a bad thing. And Grandma Pearl *did* make the best cherry pie in the whole world.

The doors at the front of the bus sucked shut and the engine started up with an almighty growl, and Ruby was relieved she still had both seats to herself. She scooched over to the window and put on the headphones for her Walkman, the orange foam tickling her ears. Her bag was filled with snacks and books and cassette tapes. She found the *Flashdance* soundtrack and inserted the cassette into the machine. Ruby had seen the movie three times with Tammy at the theater and had played the tape so much she was surprised she hadn't worn it out already. The songs were even better than those from *Fame* in her opinion, even though Tammy disagreed. They'd both been obsessed with that movie too. What they did agree on was that Irene Cara was the absolute best.

Ruby tapped her feet to the fast rhythm of Michael Sembello's "Maniac" as the bus pulled out of the station. Downtown Portland gave way to the I-5 and the Columbia River and then huge, towering sequoias. She changed buses in Seattle for the second leg of the journey to Monroe. Ruby must have dozed off because when she awoke there was no music through the headphones, just the clicking of the tape that had come to an end, and she was almost at her stop. She rubbed bleary eyes and slung her bag over her shoulder and was relieved to be able to stretch her legs after so many hours in a cramped space. The driver pulled her suitcase from the storage compartment under the bus and dumped it on the sidewalk.

Ruby looked around. Grandma Pearl had said she'd arrange a ride from the bus stop to her house, but she didn't see a cab waiting. Just an old pickup truck with the engine idling. The driver's door opened and a guy around her own age got out and broke into the most beautiful smile.

"Ruby Bryant!" he called out, as though he knew her. "Long time no see!"

"Do I know you?" she said, probably with a hint of rudeness.

"You don't remember? We used to hang out at your grandma's place all the time. Bet you could still beat me climbing that old maple tree."

Ruby squinted at him. "River Henderson?"

The beautiful smile widened. "The very same."

No, not the same, Ruby thought. The River she remembered was all awkward skinny limbs and metal braces and pimples. This grown-up version was gorgeous, with intense hazel eyes and floppy corn-colored hair. And that *smile*. Boy, those braces had really worked a treat.

"Your grandma asked me to come pick you up and take you to her place," River said, opening the passenger door for her. "Hop in. It's great to have you back in town after all these years, Ruby Bryant."

He picked up her suitcase as if it weighed nothing, and she noticed the tight definition of his muscles as he effortlessly loaded it onto the truck bed. Ruby dragged her eyes away and climbed inside the cabin before River caught her staring. She smiled to herself, figuring maybe this summer wouldn't be a complete bust after all.

If she'd known then what had just been set in motion—and where it would eventually lead her—Ruby Bryant would have turned around and gotten straight on the first bus back to Portland.

# 4

## SERENA

### NOW

Serena made her way slowly downstairs, still shaken by the encounter with the housekeeper. A set of keys had been left on the console table by the door that she assumed were for her but maybe they belonged to Wanda.

Maybe the housekeeper wasn't coming back.

Serena retrieved her bags from the car and heaved them upstairs to the bedroom. Unpacked and hung her clothes in the closet. She stripped off the now-grimy yoga pants and loose tee that she'd traveled in, and showered and pulled on a summer maxi-dress and sandals.

Her laptop and yellow notebook were both on the coffee table in the living room. She eyed them guiltily and vowed to do some work later. Right now, she needed to eat. She found the restaurant flyers Jody had given her in her purse. There was plenty of food in the house, but Serena wanted to explore the town.

And, she admitted to herself, try to find out more about the family that Wanda Stockwell had been so upset about.

Maybe something had happened to previous guests who had stayed here. Some kind of dreadful accident. The thought didn't exactly fill her with comfort.

As she drove past on her way into town, George Evans was still on his front porch. He didn't get up this time, but Serena felt his eyes boring into her until she reached a bend in the road and he vanished from her rearview mirror.

Susie's Shrimp Shack was a casual waterfront eatery painted shabby-chic blue with the restaurant's name stamped on a pink surfboard hung above the entrance.

It offered harbor views, an outdoor patio, and fresh locally caught seafood. A couple were seated at one of the outside tables under a bright yellow umbrella. They both had glasses of red wine in front of them. The man was reading a newspaper and the woman was engrossed in a mystery novel (not one of Serena's). Inside, cozy booths with picture windows overlooked the yacht-filled dock and a jukebox in the corner played "Good Vibrations" by the Beach Boys.

It was well after lunch and too early for dinner, and despite the happy hour offers, the dining room was quiet. Two older ladies sat in a back booth chatting over cocktails and big slabs of mud cake. A male diner was on his own at another table, making short work of a plateful of shrimp.

Behind the counter was a woman around Serena's age with big doe-like blue eyes and dirty-blonde hair piled on top of her head in a messy top knot. She was wearing an apron with the words "I'm all Shack up" over denim overalls. She spotted Serena and gave her a warm smile.

"Welcome to Susie's Shrimp Shack. Is it drinks only or are you dining too?"

The aroma of fried fish was making Serena's mouth water. She hadn't eaten since the bagel and latte she'd had for breakfast at the airport before dawn.

28

"Definitely food too."

The guy on his own—fair hair, mid-forties, handsome in a rugged kind of way—indicated his half-eaten meal. "I can heartily recommend Hannah's coconut shrimp. It's to die for."

The woman—presumably Hannah—shrugged in mock-modesty. "It is pretty amazing, if I do say so myself. Although Jack here is going to need an extra notch on his belt if he keeps ordering it so often."

"Hey!" Jack protested with a grin. "It's a treat on my day off."

There was something familiar about the man, but Serena couldn't put her finger on what exactly.

"Are you staying in Seaton Point or just passing through?" Hannah asked her.

"I'm renting the Cliff House." Serena watched her carefully for a reaction after the odd behavior of both the car rental guy and the housekeeper regarding her stay at the property.

But Hannah just nodded. "So you're the new guest? My mom said you'd be arriving today. You're here all summer, right?"

"Your mom?"

"Wanda Stockwell. The Cliff House is one of the rental properties she cleans. She was in town this morning to pick up the groceries."

Serena felt a hot flush crawl across her chest. Talk about awkward. "Um, I think I may have upset your mom." She grimaced. "There was some kind of misunderstanding earlier."

Hannah frowned. "Really? What happened?"

"I mentioned that I was a writer and had rented the house while working on my new book, and she seemed to think I was planning on writing about some family. She got pretty upset and left in a hurry."

Hannah looked bewildered. "That's so weird. And not like her at all. She's usually very professional."

This was Serena's chance to find out more.

"What family was your mom talking about?" she asked. "Did something happen to other Airbnb guests who were staying there? An accident or some other incident?"

She could see from the corner of her eye that the coconut shrimp guy had stopped eating and was scrolling his phone, like he was listening to their conversation but trying to appear like he wasn't.

"I don't think so," Hannah said. "There were a few short-term lets over the spring, a week or two here and there, but I don't remember hearing about any problems. And I'm sure my mom would have told me if anything had happened to any of the guests." She was silent for a moment. "Unless . . ."

"Unless what?" Serena prompted.

"Unless she was talking about the Duprie family. They used to live at the Cliff House, and then all three of them just vanished one night. Disappeared into thin air. But that was decades ago."

Serena remembered what Jody had said about folks disappearing. So much for silly ghost stories at kids' sleepovers.

Hannah must have noticed her worried expression because she gave Serena a reassuring smile.

"I'm sorry if my mom spooked you," she said. "Seaton Point is a pretty safe and friendly place. You'll love it here. Isn't that right, Jack?"

Jack looked up from his phone. "What's that?"

"I was telling . . ."

"Serena. Serena Winters."

"I was telling Serena that Seaton Point is very safe. Hardly any crime."

Jack pretended to think about it. "Well, Mrs. Kirby did report a burglary at her home on Avery Drive last week after a pack of bacon was stolen from her refrigerator. Although it turns out Mr. Kirby had a midnight snack and was too scared to confess the crime to his wife. And Hank Macaulay made another police report claiming he'd had his memory wiped by government agents again, after waking on his couch with no recollection of how he got there from O'Malley's Bar."

Serena laughed. "That story with the bacon didn't happen."

Jack grinned. "Cross my heart."

"Anyway, you came here for food, not the local crime statistics." Hannah handed Serena a menu and a wine list. "You can either eat inside or out on the patio. Your choice."

"I'll sit outside. It's such a beautiful day." Serena placed the menu on the counter unread. "I'll have the famous coconut shrimp with a side of fries and an iced tea please."

"Good choice," Hannah said. "I'll bring it out when it's ready. Shouldn't be too long."

Serena found a table shaded by an orange umbrella and pulled her cell phone from her purse. She opened Google and searched for "Duprie family disappearance Seaton Point CA."

The results threw up a couple of true crime YouTube videos from a few years back and some Reddit posts. Disappointingly, there was no Wikipedia page or any newspaper reports. Probably too long ago for those to be online.

Hannah appeared with the food and iced tea and told her to enjoy her meal. After she'd gone back inside, Serena returned to the phone. The YouTube videos were hosted by amateur sleuths recounting limited facts interspersed with stock images of crime scene tape and cop cars with flashing blue lights, all against a backdrop of cheesy dramatic music. She watched them while she ate.

This is what she learned: Bill and Dani Duprie had lived in a "big, isolated house on the edge of a cliff" in Seaton Point with their ten-year-old daughter Charlotte. (Serena sighed. Again, with the "isolated.") Bill worked in the tech industry and Dani was a stay-at-home mom. Charlotte was a quiet girl but smart, according to her teachers. The Dupries had lived in town for a few years and had mostly kept to themselves. It was believed the entire family vanished from their home in the early hours of September 21, 1994. There was no sign of foul play, and all their belongings were still at the property. No bodies, no suspects, no real leads. No one ever found out what had happened to them.

Serena felt a fizz of excitement in her belly that she hadn't experienced in a long time. Her breathing was faster, and her heart rate had kicked up a notch. It was exactly how she felt whenever she watched a great thriller or read a gripping novel, or when she knew she'd hit upon the perfect plot for her next bestseller.

Whenever there was an intriguing mystery begging to be solved.

"Tell me I was right," said a man's voice. "Wasn't that just the best coconut shrimp you've ever had in your whole entire life?"

Serena looked up, startled. The guy from inside—Jack—was standing next to her, shielding his eyes from the sun. She slammed the phone face down on the table like she was a teenage boy who'd been caught watching porn. Had he seen what she'd been looking at?

"I'm sorry? What?"

He nodded at her plate. There were only a few fries left. "The shrimp. It was good?"

"The shrimp. Right." She nodded. "Not too bad at all. Thanks for the recommendation."

Jack smiled and gave a little salute. "Glad to be of service. Maybe see you around."

She watched him go, then turned her attention to the Reddit posts. They had titles like *What happened to the Duprie family?* and *Sightings of Dani Duprie* and *Missing Duprie family theories . . .*

But Serena didn't want theories, she wanted facts.

She sighed and tucked the cell phone back into her purse, just as Hannah came out to collect the dirty plate and empty highball tumbler.

"I spoke to my mom," she said. "I think she's a little embarrassed. She was kind of friendly with Dani Duprie—that's the woman who disappeared—and she got the wrong end of the stick and overreacted. She says she'll be at the house on Monday as agreed."

"I'm glad she's okay." Serena hesitated. "But I must admit, I'm a little intrigued now by the Duprie family. Do you know much about what happened to them?"

"I was a kid at the time, so my memories are kind of hazy." Hannah gestured to the empty seat facing Serena. "May I?"

Serena nodded. "Sure."

Hannah sat down. "Charlotte, the daughter, was in my class at school," she said. "She was a sweet girl, if a little quiet. Quite studious, always reading. We had a few playdates together and there was a sleepover at my house for my birthday that year. I'd have been ten. A few friends were invited, and Charlotte was one of them. I remember her mom kept calling to make sure she was okay. Like every hour or so, the phone would ring. My mom was getting really irritated, thinking Dani didn't trust her to look after her kid.

"The next morning, Dani was at the house early to collect Charlotte even though it was a weekend. Charlotte got upset because she wasn't allowed to stay for breakfast and my mom was making her famous blueberry pancakes. I was never invited to Charlotte's house. I don't think any of the kids were. When my mom got the housekeeping gig a few years back, she told me it was the first time she'd been inside the Cliff House."

So, Wanda Stockwell hadn't known Dani Duprie well enough to be invited to her home? Yet she'd been on the verge of tears earlier about the woman vanishing three decades ago?

Strange.

"What about the disappearance?"

"Charlotte hadn't been in class for a few days, but I probably thought she was sick or something," Hannah said. "Then the police showed up, which was scary and exciting because Chief Raskin had only ever been at the school before to do talks on road safety and stranger danger. There was a lot of whispering among the adults, and I think all the teachers were questioned. I remember my mom asking me if Charlotte had been worried or scared about anything, but she'd seemed totally fine in the days beforehand."

"Did this Chief Raskin ever make any progress with the case?" Serena asked. "Any arrests or leads or theories about what might have gone down that night?"

"Not as far as I know. Their photo was in the local paper for a while and then, after a month or two, it wasn't. With no leads and nothing new to write about, I guess people around here eventually forgot about them."

Serena thanked Hannah for the food and her time and paid the check. She decided to go for a stroll along the marina and browse the nearby boutiques, try to burn off some calories after such a big meal. The sun was already beginning to set when she returned to the Shrimp Shack's parking lot. She spotted a piece of paper tucked under the Mustang's windshield wiper, and figured it was probably a flyer targeting tourists.

As she got closer, she saw that it wasn't a flyer. It was a folded sheet of lined paper. She plucked it from the wiper and opened it. There were three words written in blocky capital letters.

Serena stared at the note in disbelief.

**LEAVE TOWN NOW**

# 5
---
## SERENA
---
## NOW

By the time she reached Cliffside Drive, Serena had convinced herself the note was likely down to kids messing around. She no longer had the steering wheel in a death grip and her heart rate had just about returned to normal.

When she'd left the Shrimp Shack after her meal, there had been five or six teens hanging around the parking lot with skateboards. The Mustang had a "Dale's Rent-A-Car" sticker on the window, so it was clearly a rental being used by someone from out of town. Maybe the skateboarders had thought it would be amusing to slip a threatening note under the wiper to freak out a tourist. The group had left by the time she'd returned from her walk. Or that was what she'd thought. They could have been hiding behind a truck, waiting for her to find the note, having a good laugh as she scrunched it into a ball and tossed it into a trash can. As she gazed around the deserted lot with trepidation. They may even have filmed her on their cell phones for some dumb TikTok prank video. It seemed like the kind of thing bored kids would do for kicks.

But as the Cliff House came into view now, the short-lived relief evaporated, and Serena felt uneasy all over again.

In the sparkling sunshine earlier, the house had looked like it belonged in a photoshoot for *House Beautiful*. Now, looming big and dark against a purple twilight sky, the building seemed ominous— threatening even.

Serena shook her head as she turned into the driveway, the tires crunching noisily on gravel.

"Get a grip, Winters," she muttered.

She knew she had an overactive imagination. It was the blessing and the curse of being a writer.

Even so, she sat for a moment in the car, steadying herself. The engine ticking over as it cooled was the only sound in the silence. Even the waves were quiet tonight. She took her keys from her purse, got out, and hurried up the porch steps and into the house.

Once inside, Serena palmed the switch for the hall light and double-locked the front door, hooking the security chain into place. She made sure the kitchen door and all the downstairs windows were secured too.

She returned to the hallway and stood in front of the two doors that Wanda Stockwell hadn't opened. The first, as expected, was a closet hiding nothing more sinister than cleaning supplies. She tried the knob on the second door, but it wouldn't open. A night latch had been fitted at eye level. Serena leaned in for a closer look and saw that there were scratches around the key insert. She reached out and touched the round brass plate, feeling the scores under her fingertip. It was as though someone had tried to pick the lock. She knew there wasn't a matching key on the set Wanda Stockwell had left for her.

Serena wondered if the locked door led down to a basement. What was stored inside.

After changing into her pajamas, Serena poured herself a generous glass of Chablis and settled on the couch with the yellow notebook and her favorite fountain pen. Instead of making notes about her novel—she still had no idea what the plot was going to be—she found herself jotting down everything she'd learned so far about the Duprie family.

Her cell phone vibrated with a text from Margot: *I take it you arrived in SP okay? How's the house?*

Serena tapped out a response: *House is fab. Even better in real life than the photos I sent you.*

She decided not to tell Margot about all the weird stuff. Her agent would only think she was paranoid and try to convince her yet again to see her shrink.

Margot: *Dare I ask about the writing?*

Serena: *The words are flowing . . .*

It wasn't exactly a lie. She'd filled several pages of her notebook, after all.

Margot responded with a thumbs-up emoji.

Serena swapped the text app for a search page and found the Reddit post titled *Missing Duprie family theories . . .* She read the whole thing. The theories were as ridiculous as she'd expected them to be: abducted by aliens; joined a cult; gone into witness protection after testifying against the mob . . .

Serena looked over her notes and tried to work on a theory of her own based on the limited information she had.

There wasn't much about Bill, the husband, other than that he'd worked in the tech industry. Which told her nothing except why they'd been able to afford to live in a place as grand as the Cliff House. Dani was more interesting. She appeared to have been friendly with the other school moms without actually being friends with them. Was she simply a private person, or had she been hiding something?

Serena thought again of the locked door in the hallway.

Dani had been antsy about Charlotte spending the night at Wanda Stockwell's house. She'd clearly been very protective of her daughter. Had she been overprotective? Serena was not a mother, had no firsthand experience of caring for and loving a child, but Hannah's account of the birthday sleepover seemed to suggest that Dani's behavior had been out of the ordinary.

What was it those YouTube videos had said?

*They'd kept to themselves.*

Serena tapped the pen against her teeth, her mind racing. Then she wrote down: *Witness protection.*

It was probably nothing quite as dramatic as testifying against the mob, but it made sense. If Bill and Dani had been relocated to Seaton Point with new identities, they wouldn't have wanted anyone getting too close and asking too many questions. They certainly wouldn't have wanted folks snooping around their home. And it explained Dani's anxiety over Charlotte being away from home overnight. Hell, maybe the kid had been the key witness to the crime, rather than the parents. Their cover blown, they'd been whisked away to a new location in the dead of night and never heard of again.

Serena liked the theory. She circled the words "witness protection" then closed the notebook, clipped the pen onto the cover, and tossed it onto the coffee table.

She drained the rest of the wine and yawned. Her eyelids felt heavy and her head was fuzzy from the booze. She tapped her phone screen and saw that it was just after ten p.m. but, she reminded herself, it was after one a.m. back home. She was still on New York time and it had been a long day. A long and very strange day. She placed the empty wineglass on the table next to the notebook. Trudged upstairs and climbed into bed.

For once, Serena didn't think of Michael as she drifted off to sleep. Instead, she thought of an isolated house on a clifftop and a missing family . . .

Her eyes snapped open.

The room was shrouded in darkness. As her eyes adjusted to the gloom, unfamiliar shapes began to materialize. Panic welled up inside her. Then she remembered: she wasn't in her apartment in Manhattan, she was thousands of miles away, in a house in California.

What had woken her? Was it being in a strange bed? Yet she had spent hundreds of nights in hotel rooms in towns and cities all over the country and usually slept soundly. She sat up and tried to wind back through her subconscious brain, like rewinding an old VHS tape. Was it the crunch of gravel outside? Or the light tread of footsteps downstairs? Or the soft breath of a stranger in her room?

Serena shivered and realized how cold the bedroom was as a draft tickled her face and goosebumps prickled the bare skin of her arms. She turned on the bedside lamp and chased the shadows into the far corners. One of the French doors was ajar, letting in a stiff breeze. Serena tensed. She thought back to when she'd arrived home earlier and ensured that all the doors and windows downstairs had been locked. She hadn't checked the French doors in the bedroom because there was no way for anyone to access the balcony from the cliff-face outside. The doors likely hadn't been closed properly after Wanda Stockwell's dramatic departure and the wind had blown one of them open in the night.

The cool air and the crash of the waves had no doubt been what had woken her.

Even so.

Her cell phone told her it was 03:17. Far too early to get up and start her day, but Serena knew she wouldn't be able to go back to sleep unless she put her mind at rest first. She padded barefoot downstairs and saw that the front door's security chain was still in place. She hit the switch for the porch lights and peered out of the slim window by the door. The driveway was empty save for the Ford Mustang. The powder room was empty too. So was the utilities closet. The other door was still locked.

Serena told herself she was being ridiculous. That when your job was to write about bad people doing bad things, it started to mess with your head. But she couldn't shake the feeling that there had been a presence in this house very recently. The tiny hairs on the back of her neck stood up. Her skin crawled. She passed through the living area into the kitchen and fumbled for the light switch, illuminating the space in a sudden bright glare.

Serena froze.

Her wineglass was on the countertop. She was sure it had been on the coffee table in the other room when she'd gone to bed. She strode quickly over to the kitchen door and yanked on the handle. Locked. Ditto the windows. Serena returned to the living area and looked around. The floor-to-ceiling windows didn't open. But something still felt off. Her gaze landed on the table on which she could have sworn she'd left the wineglass.

Then she saw it.

Her favorite fountain pen, a gift from her father, was next to the notebook. Serena always clipped the pen to the cover. A cold feeling came over her. That crawling-skin sensation was back. The rational part of her brain tried to force her to think logically. The house was locked up tighter than Fort Knox. There was no sign of forced entry anywhere. No broken windows or jimmied locks. She'd been dog-tired when she'd crawled into bed and the wine had gone straight to her head. She'd probably just forgotten that she'd taken the wineglass into the kitchen. Hadn't clipped the pen onto the notebook's cover properly.

That was the most logical explanation.

Serena caught sight of her drawn face reflected in the living room window.

It was at least another hour until sunrise, but there was no point going back to bed.

There was no hope of sleep now.

# 6

## DANI

### NOVEMBER 1983

The radio alarm clock digits glowed eerie red in the gloom: 01:49.

Bill had quickly silenced his pager, but not before Dani was stirred from slumber by the annoying beeping. She'd heard the creak of the mattress, felt the shift in weight as he'd pulled back the sheets and slid out of bed. Then the soft click of the lock engaging on the front door as he'd snuck out of the apartment. Not for the first time.

Now she stared at the ceiling, wide awake. The headlights of passing cars down below intermittently lit up the bedroom, even at this hour. The occasional blast of a siren or shouts from a passerby on the street shattered the silent night. Dani hated this strange city in this unfamiliar state. Sure, the stylish rental apartment, with its stylish rental furnishings, was nice enough. Better than nice. White marble in the en suite and the main bathroom. Cream leather sofa and smoked-glass coffee table and panoramic views of downtown.

Plush carpet so thick it hid your toes. She knew she was lucky. A million people would kill to live in a place like this.

But Dani missed her sunshine-yellow Victorian house in San Francisco, the chic affluence of her Pacific Heights neighborhood. She missed her friends and retail therapy in Union Square and spa days and lunches at the Tadich Grill, where the healthy Cosmopolitan salads were cancelled out by day-drinking carafes of fine Californian wine. Dani Duprie missed the life she used to have. She was so lonely here, especially when the other side of the bed was empty and cold.

But, she reminded herself, the empty space next to her was nothing new. And, surely, it was better to know where Bill was, who he was with, why he was leaving his home and his wife in the dead of night? Better than before, when he'd be out all night, crawling clumsily into bed when dawn was starting to light the sky. Back then, she'd smell the rank liquor on his breath, feel the unnatural racing of his heart as he pulled her close, his chest pressed against her back. Whispering "I'm sorry" into her hair.

Then, after all those nights of worry, had come the shame. The arrest. His firing. Having to move away and start again. Bill had been doing so well here these past few months that Dani didn't want to risk a relapse by causing a fuss and creating a stressful situation. It was the stress, he'd said, that had led to the problems in the first place. The pressure of the job, the peer pressure of his coworkers. Coworkers who'd all deserted him when everything unraveled for Bill, like he'd been the only one partaking.

That damn bleeper, the small black device his new firm was trialing, was supposed to be for work, summoning staff to important meetings and so on, but she knew it wasn't the office calling when it went off at midnight, at one in the morning, even later . . . Bill worked in tech, for goodness' sake, he wasn't a doctor or a cop or a paramedic. It wasn't his job to save lives, but he seemed to think that it was. He claimed that's what he was trying to do: save people, help others, pay it forward. But what about Dani? What about what she wanted? What about what she *needed*?

Every single night she got down on her knees, onto the cold marble tile of the bathroom floor, and she prayed. Pleaded with God for a miracle. But it wasn't just down to God; Bill had to play his part too, and they'd never be able to overcome the challenges they'd been facing if he wasn't even in the same bed as her.

Dani punched the pillow and tried to get comfortable. Pulled the sheets up to her chin to stave off the winter chill. It was a poor substitute for the body heat of her absent husband. She should try to get some sleep. Tomorrow was her first day at her new job and she didn't want to show up looking like a zombie.

Dani didn't have to work. Bill earned more than enough money for them both. Not Silicon Valley money, not anymore, but still a hefty salary. He'd been lucky to get this job after the accident and the subsequent arrest. But he was smart, and that's why they'd taken him on despite the criminal record.

Bill had always been academic, unlike her. When they'd met, he was a student at Stanford, already acing his classes and being courted by the big tech companies. They were introduced at a party by a mutual friend who was at Berkeley. Dani didn't go to college, had got by in high school with her blonde good looks and fizzy personality, barely scraping her GED, and still hadn't figured out what she wanted to do with her life when she met Bill. He wasn't her type at all. She'd always gone for the jocks; that old cliché of the captain of the cheerleading squad dating the star of the football team. Bill was a nerd, with his big brain and thick black glasses, always shoving his hair back nervously off his face, generally awkward and no good at making small talk unless he'd had a couple of beers. The opposite of Dani, who was outgoing and bubbly and rode through life on personality rather than SAT results. But she was smart enough to realize that Bill Duprie was funny and kind and caring and that wasn't something she was used to with the boys she'd dated.

They had fallen hard for each other, got married after he graduated, bought the big house in San Francisco, and everything had been perfect. Well, almost perfect. There were the . . . challenges. Then the stress and the all-nighters, the arrest and the relocation.

Dani figured she could still be bubbly and outgoing, that her gregariousness would translate to a different state. She just needed to meet new people. So, she'd applied for the job at the bus station downtown. Selling tickets, answering customer queries, not exactly rocket science (or writing software like Bill), but it was something. Better than spending all day—and most nights—in this big, luxurious, soulless apartment on her own.

Another glance at the clock told her it was 02:21. She closed her eyes and willed sleep to come even though her husband was out there in this alien city with another woman, and Dani had never felt so alone.

# 7

## SERENA

### NOW

Serena had been in countless libraries over the years—first as a reader and then as an author—and had met library staff of all shapes and sizes. But she had never come face to face with a librarian who could have been on the cover of *Vogue* before.

That was a first.

The woman behind the front desk of the Seaton Point Public Library was around Serena's age, with long, full Afro curls framing striking features. She had the kind of dewy, flawless skin that was the result of great genes rather than expensive chemical peels. A satin khaki jumpsuit hugged her killer curves, and her slim wrists were adorned with delicate gold and diamond bangles.

Serena felt her fingers instinctively go to the fine lines creasing the corners of her own eyes. Laughter lines, people called them, although she hadn't been doing much of that lately. This morning, she'd had to dab extra concealer onto the dark smudges under her eyes following her restless night.

The woman glanced up from her computer screen as Serena approached, and did a double take. Leaned across the desk for a closer look. Then said, "Well, fuck me."

Another first.

"You *are* Serena Winters, aren't you?" she added.

Serena smiled awkwardly. "The one and only."

"I'm Cynthia Hall." The librarian stuck out a hand for Serena to shake, a gold Cartier watch glinting under the library lights. "Apologies for the cussing but an overdue book return is usually as exciting as it gets around here. Are you in Seaton Point on vacation?"

"A kind of working vacation."

"How long for?"

"All summer."

Cynthia raised a perfectly sculpted eyebrow. "Is that so? I should book you for a library event while you're in town. It's not every day we have a famous author walk through the door."

Serena gestured to a rumpled older man who was snoozing on a chair in the corner, a copy of *Nineteen Eighty-Four* by George Orwell splayed open on his lap.

"Is the audience likely to be more engaged than that gentleman?"

"I can promise butts on seats, I just can't guarantee they'll all be conscious." Cynthia shook her head. "You know, Hank has been reading that book for as long as I've worked here, which is almost three years now. He'll never finish it."

"Hank? Did a couple of government agents in black suits drop him off here?"

Cynthia laughed. "You've heard about Hank already, huh? Crazy paranoid but harmless enough. So, that library event . . . Shall we get a date in the diary?"

Serena's last author event had been the night Michael died.

"Let me think about it," she said.

"Okay, but just so you know, I'll keep on asking until you say yes. I'm like a dog with a bone. Now, what can I do for you?"

The library was very contemporary, with plush tub chairs in bright colors and gleaming white shelves, and freestanding vertical signs dotted around the room with words like "READ" and "DREAM." There was a kids' corner filled with beanbags and picture books that was currently occupied by half a dozen moms wrangling chubby, squealing toddlers. It did not look like the kind of place that housed dusty old newspapers.

"I was hoping to access some old articles from the local newspaper," Serena said. "But I'm not sure a modern library like this would have that kind of thing."

"Sure we do," Cynthia said. "We have archived editions of the *Seaton Point Sentinel* dating from 1859 to 2015."

"Really?" Serena was surprised and impressed.

"Yep, it's all on microfilm. Hundreds of historical documents too—such as church records and passenger lists—that are popular with the genealogy nerds. We have a lot of cool shit here. Who knew libraries could be so useful! What period do you need?"

Hannah from the Shrimp Shack had mentioned interest in the Dupries had started to wane after a couple of months.

"Two months, starting September 21, 1994."

"That's very specific," Cynthia observed.

"I'm looking for information about the Duprie family. The night it happened seems like the logical place to start."

"The night what happened? What did they do?"

"You don't know?"

"Nope."

Cynthia had said she'd only worked at the library for a few years, so maybe she was a more recent resident and didn't know the town's history.

"They vanished," Serena said. "The whole family. They're still missing."

"Wow—who knew sleepy little Seaton Point could be so exciting?" Cynthia smiled slyly. "Wait, is this research for a new book? You said it was a working vacation."

Serena was about to say no, and then thought about the pages of notes she'd filled about the Duprie family the night before. Their story *could* be the basis of the novel she'd been struggling with.

"I'm not writing directly about the Dupries," she said. "It's fiction, not a true crime book, but I guess you could say their story is providing the inspiration."

Serena knew lots of authors whose work was inspired by events ripped from the headlines. She'd done it herself several times in the past, when real life had provided the spark of an idea, the jumping-off point, even if the book always turned out to be very different from the source material.

It could be the same with the Dupries.

Excitement bubbled in her belly again as she followed Cynthia to a computer room with five iMacs and one microfilm reader. The boxy machine looked like a museum artifact next to the slim computers. Cynthia opened a metal file cabinet and perused a shelf filled with boxes before selecting the one containing the right film. After switching on the projector, she pulled out a tray from under a microscope, placed the film roll on a spindle and expertly fed it under the rollers to a reel on the other side. Wound the reel a few times and tapped some buttons, pushed the tray back under the microscope, and—like magic—an image appeared on the monitor.

Cynthia demonstrated how to use the rotate knob to swivel the image, and the buttons on the pullout tray to fast-forward and rewind to the desired page, and how to zoom and focus, then she left Serena on her own in the room.

After familiarizing herself with how to operate the machine, she started working her way through the pages of the newspaper. Felt a punch of nostalgia as she was transported back to the mid-1990s. A half-page advert for a local electronics store featured special offers on a portable CD player, a cordless phone, and a VHS camcorder. A TV critic offered a favorable review of a new sitcom called *Friends* that had just debuted on NBC. In the sports pages, a big boxing match between Lennox Lewis and Oliver McCall was previewed. The cinema listings for the Seaton Point Plaza included new releases *The Shawshank Redemption* and *Terminal Velocity*, as well as a last chance to see *Natural Born Killers*. Serena remembered applying a ton of makeup and tricking her way into the theater to watch the movie as a fourteen-year-old, and being traumatized for days afterward.

There were a bunch of local interest stories too—the high school debate team progressing to a state tournament, a stabbing on Point Beach, angry residents reporting illegal trash dumping. Then, in the weekend edition—on Saturday, September 24—a first mention of the Duprie family as the front-page splash. Serena studied the three faces in the photo that illustrated the article.

Bill. Dani. Charlotte.

She felt like an icy finger had touched her spine.

*What happened to you all?*

Bill was square-jawed and clean-shaven. His brown hair was cut short and neatly combed to the side, eyes dark behind black-framed glasses. Dani was the epitome of '90s glamor. Big blonde hair, frosted lipstick, a slim frame made sharper by the shoulder pads in her blouse. Charlotte was gap-toothed and freckled with a round face and braided hair that was either fair or strawberry-blonde. It was impossible to tell which in the black-and-white image.

The article had been written by Patrick Dolan, the *Sentinel*'s crime correspondent. The headline was simple and straight to the point: *SEATON POINT FAMILY MISSING*.

The Seaton Point Police Department had launched an appeal for information after a welfare check at the house on Cliffside Drive raised concerns about the wellbeing of the family of three, who had not been seen since Tuesday. Officers had searched the property on Friday afternoon after the alarm was raised by Wanda Stockwell, a friend of Dani Duprie, when her calls to the house had gone unanswered. A white Ford Taurus and a light blue Dodge Caravan, both belonging to the family, were parked in the driveway of their home. A quote from Police Chief Don Raskin stated that there were "no signs of a struggle at the house or evidence of foul play, however there were indications that the family did not leave on a planned vacation." Bill, who was employed by a San Diego software firm, had not been at his office or had any contact with coworkers for several days, which was believed to be out of character. Charlotte had also been absent from school without explanation.

Serena sat back and thought about what she'd just read. Decided the most interesting fact was that Wanda Stockwell had been the one to alert the cops.

The following days had seen more appeals for information as concerns continued to grow. Residents spoke of their shock at the disappearance. A "Missing" flyer was distributed by the cops. In other words, there wasn't a whole lot of new information. A week later, a color piece—headlined *MYSTERY OF THE "MARY CELESTE" HOUSE*—was published after the reporter apparently accessed details of the crime scene.

Patrick Dolan compared what had awaited cops at the Cliff House to the discovery of the *Mary Celeste*, the ship that was discovered adrift and deserted in the Atlantic Ocean in 1872. He wrote that chopped vegetables were found congealing in a pan on the kitchen counter, alongside a chopping board. A knife was on the floor but had no blood on it. Laundered clothes were in the dryer, its light still blinking to indicate the end of the cycle. Bill and Dani's cars were both parked in the driveway, lights were ablaze in several of the rooms, and the front door was unlocked. Suitcases were stored in the closet, the couple's clothes still hanging on the rails. Dani's cosmetics and hairdryer were on the dressing table. In Charlotte's bedroom, her homework was open on the desk. Her Barbie dolls were lined up neatly on a shelf. Her closet was filled with dresses and jeans and sweaters. The house had been abandoned, Dolan noted, just like the *Mary Celeste*. A ghost house.

A follow-up story suggested the Dupries could be in Mexico, either voluntarily or after having been kidnapped. Having accessed their financial records, investigators were "following a line of inquiry." Dani and Bill's wallets—including bank and credit cards and Dani's driver's license—had been found discarded by the side of a highway sixty miles south of Seaton Point. Authorities were working on the theory that they could have been heading for the border. There was no mention of Bill's driver's license in the story. The article ended with an appeal for information on any cars seen in the vicinity of the Duprie family home around the time of their disappearance, which was now believed to be in the early hours of September 21.

A month later, and in the absence of a breakthrough in the case, the reporter had opted for a different angle on the story, this time exploring the "dark history" of the Cliff House. The vanishing of Bill, Dani, and Charlotte Duprie was not the only tragedy to unfold at the property, he reported. Back in 1989, the original owner, Grady Hargreaves, had died within days of building work being completed and moving in. His broken body was found on the rocks fifty feet below, having fallen—or jumped—from the balcony of the main bedroom. The house had been inherited by family members who never lived there and chose to rent it out instead. The Duprie family had been the first tenants.

Serena thought of another broken body, at the foot of a staircase in a New Jersey home. She lent her elbows on the desk and closed her eyes and massaged her temples.

"Are you okay?"

Serena started at the sound of Cynthia's voice behind her. She swiveled around in the chair to face the librarian and smiled weakly. "Eyestrain from reading all that small print on the monitor."

A headache was blooming behind her eyes, and it wasn't just from the screen glare.

"Did you find what you were looking for?" Cynthia asked.

"A few articles that were interesting. Is it possible to get hard copies?"

"It is, but it'll cost you fifty cents a sheet. No freebies just because you're a big-time author."

Serena laughed. "I think I can stretch to a couple bucks."

She asked Cynthia to print out the four news stories, as well as a blown-up version of the photo of Bill, Dani, and Charlotte.

Cynthia collected the pages from the printer and studied the family portrait. "So, this is the Dupries? I can't believe I haven't heard about them before." She gazed at the photo for another moment, a small frown briefly marring her perfectly smooth forehead, and then handed the printouts to Serena.

They headed back into the main library area and Serena inquired if the offices of the *Seaton Point Sentinel* were nearby. It would be worth knowing if reporters had followed up on the case over the years—garnered any new information.

Cynthia shook her head, her curls bouncing. "The newspaper closed down years ago, before my time. I'm guessing 2015, seeing as that's the most recent microfilm we have."

"I don't suppose you know if the reporter, Patrick Dolan, is still in town? If he's even still alive, that is."

"Oh, Patrick's alive and kicking," Cynthia said. "Comes in here often. A big fan of those old PI novels by Raymond Chandler and Robert B. Parker. Don't think he's ever borrowed any of your books, though. Sorry."

"I'll get over it. Do you think he'd speak to me? Do you have a number or an address where I could reach him?"

"I don't, but I could pass on your number the next time he stops by, see if he'd be up for meeting you? Don't get your hopes up, though, he's not the most sociable of guys."

Serena rummaged in her purse and found a business card with details of her author website, social media accounts, and her public email address. She wrote her cell phone number on the back.

Cynthia took the card and slipped it into the desk drawer. "I'll pass this on to Patrick on one condition."

"What's that?"

"That library event?"

Serena glanced at where Hank Macauley was still snoozing, mouth open, snoring softly. The book had fallen from his lap onto the floor.

She sighed. "Okay. It's a deal."

Serena had planned on having a nap when she returned to the Cliff House, but when she got there the house was filled with bright sunshine. Light bounced off the white walls, shiny surfaces glimmered, and the ocean outside the windows was impossibly blue. Her fatigue and headache melted away and she felt suddenly uplifted. Her brain was buzzing, and the urge to write was strong and compelling. It was the perfect day for working outside on the balcony, but knowing the previous owner had met his demise from that very spot chilled her and she didn't want anything to darken her good mood.

The middle-sized bedroom overlooked the front of the house with not much to see other than a road and a gravel driveway, but the smallest room had a desk and an ocean view—without the close proximity to Grady Hargreaves's fall—and Serena promptly turned it into a makeshift office with laptop, notebook, pens, and the *Seaton Point Sentinel* printouts from the library. She Scotch-taped the photo of the family to the wall.

Then she opened her laptop and started writing.

Yesterday, she'd told Margot the words were flowing. This time it was true. Her fingers flew across the keyboard, trying to keep up with the words that were pouring out of her. She lost herself in the story of Layne Farraday's latest investigation as hours passed by unnoticed.

That night, she slept soundly and woke feeling refreshed, the heat of the day already warming the bedroom, shards of light slashing across the wooden floor. There had been no incidents in the night to disturb her slumber or items inexplicably moving around.

By late Saturday afternoon, Serena had the prologue and first two chapters down. She was considering what to make for dinner when a text arrived from Cynthia:

*Patrick Dolan was in the library earlier. He'll be in touch.*

An hour later, her cell phone buzzed with a message from an unknown number:

*My boat at the marina. Noon tomorrow. I'll tell you what I know about that family.*

# 8

## SERENA

### NOW

Sunday dawned bright and glorious, a clear azure sky unblemished by clouds, the temperature hovering pleasantly in the mid-seventies. The harbor was busy with families and couples, clutching ice creams and takeout coffees, eager to take advantage of the rest of the warm weekend weather.

Serena strolled past the waterfront eateries and made her way down a ramp to the wooden dock. A few hundred yachts, boats, and sailboats were moored in the marina, and she realized she had no idea how to find the one belonging to Patrick Dolan. She kept on walking until she spotted a man on the deck of a pocket yacht holding a rope.

"Excuse me, sir," she called, raising a hand to shield her eyes from the sun. "Do you happen to know where I can find Patrick Dolan?"

"Sure." He pointed east. "Head toward Seaton Wharf, where the sportfishing and whale-watching tours are booked. After about a hundred yards, you'll find Dolan's slip. His cruiser is the *Miss Misty*."

Serena thanked him and followed his directions, the midday sun warm on her bare arms, the scent of salt and fish hanging in the air. As she passed by each boat, she read the name etched on the side, wondering about the significance of the monikers that had been carefully chosen.

Then she spotted *Miss Misty*.

The cruiser was gleaming white and around twenty-eight feet in length. Bigger than she'd expected. Librarians wearing Cartier watches . . . Ex-newspaper hacks whiling away lazy Sundays on yachts . . . Seaton Point was even more affluent than she'd first thought.

"Hello?" she yelled. "Mr. Dolan?"

Nothing. No response.

She called out again, louder this time. There was the sound of shuffling and then a man in his sixties emerged from the cabin, dressed in deck shorts and an open plaid shirt over a white under-shirt. Tufts of steel-gray hair escaped from under a ball cap. He reminded her of Quint, the shark hunter from *Jaws*, but without the mustache.

The man—presumably Dolan—stared down at her. "Are you the writer?"

"I am. Serena Winters."

He nodded curtly. "Permission granted to come aboard."

Dolan moved to the starboard and held out a hand to assist her, his skin rough and callused against her own. Up close, the apples of his cheeks were cherry-red and weather-beaten, his eyes a cool blue like the water that surrounded them. Serena was glad she'd dressed appropriately, in capri pants and sneakers, but still managed to clamber on board ungracefully. He led her to a small seating area at the stern and gestured vaguely around him.

"Welcome to my humble abode."

His voice was sandpaper-rough, like his hands.

"You live here?"

Serena had initially thought of the cruiser as being big and extravagant—a symbol of his wealth—but now that she knew it was his home, it seemed tiny.

As though reading her thoughts, Dolan said, "When my wife, Misty, passed, I sold the house and sunk everything I had into this little liveaboard." He grimaced. "Bad choice of phrasing, but it was the best thing I ever did."

He told her to take a seat and offered her a beer from a well-stocked cooler. Serena figured Dolan was the kind of man who felt most comfortable sharing war stories over a drink. She accepted and he twisted the tops off two bottles of Budweiser. A couple of paperbacks were stacked next to the cooler. A Robert Crais novel and one of her own: *Dead Before Dawn*.

Dolan noticed her noticing and a hint of a smile played on his lips as he took a pull from the cold beer. "Cynthia sold you as a world-famous mystery author," he said. "I wanted to see what all the fuss was about."

He didn't offer an opinion on her work even though a bookmark poking out from the pages suggested he was almost halfway through the novel.

Instead, he said, "So, you're writing a book about the Duprie family."

Serena's response echoed what she'd told Cynthia. "It's not a true crime book, it's a work of fiction. But, yes, their story is providing some of the inspiration. And, having looked into the Dupries some more, I'm intrigued."

Dolan stroked his heavy gray stubble. "You know, I always thought I might write a book about them one day. I guess you beat me to it."

"Why didn't you?"

He set the bottle at his feet and took a crumpled pack of Marlboro Reds and a cheap plastic lighter from his breast pocket. "A story needs a beginning, a middle, and an end. I only ever had the middle. I never found out what came before or after that night."

"What do you think happened?"

Dolan placed a cigarette between his lips and lit it. Blew out a plume of dirty gray smoke. "I think they were running from something—or someone. Hiding from their past. And it caught up with them."

"Why do you think that?" Serena asked.

"I spoke to a lot of people after they vanished. They all said the same thing. Nice couple but kept to themselves. People knew them without really knowing them. They were friendly without having any real friends. Bill didn't go for after-work drinks. Dani didn't have girlfriends over for dinner. The kid never invited friends from school to the house. That tells me that whatever trouble they were in, it started long before that night. Probably before they moved here. They didn't want anyone getting too close and there had to be a reason for that."

Serena told him her witness protection theory. Dolan shot it down immediately.

"If they'd been in the program when they landed in Seaton Point, they would have had new identities," he said. "That wasn't the case. I dug into Bill Duprie's background. Found a source at the tech company where he worked who got me a look at his résumé. Everything checked out. He went to school at Stanford, began his career in Silicon Valley, then had a bunch of other jobs. William Duprie was not an alias. Dani was more of a mystery; a home-maker, so no coworkers to pump for information. The other moms said she'd mentioned having a few part-time jobs in the past, but she never went into detail. Dani told them she'd been a stay-at-home mom since the kid came along."

Serena took a sip of beer and nodded. "Okay, so what if they went into witness protection later? As in, that night? That's why they disappeared. The Dupries witnessed a crime and had to leave in a hurry."

Dolan smoked and considered it for a moment. Then he shook his head. "The police chief, Don Raskin, never gave up on the case. He worked it hard, kept poking at it for years. I don't know for sure, but I reckon someone from the US Marshals would have had a quiet word in his ear and told him to stop looking if they'd gone into the program."

Serena gazed out at the water. A group of paddleboarders worked the waves. A whale-watching charter set off from the wharf. A nearby radio played "The Reflex" by Duran Duran. The scene reminded her of vacations in Key West as a kid. A wistful nostalgia washed over her, same as when she'd browsed those old newspaper articles.

"I read the stories you wrote about them," she said.

"The *Mary Celeste* one too?"

"Yes."

Dolan looked embarrassed. "That analogy was kind of bull-shit. The whole table-being-set-for-dinner thing when the ship was found abandoned, that wasn't true. It was a myth. But it's what people think of when they hear the name *Mary Celeste*—and it's what I thought of when I saw those photos. I wanted to get that sense of eeriness across to our readers."

Serena was surprised. "Wait—Raskin showed you the crime scene photos?"

Dolan crushed the cigarette butt into a metal tin. "He was desperate. He'd had no breaks in the case. I told him I needed something new to keep their names in the paper, so he showed me the photos."

He drained the beer bottle, cracked open a fresh one. "When you work the crime beat as long as I did, you see a lot of horrible shit; bear witness to all the awful things people do to each other. But something about those photos chilled me—especially the little girl's bedroom with the homework open on the desk—and I don't spook easily."

"I also read the article about their finances leading to a line of inquiry and the theory that they could have been heading for Mexico."

"I knew something had shown up in those bank statements, but Raskin wouldn't tell me what," Dolan said. "He said if the Dupries were involved in something big, he didn't want it all over the papers until he knew what he was dealing with. I tried the bank too, but the manager was a stick-up-the-ass, by-the-book type and refused to talk on or off the record."

"Did you ever find out?"

Dolan nodded. "Me and Raskin weren't ever what you'd call friends. He was a cop and I was a reporter and that's like oil and water—they don't mix. But, years later when we were both retired, we'd meet up occasionally for a beer. Talk shop, old cases, old stories. Raskin told me the wife had emptied their checking and savings accounts the day they vanished."

"How much?"

"Fifty grand."

Serena whistled. "I'm assuming the money wasn't at the house when the cops searched the place?"

"Not a single dollar."

"A ransom for the daughter who was kidnapped?" she suggested.

Dolan shrugged. "Or a drug deal went bad, and they fled to Mexico with all their cash. The money was clean, by the way. Bill Duprie had a good job, a big salary."

"Why drugs?" Serena asked doubtfully.

"Bill Duprie had a record. Possession of cocaine and drug driving after crashing his Beamer. This was back in the eighties, when all those yuppie-types were shoveling that shit up their noses. He'd been clean since then and there was no indication that he was involved in anything criminal, but . . ."

Dolan let the suggestion hang between them.

"You think he relapsed," Serena said. "Got in with a bad crowd and that led to a bad situation."

"Maybe. Who knows? It's one theory. There were lots of theories. Murder–suicide was another one. All three of them went over the bedroom balcony, just like Grady Hargreaves, only their bodies washed out to sea and were never found. There were sightings too. Tijuana, Nevada, San Francisco, all over the place . . . None of them ever came to anything."

"Do you think Don Raskin would speak to me?" Serena asked.

"Not unless you own a Ouija board."

"He's dead?"

She wasn't sure why she was surprised. If Raskin had been chief of police three decades ago, he would have been an old man by now.

"Died two years ago," Dolan confirmed. "He never gave up on looking for the truth, right up until the end. Reckoned he had a lead on an old case but wouldn't say any more about it, or even what case it was, but I always figured it was the Dupries he was talking about."

"But you never knew for sure?"

"Nope. A few days later they pulled his body out of the water." Dolan swiped a hand in a westerly direction. "A couple hundred yards that way."

"What happened?"

"He'd been drinking all evening in O'Malley's with Hank Macaulay. Decided to take a walk down by the marina on his own late at night. Three sheets to the wind, and I'm not talking about the sails on the boats down here." Dolan fixed Serena with his cold blue eyes. "A freak accident. Or, at least, that's what the cops said."

# 9

## SERENA

### NOW

Serena woke with a start.

Her heart hammered as she sat up in bed. What had torn her from sleep this time? The answer came to her quickly in the dark room, its echo still lingering at the edge of her consciousness.

A noise.

Loud.

Like a door slamming shut.

Had it been part of a dream? Or had she heard it for real?

Her imagination was likely in overdrive, she conceded, even when she was sleeping. When she'd returned from Patrick Dolan's boat, her head had been spinning with all the new nuggets of information.

The missing fifty grand.

Bill Duprie's criminal past.

Don Raskin's death.

Especially that last one.

Raskin had claimed he'd made a breakthrough in a case and was then found dead a few days later. It was clear Dolan didn't buy the accidental death verdict delivered by the cops—Raskin's old colleagues—even though he hadn't said as much. Dolan had brought the meeting to an end soon after and Serena had returned to the Cliff House and pondered awhile.

Then she'd spent the evening writing. Another couple of chapters in the bag. All good words. Even though Dolan had dismissed her witness protection theory, it was an angle she was exploring in the novel. A young girl who witnessed a terrible crime; her parents faced with an impossible choice. *Do they do the right thing and go to the police and potentially put their daughter in danger? Or do they say nothing and allow a criminal to roam free and strike again?* Decades later, intrepid investigator Layne Farraday had started picking apart the family's mysterious disappearance.

When Serena had finally climbed into bed, sleep had come quickly. Her dreams were haunted by the faces of Bill, Dani, and Charlotte, merging with macabre images of a wrecked corpse on the rocks and a bloated body being fished out of the water like a giant trout.

Now there was the noise that had woken her.

The lingering fragments of a dream, or something more sinister?

Serena reached for the lamp on the nightstand. In the dull ochre glow, she saw that the balcony doors were shut. The night was pitch-black beyond the glass, the sun yet to begin its ascent. The only sounds were the whooshing of the waves against the rocks and her pulse thrumming in her ears. Her phone screen told her it was just after three in the morning.

After practicing some breathing techniques she'd learned in a meditation class she'd attended with Margot after Michael's accident, Serena's heartbeat gradually slowed to a regular rhythm. But she still couldn't shake the sense of unease. She got out of bed. The soft light of the bedroom lamp illuminated the way as she started downstairs.

*Creeeeaaaak.*

Serena froze. Her heart leapt into her mouth. Then she realized she'd trodden on a creaky step and let out a nervous laugh. Jeez, her nerves were shot. She listened for a long moment, and when she was satisfied there had been no other sounds or movement in the house, she continued her descent in the half-light. The security chain was still in place and the front door was locked up tight. She peered out of one of the side windows, while flipping the switch for the porch lights.

Nothing happened.

The porch and the driveway and the road beyond were hidden in the shadows of the predawn night. She toggled the switch another couple of times with the same result. Then she hit the switch in the hallway and was bathed in sudden bright light. So not a power outage affecting only the first floor then.

After a moment's hesitation, Serena unhooked the security chain, unlocked the front door, and warily stepped outside onto the cold concrete of the porch. A cool breeze blew in from the ocean and she shivered in her pajamas and hugged her arms around her body for warmth. The sky was a canvas of black and gray and empty of stars. Not even a sliver of moon. Far off in the distance was a pinprick of light that she guessed was George Evans's house. Otherwise, it was too dark to see anything. Even so, she had the unnerving feeling that someone could see her, backlit against the light from the hallway.

"Hello?" she called out. "Is anyone there?"

Serena felt foolish. If someone *was* hiding in the scrubland, watching the house, watching *her,* they were hardly going to reveal themselves, were they? The only sound was the frenetic chirping of unseen crickets. She took another tentative step forward, and yelped in pain as something sharp speared the sole of her bare foot. She balanced on the other foot, lifted the wounded one, and plucked out a shard of glass. Bent down and noticed more broken glass directly beneath the porch light. Slivers of glass lay beneath the matching light too.

Both bulbs had shattered.

"What the . . . ?"

Serena went back inside and secured the door behind her, then hobbled to the kitchen where she found a first-aid kit under the sink. After cleaning and dressing the cut, she carried out an inspection of the kitchen and living area. The kitchen door was locked. Nothing appeared to be amiss. No items had been moved around. She retrieved a dustpan and brush from the utility closet in the hall. Took a deep, steadying breath and opened the front door. Quickly swept up the broken glass on the porch, and felt relief wash over her once she was safely back inside and the debris had been dispatched in the trash.

She drank a glass of water from the tap, turned off the lights, and returned to bed. Lay there for a while, staring at the ceiling, wondering what the hell was wrong with this house.

Had someone tampered with the porch lights, or was it simply a case of a blown fuse or some other innocent explanation?

Serena must have drifted off eventually, because when she opened her eyes again the bedroom was filled with daylight and there was a noise inside the house that wasn't dreamed or imagined.

The droning of a vacuum cleaner.

She was momentarily confused until she remembered it was Monday. Wanda Stockwell's day for housekeeping duties. But the woman wasn't supposed to be here until ten. Serena rubbed the sleep from her eyes and picked up her cell phone. Gasped when she saw it was almost eleven and that she'd overslept. Surprise rapidly gave way to embarrassment as she realized Wanda must have been dusting and cleaning—and now vacuuming the large rug in the living area—for almost an hour while Serena was still in bed. She threw off the covers and crossed the landing to the main bathroom, where she noticed Wanda had already replaced the towels with fresh ones. She peed, showered, and dressed quickly.

Downstairs, Wanda had finished vacuuming and was now on her knees polishing the glass on the coffee table, a plastic caddy stuffed full of cloths and cleaning products on the floor next to her. She wore a pink apron embroidered with the words "Stockwell Home Services" over her blouse. She spotted Serena hovering in the doorway.

"I hope I didn't wake you with the vacuum cleaner," she said. "I knocked on your bedroom door and there was no answer. I didn't want to disturb you, so I did the other upstairs rooms, then made a start down here. I'll change the bedsheets before I leave if that's okay?"

Serena's cheeks burned. "Yes, of course." Feeling the need to offer an explanation, she added, "I was working late and then had a very unsettled night. I don't usually sleep until mid-morning."

"No need to explain. Guests are free to come and go as they please."

Serena hesitated. "I also wanted to apologize for getting off on the wrong foot the other day."

Wanda batted away the apology like she was swatting a fly. "I'm the one who should be apologizing. My conduct was unprofessional . . ." She looked like she wanted to say something else, then shook her head and resumed the vigorous polishing.

Serena said, "Something strange happened last night."

"Oh?" The cloth stilled and Wanda stared at her. "Strange how?"

Was there a hint of fear in her eyes?

Serena told her about being woken in the night by a noise and then discovering the broken porch lightbulbs.

Wanda got up slowly from the floor, bones cracking audibly, and dusted off the knees of her slacks. She looked worried. "I think you should tell the police."

"Really?" Serena was surprised. "Isn't that a little extreme? I'm sure there's an innocent explanation."

But was she sure?

"I'm sure there is," Wanda agreed. "But you should make a report anyway. Ask Chief Beaumont to check it out. You'll feel better if you do."

"I'll think about it."

She debated telling Wanda about the other incidents too—finding the balcony doors open in the middle of the night, the wineglass and pen being in different places from where she thought she'd left them—then decided against it. She didn't want the woman to think she was crazy. There was no way anyone could have been inside the house. Unless . . .

"Who has keys to the Cliff House?" she asked.

"The guests and myself."

"No one else?"

"No."

"Not even the owner?"

Wanda considered. "Well, yes, I suppose they would have a set too. Although the Hargreaves family live out of state and never visit the property. Why?"

Serena didn't answer. Instead, she asked another question.

"Where does the locked door in the hallway lead to?"

"The basement."

"There's no key for that door on the set I was given."

"Guests don't have a key for the basement, and neither do I." Wanda gave Serena a pointed look, her lips a thin white line. "There's no reason for anyone to go snooping around down there."

*Snooping.*

It felt like something had shifted between them, like the tension from their first meeting was back again.

Wanda said, "You told me you weren't writing a book about the Dupries. But apparently you are."

Serena was starting to feel like a broken record.

"It's not about them directly," she said wearily. "It's a fictional novel about a missing family. I thought it would be beneficial to find out more about the Dupries as part of my research."

Serena had quizzed Hannah for information while dining at the Shrimp Shack, but she hadn't told her she was basing a book on the Dupries—so how did Wanda Stockwell know?

Then it dawned on her. Wanda had already been upstairs.

"Did you clean the office?"

Wanda's brow furrowed. "The office?"

"The small bedroom. I'm using it as a workplace."

"Oh, right. Yes, I did."

"So you saw the photo of Bill, Dani, and Charlotte, and thought I'd lied to you about them being the reason why I'm here. I promise, I knew nothing about them when I arrived in Seaton Point."

"I don't know what photo you're talking about," Wanda said defensively. "I didn't look through any of your work and I didn't touch anything on the desk. I dusted around everything."

"I'm talking about the photo taped to the wall," Serena said. "You can't miss it."

"I didn't see any photo."

"The family portrait? From the newspaper clipping?"

Wanda gave her a blank look.

68

Serena sighed, exasperated. "Come with me and I'll show you."

They made their way upstairs to the second floor. Serena pushed open the door of the office—and stopped dead. The blood in her veins turned to ice.

"Wait . . . *what?*"

On the desk was the laptop, yellow notebook, pen, and printed newspaper stories. Above the laptop, the wall was bare.

The photo was gone.

# 10

---

## RUBY

---

## SUMMER 1983

Ruby and River made a great team. They even *sounded* good together. Ruby and River. River and Ruby. He mowed the lawn and trimmed the rosebushes and fixed the old barn's rickety door, while she dusted the ornaments and polished the furniture and laundered and ironed.

Grandma Pearl was frailer than when Ruby had last visited. Her soft plumpness had melted away to reveal a sharper, skinnier frame, her shoulders were stooped, and her hair was now more snow-white than fire-red. Like Ruby's mom, Pearl had never married, and her pregnancy had been an accident. But unlike Coral, she'd been an older mom, who'd long given up hope of having kids, and had welcomed the unexpected blessing. Ruby was glad to note that, despite her advanced years, Grandma Pearl's eyes hadn't lost any of their sparkle.

"You know, I only pay River to do odd jobs twice a month," she remarked one day, a few weeks after Ruby had arrived in town. "It's all I can afford and, even then, it's nowhere near enough for all the work he does for me." She smiled mischievously. "But I can't help noticing he's been at the ranch house almost every day since you got here."

"I'm sure he just enjoys helping you out," Ruby said, her face burning like she had a fever. "Oh, and your cherry pie too! That'll keep him coming back."

Grandma Pearl winked. "The pie's good but it's not that good, sweetheart. And there's only so much pruning my rosebushes can take."

The truth was, Ruby was crazy about River Henderson. She'd had crushes before but nothing like this. He was all she thought about. She even dreamed about him. Felt her heart leap every time his truck pulled into the driveway. She hadn't dared hope he might feel the same way about her, but Grandma Pearl was right. He *had* been spending a lot of time at the house . . .

A couple of days later, River was back, up a ladder, clearing the roof gutters. Ruby sat cross-legged on the big swing seat on the porch, trying to read a book, trying not to watch him while he worked. When he was done, he flopped down beside her. The armpits and neckline of his t-shirt were darkened by perspiration and Ruby would usually find being that close to someone else's sweat disgusting—but not his. It was kind of . . . hot?

"What're you reading?" he asked.

The book was face down on her lap and she picked it up and showed him. *Christine* by Stephen King.

River studied the cover. "The title looks like a car logo from the fifties," he said. "Very cool. Is it about cars?"

She smiled. "Kind of. It's about a '58 Plymouth Fury called Christine that's possessed by supernatural forces."

"Sounds freaky. You're a big reader, huh? I've noticed you spend a lot of time out here with your books."

71

Ruby nodded. "I love the way stories transport you to a totally different time and place; how they can provide an escape from the real world for a while." Realizing how serious that sounded, she added, "And I especially like horror books because I guess I like to be scared shitless."

There had been no books in the apartment when Ruby was growing up—not Coral's thing at all—but Grandma Pearl had a shelf stuffed full of dog-eared old paperbacks. Ruby had blasted through half of them during that last summer she'd spent here. When she'd returned to Portland, she'd gotten a library card and read every Judy Blume novel she could get her hands on, which had certainly been an eye-opening experience.

"Do you like to read?" she asked River.

"Nah, I prefer to work with my hands, do practical tasks. I like messing around with car engines and figure I might try to line up a job at an auto repair shop when summer is over." He hesitated, suddenly awkward. "Pammy likes to read, though. Not scary stuff like you. More like romances."

Ruby frowned. "Pammy? Who's Pammy?"

"You remember Pammy, right? She used to hang out with us too when we were kids."

Pamela Gleeson. Ruby had forgotten all about her. The third member of their gang, although a less enthusiastic participant in most of their escapades. Pretty, petite, and naturally sun-kissed blonde. Didn't like being dirty or climbing trees or fishing or getting her hair wet swimming in the lake. Pamela Gleeson had mostly lazed around the yard sunbathing and, yes, reading books. Old tween romances by the likes of Rosamond du Jardin and Janet Lambert, if Ruby remembered correctly. Pamela's and River's moms were best friends, which is why their kids were buddies too, although Ruby didn't recall her ever being referred to as "Pammy" back then.

"Sure, I remember her."

"She's uh, my . . . Well, I guess you could say we've been dating for a while."

Ruby felt like Cujo, the rabid Saint Bernard from another Stephen King novel, had just clamped its teeth around her heart and ripped it into tiny, bloody pieces.

"Oh, that's nice," she said, returning her attention to *Christine*. Ruby tried desperately to hold back the hot tears that threatened to spill over; tried to act like she couldn't care less that River had a girlfriend. Of course he did, a catch like him. How stupid of her to even think she stood a chance.

River didn't return to the ranch house for a whole week, and Ruby was starting to think he was never coming back. Her heart pounded like a drum when she finally heard his truck trundling along the dirt track, and she berated herself for still caring. She was sitting under the old maple tree, reading as usual, and acting like she hadn't noticed him. River dropped onto the patch of dried grass next to her, close enough for her to feel his body heat.

"What're you reading?" he asked.

Ruby showed him the cover. *Phantoms* by Dean Koontz. Dolores at the library back home had allowed her to borrow six books for the whole summer, even though the limit was thirty days. Reckoned Ruby would like Koontz, seeing as she was such a big fan of King. Dolores was right. The story had provided a welcome distraction from Ruby's broken heart—until now.

"Another scary book?" River asked.

"More weird than scary, but still spectacularly good all the same."

"I think you're spectacularly good, Ruby Bryant," he blurted out. He shook his head, embarrassed. "Wow, how corny was that line?"

Ruby was speechless. Before she could answer, River leaned over and kissed her. His lips were soft, his tongue gently probing, and it felt like a thousand fireworks had gone off in her belly. It was just as well she was sitting down, otherwise her legs might have given out from under her. When they finally pulled apart, she felt slightly breathless and lightheaded.

"What about Pamela?" she said.

Ruby refused to call her Pammy.

"We broke up," River said. "I've been wanting to kiss you since the first moment I saw you get off that bus."

"Is that why you stayed away this past week?" Ruby asked. "Because you were breaking up with Pamela?"

River nodded and smiled wryly. "And trying to smooth things over with my mom."

"Your mom?"

"I think she was more upset by the breakup than Pammy was. Always figured we'd get together, get married, have kids one day. She's made it clear she doesn't approve of my choices."

Ruby wasn't surprised. Tonya Henderson, with her honeyed hair and too much blue eyeshadow and frosted pink lipstick, had never been her biggest fan. Always wrinkling her nose at Ruby's skinned elbows and muddy knees and messy braids as a kid. But all thoughts of Tonya Henderson and Pamela Gleeson evaporated as River pulled her close and kissed her again.

Ruby and River were inseparable from then on. They hiked and biked around Lake Tye Park, made out at the beach a lot, ate burgers and pizzas at Jeno's, and saw *National Lampoon's Vacation* and *Risky Business* and the movie adaptation of *Cujo* on the big screen.

On her eighteenth birthday, Grandma Pearl presented Ruby with a velvet box containing a gold necklace with a red stone at the center that shimmered under the kitchen light.

"It's a real ruby," she said, a tiny mother-of-pearl pendant hanging around her own neck. "I saved a long time for this day. A precious gem for a precious gem."

Tears streamed down Ruby's face as Grandma Pearl lifted her hair and fastened the delicate chain in place. There had been no gift or card or even a phone call from her mom. Coral had been given a coral necklace for her own eighteenth but had never worn it, dismissing the jewelry as cheap junk.

It was Grandma Pearl who'd wanted to carry on the tradition of women in the family being named after gemstones. Ruby's mom had planned on naming her daughter Brittany, and Ruby guessed she hadn't cared enough to argue when Grandma Pearl had suggested an alternative.

"I should have called your mom Jet or Onyx," Grandma Pearl said when Coral didn't call to wish Ruby a happy birthday. "That woman has a heart as black as coal."

That night, River shyly handed over a gift wrapped in tissue paper. It was a first edition of *The Shining* and Ruby cried again. More happy tears. Then he took her by the hand and led her into the barn. They made out with an intensity and hunger that felt different from all the other times.

"Are you sure?" he whispered, his eyes locked on hers.

Ruby nodded. She'd never been surer of anything in her life. He slowly undressed her until all she was wearing was the ruby necklace. They lay on a bed of hay, and he moved gently on top of her, and it was both painful and amazing. Afterwards, they held each other, trembling, skin against skin, hearts racing, slick with sweat. Through the hole in the barn roof, the velvet night sky was filled with a million clear stars. River told her he loved her. She loved him too. Of course she did. Ruby thought she might explode with happiness. She wanted to stay here forever, wrapped in River Henderson's arms.

Ruby didn't want to think about what would happen now that summer was coming to an end.

# 11

## SERENA

### NOW

The Seaton Point police station was located in the heart of downtown, in a neat single-story terracotta building with a red stucco roof and manicured front lawn, right across the street from McDonald's and Starbucks. The carport reserved for six cruisers was empty, save for an unmarked black Ford Escape.

Serena had decided to take Wanda Stockwell's advice and pay a visit to the cops, even though there had been even more tension between them by the time the housekeeper left the Cliff House earlier. Wanda was still adamant that she'd never seen the newspaper photo of the Dupries—which left Serena with three possible scenarios:

One: Wanda Stockwell was lying. She'd spotted the picture while dusting in the office and had ripped it from the wall in a fit of rage, and now didn't want to admit what she'd done. Serena had waited until Wanda was gone, then she'd rifled through the trash bag that the housekeeper had taken from the kitchen to the garbage receptacle outside on the patio. But she had found only empty food packets, soiled paper napkins, and the bloodied cotton ball she'd used to clean the wound on her foot the night before. No discarded family photo. Which proved nothing. Wanda could have hidden it in the pocket of her slacks or stuffed it inside her cleaning caddy to dispose of later.

Two: Serena was losing her mind. The guilt and grief over Michael's death, the stress of her writer's block, the lack of sleep, and the strange history of the Cliff House had all led to her mind playing tricks on her. The sticky residue on the wall from the Scotch tape confirmed that she *had* taped the photo there. But maybe she'd taken it down herself and forgotten, or had torn it from the wall while sleepwalking. But she'd never sleepwalked before, and the picture wasn't anywhere she might conceivably have put it.

Three: Someone else—an unknown third party—had been inside the house and stolen the photo.

If it had been an isolated incident, without all the other weird shit that had been going on since she'd arrived in Seaton Point, her money would have been firmly on Wanda Stockwell. But add in the threatening note, items being moved around, doors left open, smashed porch lights, and strange noises in the night, and Serena was veering wildly between options two and three.

On her way into town, George Evans had been on his porch again, brandishing the binoculars and notebook, like a one-man Neighborhood Watch. Already pissed, Serena had been tempted to lean on the Mustang's horn or flip him the bird—give him something to write in his stupid book—but figured she should try to be a responsible adult instead.

Even so, the sight of the old-timer had got her thinking about the lights being on in his house well after three a.m. Maybe he always kept a lamp burning at night or he was an insomniac or he needed to get up five times a night to pee. Or maybe he was up to no good. A mile wasn't too far to walk between the two properties, and he'd be familiar with the terrain. But why would George Evans be creeping around outside her vacation rental?

Then again, why did he watch her car through his binoculars every time she drove past?

Serena pushed open the door to the SPPD building and was hit by a blast of cool air when she stepped inside. The waiting area comprised two rows of five black plastic chairs nailed to the floor—all unoccupied—either side of a low wooden coffee table with no reading material. A giant plastic cheese plant dominated one corner of the room; a water cooler stood in the other. The bulletin board was filled with overlapping posters and flyers but none of them was a faded thirty-year-old "Missing" poster for the Dupries.

A young woman sat behind the front desk, tapping at a computer keyboard with cerise acrylic nails that should have been too long for the task. The light tapping was the only sound in the room. No raging drunks being carted off to the cells, or victims of crime demanding attention, or phones ringing with urgent calls. It was quieter than the library.

The woman was pretty, with razorblade cheekbones and cotton-candy pink hair teased into loose curls and the most mesmerizing blue eyes that Serena had ever seen. Serena didn't think she was a cop, unless she was a super-stylish detective with a taste for tight leather pants and off-the-shoulder designer tops.

Behind the woman were four empty desks stacked with files and a closed office door with "Chief Beaumont" engraved on the silver metal sign affixed to the front, the window blinds pulled tightly shut.

Serena hesitantly approached the front desk.

"Good afternoon," the maybe-receptionist said pleasantly. "How may I help you?"

"Uh, I'm staying at the Cliff House, up on Cliffside Drive, and . . ."

And what? Had there even been a crime committed? Serena wasn't sure.

Before she could say anything else, the woman's bright blue eyes widened, and she broke into a beaming smile.

"You're the famous author? Serena Winters? I was hoping I'd bump into you at some point." She opened a drawer and produced a copy of *Murder After Midnight* and waved it in the air. "I've been reading it on my lunch breaks, and I'm totally hooked. Layne Farraday is such a badass!"

"Thank you," Serena said.

She was starting to wish she'd never come here.

The paperback had been purchased from a store, rather than borrowed from the local library, and the woman asked Serena to sign it and dedicate it to "Kelly."

"So, what can I do for you, Ms. Winters?" Kelly asked, once the book and Sharpie had both been returned to the drawer.

Serena told her about the note that had been left on her car, and the loud noise she'd heard in the middle of the night, and the broken porch lights, and the missing photo. She decided to leave out the other stuff—the balcony door and the pen and the wineglass—because she couldn't be certain those weren't down to her own forgetfulness.

Kelly glanced up from the notes she was taking. "Was the photo frame valuable?"

"Oh, no. There was no frame. It was a printout from a newspaper that I'd taped to the wall of my office."

"Okay." Kelly's brow puckered briefly in confusion. "Have any valuables been taken from the property, such as cash, credit cards, jewelry, or electronic devices?"

"Um, no. The only thing that's missing is the photo."

"The one from the newspaper?"

"Yes. Look, I shouldn't have come here," Serena said, feeling foolish. "I'm wasting your time."

Kelly smiled reassuringly. "You're not wasting anyone's time. I'll pass on the information you've given me to Chief Beaumont and ask him to stop by the house, check the place over for you."

"The chief of police?" Serena was aghast. "I really don't think there's any need for—"

"Ms. Winters," Kelly interrupted firmly. "You're a visitor to Seaton Point and it's important that our visitors feel safe and protected while they're here. Chief Beaumont will come see you, no problem at all."

Serena thanked her and was about to leave when Kelly spoke again.

"I heard you're writing a book about the Duprie family."

Serena suppressed a sigh. Not again. "Sort of."

"I'd totally read it," Kelly said enthusiastically. "I love all that true crime stuff. *My Favorite Murder, Serial, The Staircase, The Tinder Swindler* . . . You name it, I've binged it. I've always been kind of disappointed that no one ever made a podcast or documentary about the Dupries."

"How did you know about the novel I'm writing?"

Kelly laughed. "It's a tight-knit community. Word gets around and people talk. Especially when a famous writer is in town."

Serena felt uncomfortable, knowing people were talking about her. But maybe Kelly would have information about the Dupries, seeing as she was a self-confessed true crime nut who worked in the local police station.

"Do you know much about the case?" she asked.

"Mostly just what I've read online and what people have said over the years. I was a couple years younger than the daughter, so we weren't friends or anything, and I don't really remember the family at all. But, like everyone else, I've heard all the theories."

"What did you hear?"

Kelly held up a hot-pink-tipped finger for each one. "Murder–suicide. Kidnapped by the mob. Robbed a bank and disappeared with all the cash . . . Personally, I think the cult theory is the most likely."

Serena remembered a cult being mentioned in some of the Reddit posts, but had written it off as nonsense.

Kelly must have noticed her doubtful expression because she hastily added, "The cult is real. It's not some urban myth. It really exists. Cedarwood Farm. Just outside the town."

"And it's definitely a cult?" Serena wasn't convinced. It didn't sound very cult-like. *Cedarwood Farm.* It sounded quite . . . pleasant.

Kelly shrugged. "That's what folks around here say. And I know for a fact that Bill Duprie spent a lot of time there in the months leading up to the family's disappearance."

"How do you know that?"

"My dad told me. He saw it with his own eyes—Bill Duprie's white Ford Taurus going down the dirt road to that farm a bunch of times. Once, he thought the daughter might have been in the car too. I know what you're thinking, just local gossip, right? But the cops must have been interested enough to head on out to Cedarwood Farm and question the people who run the place."

"Did anything ever come of it?" Serena asked, more interested now. Maybe the crazy cult theory wasn't quite so crazy after all.

"I don't think so," Kelly admitted. "Chief Raskin didn't have enough evidence to get a search warrant and those places are very secretive and notoriously difficult to gain access to. That doesn't mean they weren't involved, though."

"I guess so."

Kelly leaned across the desk, her blue eyes shining. "You ask me, the Duprie family never really left Seaton Point. I think they've been hiding at Cedarwood Farm all this time."

# 12

## SERENA

## NOW

Serena sat in front of her laptop in the office, trying to avoid looking at the blank section of wall where the missing photo had been, focusing her efforts instead on the words she was trying to write.

She replayed the conversation with Kelly over in her mind again. Could the Dupries really have been involved with a cult? It seemed unlikely but, assuming Kelly's father was telling the truth, why had Bill Duprie been spending so much time at Cedarwood Farm?

A loud double chime echoing throughout the house jolted Serena from her thoughts. She needed a moment to figure out what the hell the noise was.

The doorbell.

She realized it was the first time she'd heard it. Another realization followed swiftly on its heels. Other than Wanda Stockwell, who had her own key, Serena had had no visitors to the Cliff House.

Just like the Dupries.

She made her way downstairs and opened the front door and was momentarily puzzled to find a vaguely familiar man standing on the porch. He was tall and broad-shouldered. Good-looking, with a square jaw, fair hair cut short at the sides and longer on top, and nice cocoa-colored eyes. It took a beat for Serena to place him. The diner from Susie's Shrimp Shack. The coconut shrimp guy. Or Jack, as he'd probably prefer to be known. Or Police Chief Beaumont? Instead of the blue jeans and plaid shirt he'd been wearing the other day, he was now dressed in neatly pressed forest-green pants and a matching shirt with the sleeves rolled up, showing off toned, tanned forearms with little sun-bleached blond hairs. A thick black leather gun belt was looped around his narrow waist. Behind him, an SUV police cruiser was parked next to the Mustang.

"*You're* Chief Beaumont?" she asked.

"Guilty as charged."

He grinned and she was hit by that sense of familiarity again—same as when she'd first met him at the restaurant—but the sensation was fleeting, like trying to remember a fast-fading dream. Then the grin was replaced by a concerned frown.

"My office manager, Kelly Dunne, said you reported having some problems at the house?"

"That's right."

"Is now a good time to talk me through what's been going on?"

"Sure. Come on in."

Serena ushered him inside and led him through the house and into the kitchen. "Can I get you something to drink? Coffee? Soda?"

"I'm good just now."

They both sat at the kitchen table across from each other, and Beaumont removed a small notepad and pen from his breast pocket.

"So, you believe someone's been harassing you?" he prompted, opening the pad to a fresh page.

"It started the first day I arrived in Seaton Point," Serena explained. "The same day we met at the restaurant. I went for a walk after dinner, then found a note slipped under my windshield wiper when I returned to the parking lot. It was handwritten and said: *Leave town now*."

"Do you still have the note?"

Serena shook her head. "I trashed it there and then. Assumed it was kids pranking a tourist. Filming it for TikTok or just doing it for shits and giggles."

She told him about the gang of teens with skateboards who had been hanging around the parking lot earlier.

Beaumont said, "I know the group you mean. I have to say, the skateboarders are pretty good kids, they've never been in any trouble. I really don't think they would have been behind the note."

"Have any other visitors to the town reported receiving threatening messages?"

He shook his head. "No, this isn't a problem we've had before. Not until now. Do you want to talk me through what else has happened?"

Serena quickly filled Beaumont in. He listened, jotted down some notes, then asked if he could look around. He did a recce of the inside of the property and then the grounds outside. He found a box of spare lightbulbs in the utility closet and, when he returned to the kitchen, reported that the porch lights were working again.

"The bulbs had blown," he said.

"Both at the same time?" Serena asked doubtfully.

"I'm no electrician, but I guess it can happen. When you hit the switch and send a power surge, it's possible it could blow both together."

Beaumont also confirmed what she'd already known—that there was no way to access the house other than through the front door, kitchen door, and windows, or the front-facing bedroom window on the second floor.

Serena said, "I don't use that bedroom, so the window is never open. And I always fasten the security chain in place on the front door whenever I lock up."

Beaumont rubbed his stubble thoughtfully. "So the kitchen is the most likely point of entry for an intruder. And probably the door leading off the patio, because those windows would be a tight squeeze for anyone bigger than a child."

"That would make sense," Serena agreed. She shivered despite the heat coming in through the windows from the late-afternoon sun.

Beaumont unlocked the kitchen door, took a Maglite from his belt, and crouched down to inspect the lock. "No indication that it's been jimmied or even picked. It's a puzzling one all right."

"It's been driving me crazy." Serena got up from where she was still sitting at the table, needing something to do. "I'm going to put some coffee on. Would you like one now?"

"Please. Cream, no sugar."

She got to work with the coffee maker, as Beaumont returned to the table. While she waited for the water to drip down through the coffee filter, she said, "Have any other guests had problems while staying here? People creeping around the house? Things going missing?"

"No, you're the first."

"How long has the Cliff House been a vacation rental?"

Beaumont thought about it. "A few years, I think."

Serena wondered if he believed her or thought she was crazy or making it all up. A writer trying to live inside her own dramatic story. She filled two mugs, added cream to one, and set them on the kitchen table. Dropped wearily back into the chair.

"So, why me? What's so special about me?"

Beaumont shook his head. "Beats me."

But Serena thought she knew the answer—she was likely the only guest who'd decided to poke around into the missing family who used to live at the house. The only one trying to dig up the past, as Wanda Stockwell had put it.

"One thing's for sure," she said. "It's clear that I'm not wanted here."

Beaumont smiled kindly. "I don't think that's true at all." Then he surprised her by saying, "I know one person who's pleased you're here. My son."

"Your son?" she asked, bewildered.

"You met him when you first got here. Jody. He works at Dale's Rent-A-Car."

Now Serena knew why Beaumont had seemed so familiar. That grin. It was almost identical to the surfer kid's, just not quite as megawatt bright.

"I should have guessed. I can see the family resemblance."

He nodded, pleased by the comment. "Jody got a good bonus from his boss, Dale, thanks to your long-term rental and you opting for one of the premium selections. Both Dale and Jody were stoked, apparently. That was Jody's word, not mine." Then he added, "You've met his mom too."

"I have?"

"Hannah. At the Shrimp Shack."

Serena felt heat rise to her cheeks and wasn't sure why. She tried to mask the blush by drinking some coffee even though it was too hot and scalded her tongue.

"Oh, right," she said casually. "I didn't realize you were together."

"We're not," Beaumont said quickly. "We had a summer fling twenty years ago and Jody was the result—and the best thing that ever happened to me—but it was never going to work out between us. We've remained good friends. Hannah is married, has two other kids with her husband, Antonio."

A thought occurred to Serena. "So Wanda Stockwell is Jody's grandmother?"

Which made Wanda and the chief of police practically family. Serena was glad she hadn't mentioned any doubts she had about the housekeeper or made any accusations against her.

Beaumont nodded. "As well as his part-time job at Dale's, he also helps out his grandma at Stockwell Home Services. Grocery shopping, any repairs that need doing, that kind of thing. He's a good kid."

The number of folks who could have access to the other set of keys to the Cliff House had just potentially tripled—Wanda, Hannah, and Jody. Maybe even Antonio, the husband. Serena kept that thought to herself. Instead, she steered the subject onto the Dupries.

"You may have heard already that I'm working on a novel while I'm staying here," she said. "That's the reason I rented the Cliff House for the summer. A kind of writing retreat. It's about a missing family, so I've been doing some research into the Dupries, who vanished from this house, and I wonder if that's maybe the reason why I'm being . . . targeted."

Beaumont frowned. "I don't see why. That family's been missing for decades."

"Have there been any follow-ups over the years? Are you still investigating their disappearance?"

"The case is technically still open and, of course, we'll investigate any new leads that we get, but realistically it's colder than a crateful of Coors in an igloo."

"What about your predecessor, Chief Raskin? Did he make any big breakthroughs at all?"

"Not that I'm aware of. Raskin and I would speak about the case occasionally, bounce around some ideas and theories, but there was no new information."

Serena studied Beaumont's face. She didn't think he was lying. Maybe Patrick Dolan had gotten it wrong about Raskin's exciting new lead being related to the Dupries.

"Did Raskin interview the cult about the disappearances?"

Beaumont chuckled. "The cult?"

"The folks at Cedarwood Farm."

"Maybe. Raskin spoke to a lot of people. I'd need to check the file."

"So, you do still have the file?" Serena asked.

"Yes, although it's probably in storage. I'm not sure cases that far back would be digitized and on the computer system." He peered at her over the rim of his mug with mock suspicion. "Why?"

"Could I see it?"

He laughed and shook his head. "Nice try. But not gonna happen."

"Why not? You said it yourself: they vanished decades ago. Where's the harm in having a look?"

"Like I said, it's still technically a live case. Plus, there's lots of confidential information contained in that file, such as names and addresses of witnesses."

"Yeah, I guess so," Serena conceded. Then she asked hopefully, "But could you let me pick your brains? Tell me only the information that you feel would be appropriate to share?"

Beaumont drained the last of his coffee and stood up. "As much as having my brains picked sounds delightful, I'm afraid it's time for me to go. I'm on duty until ten and have some other calls to carry out."

"Another time?"

"Let me think about it, okay?" He took a business card from his pocket and offered it to her. "My cell phone number is on there. If you have any more problems here at the house, give me a call. I'll come check it out straightaway."

Serena took the card. "Thank you. I will."

Beaumont said, "I noticed the property has no home security system or cameras. You should consider asking the owners to upgrade their security. Get some cameras installed. It's pretty isolated up here and I'm sure their guests would feel safer."

Any requests would have to go through Wanda Stockwell, and Serena still wasn't sure if she could trust the woman.

"I guess I could ask, although it could take a while to arrange. I'm not sure how hands-on the owners are or if they have much to do with the day-to-day running of the place."

Beaumont thought for a moment, then said, "If you're willing to spend a little money yourself, you could try a trail camera?"

"A trail camera? What's that?"

"It's a weatherproof motion-activated camera that's used in remote areas to capture images and video of wildlife. Works at night as well as in daylight hours. It can be discreetly attached to, say, a tree trunk, so it wouldn't cause any damage or make any permanent changes to the property. Let's go take a look."

Serena followed Beaumont outside. They crossed the patio, walked past the barbecue and pizza oven and outdoor furniture, and went down a couple of steps onto the natural terrain, dry grass and twigs rustling and snapping under their feet. The sky had deepened from cornflower to navy. Beaumont strode over to a cluster of tall fir trees and patted one of them.

"If you strapped a trail camera to this bad boy's trunk, it should provide a good view of the patio and kitchen door. They're not really meant for security purposes, but it could give you some peace of mind."

Serena nodded grimly. It was a good idea. The camera might capture nothing more sinister than a curious coyote or a hungry bobcat.

Or it could provide hard evidence of something—or someone—more dangerous.

# 13

## SERENA

## NOW

Tuesday morning.

The dirt track leading to Cedarwood Farm was so inconspic-uous that Serena drove past it twice. She found it on the third attempt, located just off the main highway, about a quarter-mile beyond a roadside sign declaring: *You are now leaving Seaton Point—come back soon!*

Serena was tempted to stamp on the gas pedal and keep on going. Leave this town in her rearview mirror and not look back. But her curiosity was stronger than her desire to flee, and the need for answers won out.

The single-lane track was rocky and uneven, and the Mustang bounced along it like a fairground bumper car. She reduced her speed to almost a crawl. Jody's boss wouldn't be so stoked if she wrecked the Ford's suspension. Thirty-foot-tall fir trees lined the path, and with the top down the air was heavy with the scent of dried bark and wildflowers. Even though the highway wasn't too far behind her, the roar of traffic had faded completely and all she heard now was birdsong.

She had googled Cedarwood Farm before setting off. As one might expect from a super-secretive cult, there wasn't a whole lot of information to be found online. Of course, they didn't call themselves a cult. Cedarwood Farm was described as an "intentional community," a place to enhance spiritual and meditation practices. They were not currently accepting new members and rarely accepted visitors. Serena didn't like her chances of getting past the front gates, which loomed large and imposing up ahead.

The grand wooden double gates sat between two ornate pebbled pillars. A six-foot fence disappeared into the thickness of the trees and presumably ringed the entire perimeter of the property. A metal intercom box was attached to the gate. Serena didn't spot any cameras, but she was betting they were there, discreet and camouflaged. Not unlike the trail camera she had ordered from Amazon after Beaumont had left the night before.

Serena got out of the car and pushed the button on the intercom. Waited. No response. She pressed again, holding the button down longer this time. A click was followed by a burst of static and then a tinny-sounding female voice which uttered a single word.

"Yes?"

"Um, my name is Serena Winters and I'm a writer—"

The tinny voice interrupted. "I'm sorry, but we don't give interviews to journalists."

"I'm not a journalist. I'm a novelist. I'd like to speak to someone about Bill Duprie."

There was a pause and another crackle of static. Then, "Please wait a moment."

It was a long moment.

Serena was debating whether to press the intercom button again or return to the car and get the hell out of there, when the gates started slowly swinging inward. She got back behind the wheel, briefly questioned whether the visit was a good idea, then started the car and drove through. Once she was clear, the gates immediately closed behind her.

The dirt track led into a dusty, sunbaked clearing that was being used as a parking lot. Serena parked next to the other cars: two rusty pickup trucks, and a station wagon with wood side panels that looked so old Bill Duprie could have been driving it the night he disappeared. The gleaming Mustang stood out like a tiara at a wake. Gaudy and inappropriate in the surroundings.

Beyond the clearing lay a forested area of several acres with a half-dozen large log cabins sprinkled around a huge ranch-style house. Serena got out of the car and headed for the house, which she assumed to be the intentional community's main hub.

A rakish man with snow-white hair scraped back into a ponytail and too-big jeans cinched tightly by a worn leather belt was up a ladder carrying out repairs to the roof of one of the cabins. He watched her with open curiosity but didn't say anything. When she'd almost reached the ranch house, the front door opened, and a woman who was probably in her seventies gracefully descended the steps to greet her.

"Ms. Winters?"

Even without the static and tinniness, Serena was certain it was the same voice she'd heard over the intercom. The woman extended a hand for Serena to shake, her skin buttery smooth and her long slim fingers adorned with silver and gemstone rings.

"I'm Mariposa," she said, her voice soft and serene. "Cedarwood Farm's identified leader."

She was dressed in loose cream linen pants and a yellow linen top and white Birkenstocks, and could have been mistaken for a senior on a cruise. Her makeup was light over an unblemished and remarkably unwrinkled complexion, and her silver braided hair almost reached her waist. Like the man up the ladder, she wore regular attire. No sign of matching black sweatpants and white Nike sneakers like those worn by the Heaven's Gate members, or any other weird uniforms.

Mariposa gestured to a table and chairs on the porch. "Come sit, and let's talk."

They climbed the wooden steps that creaked and groaned but held firm, and settled into wicker seats made more comfortable by crocheted throws and pillows in cheerful rainbow hues. A young brunette emerged from the house and asked if they would like anything to drink. She wore a floral sundress that fell just below the knee and strappy flat sandals. Again—regular, everyday clothes.

"I'm afraid we're all out of Kool-Aid," Mariposa deadpanned, as though reading Serena's thoughts. "But you should try the passionflower tea. It'll do wonders for alleviating any stress that you're experiencing."

Serena hesitated, then accepted. The younger woman went back inside.

"You're a novelist," Mariposa stated. "You write a fictional mystery series. And a very successful one it is too. So, why the interest in Bill Duprie?"

Serena looked at her in surprise.

"I googled you," Mariposa said.

"You have internet here?"

The woman smiled, amused. "We do."

Serena told her about renting the Cliff House for the summer while writing her next novel and discovering the house's tragic past. How, at first, she'd been intrigued, excited to learn about the mystery attached to the property.

"And now?"

Serena realized it was now about more than just a novel, about more than solving a mystery. Something had shifted when she'd first seen that photo of Bill, Dani, and Charlotte in the *Seaton Point*

*Sentinel.* This was real life—real *lives*—and she needed to know what had happened to those people.

"I want to know the truth."

Mariposa nodded thoughtfully. "And you think you'll find the truth here?"

"There are people in Seaton Point who think so. They say that Bill Duprie and his family could have been hiding out at Cedarwood Farm all this time."

"Would it be so bad if they were? Returned to the land, free of the stresses of modern life, self-sufficient, healthy, happy . . ."

From their elevated position, Serena could see hoop-house greenhouses, an easel and canvas set up among a garden of wild-flowers, and, through the trees, glimpses of a lake shimmering in the sunlight.

Maybe the old hippy had a point.

Because that's exactly what Cedarwood Farm appeared to be. One of the remaining California hippy communes from a generation ago that was still clinging onto the idea of peace, love, and harmony. Not a cult. But somewhere to escape to all the same.

"Are the Dupries here?" she asked.

"No."

The brunette returned just then with a tray holding two steaming cups, which she carefully placed on the table. Mariposa thanked her and she left quickly and quietly.

The tea's aroma was enticing, and the taste was even better. Serena took a long drink and almost immediately felt the tension that had been bunching up her muscles begin to loosen. Like drinking a large glass of Chablis but without the fuzzy head.

"Are you sure it's only passionflower in this tea?" she said.

"It's good, isn't it? I'll give you some to take home. The tea will help you."

Serena gave her a quizzical look. "Help me with what?"

"There's a tension in your shoulders and sadness in your eyes. You're wound up tighter than a coiled spring. Something is clearly troubling you."

Serena didn't know what to say.

Then Mariposa added, "It was the same with Bill."

"Something was troubling him?"

The older woman stared off into the distance, or maybe she was gazing into the past, dusting off old memories. "Yes, I believe so."

"What?"

Mariposa took a sip of tea. "We know what the townspeople say about us," she said. "That we're a cult. That we brainwash people and keep them locked up here. But those big wooden gates are to keep the looky-loos and trespassers out, not to keep our members in. Our residents are free to come and go as they please and some of them do. But this is private land, and we are a private community." She fixed Serena with a firm look. "I don't want anything you see or hear today to end up in the pages of a book. Is that understood?"

Serena nodded. "Understood." Guitar music drifted from one of the cabins. An old Beatles song. One of the George Harrison ones. "Did Chief Raskin come here and interview the residents after the family's disappearance?" she asked.

A small smile tugged at the edges of Mariposa's mouth. "He tried. Didn't get beyond the gates. We don't recognize outside law enforcement at Cedarwood Farm. We govern ourselves by community consensus."

"And Chief Raskin just accepted that?"

"He had no choice. There were no grounds to question our residents or search our property and land."

"Was Bill Duprie a member of the community?"

"Not officially."

"But he did visit?"

"Yes," Mariposa confirmed. "I already told you he was a troubled soul. He sought us out for the purposes of peace and wellbeing."

"What was troubling him?"

"That I don't know. The pressures of his job, perhaps. Bill was a very clever man with a high-flying career. Or maybe it was the weight of responsibility that comes with providing for a young family. Nothing meant more to him than his wife and child. But . . ."

"But?" Serena prompted.

"I sensed it was something else. Something bigger. Something with deep roots in the past. But he never shared his burden with me or anyone else within the community."

"So, why come here?"

Mariposa drank from her teacup, and took her time replacing it on the table. "Bill was a drug addict," she said finally. "He used to regularly attend Narcotics Anonymous meetings. Those meetings stopped long before he moved to Seaton Point." She raised a hand, silver bangles jangling. "Before you ask, I don't know why."

Serena remembered Patrick Dolan telling her that Bill Duprie had a criminal record for drug offenses, but it had sounded like minor stuff, no different to all those other yuppies in the eighties who'd snorted a line of coke after a tough day at the office making millions. But Bill Duprie's relationship with drugs had clearly been more serious. An addiction, rather than an occasional indulgence. She wondered now if there was any truth in the theory of a drug deal gone bad.

Mariposa went on: "Bill came to Cedarwood Farm for herbal remedies and meditation techniques to alleviate stress and anxiety. Prescription medication was not an option for him. I want you to understand, Ms. Winters, that whatever demons Bill was struggling with, he was a good, decent man. He would have done anything for his family."

"Did his family ever visit Cedarwood Farm, or did Bill always come alone?"

"His daughter accompanied him once. A delightful child. Smart like her father. She loved playing with the residents' children down by the lake." Mariposa stood, indicating that their talk was coming to an end. "I have an art therapy workshop about to begin. But before you go . . ."

She glided into the house, and returned a few moments later with a small metal tin that she thrust into Serena's hands. "That tea I promised you." Then she looked at Serena with an intensity that felt like she could see right into her soul. "Bill never shared his worries, but I think you should. Confide in someone you trust, Ms. Winters. Unburden yourself. I promise, you will feel lighter if you do."

Serena thanked Mariposa for the tea and made to leave. Then she stopped, turned around, and said, "Why did you agree to speak to me about Bill Duprie?"

"For the same reason you wanted to talk to us—to find out the truth."

When Serena returned to her car, she saw that she had a text from Jack Beaumont.

*If you're going to pick my brain, why don't we do it over dinner tomorrow night?*

Her stomach did a weird, unexpected little flip and she tossed the phone back into her purse.

*Was Jack Beaumont asking her on a date?*

Serena started the engine and navigated the bumpy trail again. The wooden gates groaned open up ahead. She hit the blinker and turned onto the highway, heading back in the direction of Seaton Point and all its secrets.

She didn't notice the car concealed by foliage at the side of the road, or the driver behind the wheel who was watching her.

# 14

## DANI

## DECEMBER 1983

Dani ripped off the wrapping paper like an excited kid, and squealed when she saw what Bill had bought her.

"You didn't!"

He shrugged, and grinned. "Yeah, I guess I did. You deserve it, honey."

The Hermès purse was stunning, and must have cost a fortune. Black leather with brown trim and a discreet gold hardware fastening. A long slim strap so she could sling it over her shoulder and free up her hands for drinks and canapés at parties. Dani held the bag to her nose and sniffed it, inhaling the gorgeous new-leather smell.

*Yeah, but where are you going to wear it?* a little voice whispered at the back of her head. *You don't go anywhere other than work, and a French designer purse is hardly going to match the Greyhound uniform, is it?*

Dani pushed the thought away; didn't want anything to ruin the day.

"Your turn!" she said, handing over a gift with a huge gold bow.

Bill fingered the squishy parcel. "Let me guess . . . Is it golf clubs? A baseball bat?"

She swiped at him playfully. "Just open it, will you?"

Dani had bought the camel-colored cashmere sweater with her first paycheck (albeit she'd had to use some of the housekeeping money Bill gave her to make up the difference). She was determined to get their relationship back on track, and that started with paying attention to one another again—being thoughtful to each other.

"Oh honey, I love it." Bill held the sweater up in front of him. "Perfect fit too by the looks of it."

"It really makes your eyes pop," she said, delighted by his reaction.

They spent the rest of the morning in their pajamas, opening more gifts, Christmas movies playing on the TV in the background. Dani popped a bottle of champagne and made a mimosa for herself and a virgin version for Bill, and served both in nice glasses even though his was just orange juice. The seven-foot-tall real tree in the bay window and the bright tinsel and paper decorations strung around the room lent the apartment a coziness that made it almost feel like a home.

Later, Dani picked out a polka-dot dress with a big lace collar and a skinny belt from her closet, and pulled on knee-high boots that were a perfect match for the new Hermès purse. She strutted up and down the living room like she was Christie Brinkley on a runway, and Bill whooped and cheered and they laughed at their silliness.

Bill set the table with their best cutlery, and rolled linen napkins that matched the tablecloth into metal rings, and lit some candles, before Dani served up a shrimp cocktail to start, followed by turkey with all the trimmings, and pie for dessert. Their bellies full,

Bill did the dishes and Dani stored the leftovers in the refrigerator, and then they snuggled up on the couch to watch *It's a Wonderful Life* for the millionth time.

It had been the perfect day, the happiest Dani had been in a long time, and she dared to hope that next year might be even better if they had someone else to share it with . . .

Then it all went to shit.

The opening credits of the movie had barely begun to roll when Bill's pager started bleeping. It was still evening, the earliest it had ever gone off, but Dani knew exactly who it was. Not the office, that was for sure. She ducked out from under the arm draped around her shoulders and glared at Bill.

"Why is that damn thing on?" she demanded.

"Uh, I didn't know that it was," he said.

Dani knew he was lying.

"Ignore it," she said.

But Bill was already checking the phone number on the display. "I'm so sorry, honey." He grimaced. "But I need to go."

Dani angrily muted the TV. "Are you fucking kidding me? It's Christmas!"

He looked torn. "Exactly. This time of year, it's tough for her. She must be struggling badly to page me right now." He got to his feet. "I'll be back as soon as I can."

Dani didn't answer him. She stabbed at the remote control and turned the volume up way too high. Stared at the TV screen with her arms folded across her chest while he fumbled around in the entryway, pulling on boots and a heavy coat. She spent the rest of the evening furiously eating the entire box of chocolates he'd gifted her and smoking a full pack of cigarettes and finishing off what was left of the champagne.

It was after midnight, Christmas officially over, when she heard Bill's key in the lock. Dani was still on the couch, waiting for him.

She'd refused to go to bed and pretend to be asleep. Not this time. He came into the living room, bringing the cold in with him, his cheeks red from the biting chill.

"We need to talk," she said.

He sat on the edge of the couch, still wearing the boots and the coat. "I know. I'm sorry."

"You've done so well these past months," Dani said. "You've been so strong and shown such incredible willpower. I'm proud of you and I want you to know that."

He nodded. "Thank you. That means a lot, honey."

"But meeting her has got to stop. You've barely begun your own recovery journey and you're not her sponsor. She's not your responsibility."

"I know, but we just kind of clicked, and she doesn't get on so well with Glenn . . ."

"I don't care. Glenn is the group sponsor, not you. You need to focus on yourself." Bill went to speak again, and Dani held up a hand to silence him. "And you need to focus on *us*. This was supposed to be a fresh start, coming here, but you're spending more time with a stranger than your own wife."

Bill looked pained. "You know there's nothing going on between us, right? You know you have nothing to worry about?"

"I know," Dani said.

But did she know? A much younger woman who'd decided to attach herself to a handsome, kind, rich, vulnerable man. Did Dani really have nothing to worry about?

She went on, "That's not the point, Bill. Do you realize how lonely I've been here? That the reason for taking the job at the bus station is so I don't have to spend so much time in this apartment by myself?"

Bill dropped his head into his hands. "I'm a pathetic excuse for a husband. First all that stuff back in San Francisco, and then forcing you to move here, and then I just abandon you . . . It's just that she needs me . . ."

He looked up at her helplessly.

"No, I need you," Dani said firmly. "When was the last time we made love? How are we ever going to get pregnant when you're never here?"

"You're right." Shame was written all over his face. "I should be putting you first. You know you mean the world to me, don't you?"

He held out his hands to her. After a beat, she took them in her own. They were still freezing.

"Promise me you'll stop seeing her."

Bill nodded. "I promise."

But Dani noticed he couldn't look her in the eye when he said the words.

# 15

## SERENA

### NOW

Jack Beaumont had suggested an Italian restaurant down by the marina for their dinner date.

No, not a date. A meeting for research purposes with the added bonus of some good food thrown in, that was all. No different from the times Serena had consulted with a medical examiner and a ballistics expert and a hostage negotiator for previous novels. Hell, she'd probably be able to claim the meal as a business expense on her tax return.

Definitely not a date.

Even so, she'd spent a full half hour deciding what to wear and had made two outfit changes before settling on black slim-fit pants and a gold satin blouse. There was a fluttering of anticipation in her belly that she hadn't experienced since first dates back in high school and college. A large helping of guilt too. It felt like she was cheating on Michael even though he was dead, and she'd been the only faithful partner in that relationship.

Lavente's was located just yards from Susie's Shrimp Shack, but it was a million miles away in terms of style and ambience. Instead of bright lights and surfboards and a jukebox playing old pop classics, there were candlelit tables dressed in white linen and enclosed in intimate burgundy leather booths, with "I've Got You Under My Skin" by Frank Sinatra playing softly in the background.

Serena was led to a corner table for two by the window. Beaumont was already there, and stood as she approached. He looked—and smelled—good. Dark-wash jeans and a navy shirt and a hint of musky cologne. Her stomach flip-flopped again as she settled into the seat facing him. It was a table overlooking the boats in the marina as dusk began to fall.

"Such a beautiful view," she commented.

Beaumont seemed surprisingly nervous. "Is this place okay? I wasn't sure if it was the right choice . . ."

"It's perfect."

He grinned and appeared slightly embarrassed. "It's a long time since I've been out to dinner with a woman."

"You don't have a wife or partner?" Serena asked casually.

*What does it even matter?*

Beaumont shook his head. "A couple of close calls but I never quite made it down the aisle. Maybe one day. Who knows?"

Their server arrived just then with menus and a wine list. They decided to share a bottle of Californian Pinot Noir. Once the wine had been poured and their food orders taken, Beaumont said, "What about you? Ever been married? Kids?"

"Nope and nope."

"But you, uh, did have a partner? He passed recently, didn't he?"

Serena had been fidgeting with the cutlery. Now her head snapped up. "How do you know about Michael?"

"I looked you up," Beaumont said sheepishly. "After I heard you telling Hannah you were a writer." He smiled. "I promise, I'm not a stalker. I was just curious."

Serena didn't return the smile. Her heart was pounding. She wiped her palms on her pants.

*What does Jack Beaumont know about Michael's accident? What if he's figured out the truth?*

"You ran a police check on me?" she asked coldly.

"What? No! I googled you is all. I wanted to see what books you'd written. There was a news story about your partner's death. I'm sorry, I shouldn't have said anything."

Serena took a long drink of wine. "It's fine." The tremor in her voice indicated otherwise.

"How have things been at the house?" Beaumont asked, clearly trying to steer the conversation onto a less sensitive subject. "Any more problems?"

Serena shook her head. "Not since your visit. I fitted a trail camera like you suggested."

"That's good. Hopefully it'll give you some peace of mind. Either that or some great wildlife photos."

This time Serena did match his smile. The shock of Michael's accident being brought up was starting to wear off.

Then Beaumont said, "I have a confession to make."

"Oh?"

"I feel like I've gotten you here under false pretenses."

Serena pursed her lips. "Okay . . ."

"I looked for the Duprie case file earlier. I wanted to refresh my memory before meeting you tonight. But there's a slight problem."

"What problem?"

Tony Bennett was now crooning about leaving his heart in San Francisco.

105

Beaumont took a gulp of wine. "The file is gone."

Serena frowned. "Gone? Gone where?"

"I don't know for sure," he admitted. "But I have an idea. I think Don Raskin took it when he retired. Maybe he took some other files too. The cases he never closed."

"Do you think he was still working the Duprie case unofficially?"

"Maybe. I don't know. If he was, he never told me. But it seems the most likely explanation for the missing file."

Serena told Beaumont about meeting Patrick Dolan on his boat and how the old reporter had claimed Raskin had a big lead on an old case, but Dolan never found out what it was because Raskin was found dead just days later.

"Dolan thought the breakthrough was related to the Dupries." Serena hesitated. Now she was the one feeling awkward. "And I got the impression he didn't think Raskin's death was an accident."

Before Beaumont could answer, the food arrived. They ate in silence for a few minutes. Finally, he spoke. "Raskin was my mentor. I also considered him to be a friend. His death was investigated properly and thoroughly."

"I'm sure it was."

*So why didn't Raskin tell you what he'd found out if you were so close?*

Beaumont met her gaze, the reflection of the candlelight dancing in his dark eyes. "What happened to Don was an accident."

"I didn't say it wasn't."

"But that's what you're thinking, right? That he came across some information and it got him killed."

It was exactly what Serena was thinking.

"Is it possible?" she asked.

"I don't think so."

"What about Raskin's cell phone? Were there any unusual calls or messages before he died? Any information about the Dupries on it?"

"His cell phone was never recovered. Likewise, his house keys. Only his wallet was on him when he was found."

Serena looked up from the pasta she was spearing with her fork. "Don't you think that's odd? That his phone was missing?"

Beaumont frowned. "Not really. He was in the water, remember? The phone and keys probably fell out of his pockets and wound up on the seabed. Or maybe he lost the phone on the way to the marina, and someone found it and sold it."

"I guess," Serena said, raising her wineglass to her lips.

She wasn't convinced, but she didn't say so.

Beaumont said, "Look, Raskin was . . . I don't know . . . *troubled* before his death. He didn't take to retirement well at all. Felt kind of at a loss, like he had no purpose anymore. That's why I think he took that file." He sighed and shook his head sadly. "Don wasn't in a good place toward the end. He'd started hitting the bottle pretty hard after pulling the pin. He'd often drop by the station with coffee and donuts, and we'd sit in my office and put the world to rights. One day, he showed up looking like he'd seen a ghost. He was pale and trembling. Dumped the food on my desk and told me he had to go. That was the last time I saw him."

"You mentioned he was troubled, but you ruled out suicide?"

"Raskin didn't take his own life," Beaumont stated without hesitation. "It just wasn't in his DNA. Even if it was, drowning himself was not the way he'd have chosen to end it all."

He drained his glass and stared out of the window. Serena felt like he wanted to say more. She waited. Eventually, he turned to face her.

"It wasn't the first time," he said. "Don getting wasted and taking an unplanned swim during a midnight stroll . . . He'd done it once before. He was embarrassed afterward, didn't want the townsfolk to know, hated the thought of his reputation as chief of police for decades being tarnished. There was a police report, of course—and the harbor patrol officer who pulled him out of the water was obviously aware of the incident—but we all agreed to keep it quiet. The night he died, he'd had a skinful at O'Malley's. Likely got disoriented and fell in the water, same as before, but with a different outcome. It's sad, but that's really all there is to it. No big conspiracy, no matter what Patrick Dolan might think."

"Was Raskin married?" Serena asked. "What happened to his house and belongings after he died? I'm wondering where the Duprie file would be now if he did take it."

"He split from Patsy years ago. That old cop cliché about being married to the job more than he was to his wife. His daughter cleared out the house. I've left a message with her asking if she came across any old police files."

"But you and Raskin spoke about the case, right?" Serena said. "Right."

"What did Raskin think happened to the Duprie family? Forget all the theories about cults and drug deals and fleeing to Mexico. What did his gut tell him?"

Beaumont refilled their wineglasses. "He was convinced they'd gone on the run."

Serena nodded. "The fifty grand that Dani Duprie withdrew from the bank the day they vanished."

He looked at her, surprised. "Wow, you have been doing your homework. I'm impressed. The money was part of it, yes. There was also the potential sighting of Dani Duprie at a gas station in Nevada."

"Weren't there lots of so-called sightings, though?"

"There were, but Raskin took this one seriously enough to head on out there himself after he was sent the security footage,"

Beaumont said. "The hair was a different color, and the woman was wearing big sunglasses, but he thought it could have been her. From what I remember, the car was a dark blue station wagon. Possibly a Volvo. The gas station attendant thought someone else must have been driving, because she got out of the passenger side. He didn't notice the plates or if they were from out of state or not. There were no cameras covering the pumps, only the front counter. The woman paid cash, so no credit card record either. Raskin asked around town, but no one remembered seeing the woman or the car."

"He never found out if it was Dani Duprie or not?"

"He didn't. But, a year later, Raskin was back in Nevada. Female remains were discovered in the desert about forty miles south of the gas station. He was convinced they belonged to Dani Duprie."

"But they didn't."

It was a statement, not a question. If the dead body *had* been Dani, part of the mystery would have been solved years ago.

Beaumont said, "Dental records confirmed it wasn't her."

"Did they ever identify the remains?"

"Honestly? I don't know. Once Raskin discovered it wasn't his missing person, it was no longer of interest to the SPPD. The cops in Nevada wouldn't have felt obligated to update him on any further developments. Their victim, their case."

"That footage of the mystery woman at the gas station—would there have been stills of those images?" Serena wanted to see for herself if it could have been Dani Duprie in that dark blue station wagon at the Nevada gas station.

"There would have been. In the police file."

Serena nodded. "The file that's missing."

# 16

## SERENA

### NOW

The next few days passed without incident.

Serena spent a lot of time writing. When she wasn't in her office, she strolled along Point Beach, relishing the feel of the sand between her toes and the foamy surf lapping against her bare feet. She soaked up the sun and was calmed by the sound of the waves while sitting on the balcony, having decided she wouldn't allow Grady Hargreaves's tragic demise decades earlier to deprive her of such a stunning view. It was exactly what Serena had imagined this working vacation to be like when she'd first booked the Cliff House, before all the unpleasantness had sullied the experience.

She checked the trail camera only once. There were no shadowy figures hiding in the trees or intruders trying to gain access through the kitchen door. Only a shot of a coyote scavenging unsuccessfully for food, and a pretty fuchsia-and-emerald bird that she thought might have been some kind of hummingbird, caught majestically in mid-flight. Jack Beaumont had been right about the impressive wildlife captures.

Beaumont.

He had been on her mind a lot since their dinner—and not just because of the information she had gleaned from him. After the meal, he'd stood with her outside the restaurant while she waited for her ride home, the night air still warm, the lights from the eateries shimmering on the dark water. When her Uber arrived, Beaumont had leaned in close and brushed his lips against her cheek, and she'd thought he might move his mouth to cover her own. Then the driver had wound down his window and yelled her name and the moment was gone.

If Serena were being honest with herself, she was attracted to the police chief and a part of her had wanted him to kiss her properly— but she wasn't entirely sure she could trust him.

She didn't trust anyone in Seaton Point.

Saturday afternoon was spent giving a talk at the library. To be fair to Cynthia Hall, she had managed to pull in quite a crowd at short notice. Probably around fifty butts on seats. Other than Cynthia, there was just one familiar face, sitting on his own in the back row.

Hank Macaulay.

He looked like he had slept in his clothes, but he was awake and alert and seemed interested in what she had to say. Serena wanted to speak to him about the night Don Raskin had died, seeing as Macaulay had been one of the last people to see him alive.

She spoke for around an hour about her novels, including a Q&A with the audience. There were the usual questions: Where did she get her ideas from? Was Layne Farraday based on herself? Who would she like to see play Layne on the big screen?

An enthusiastic fan in the front row—who reminded her of Lenora from Louisiana—demanded to know what she was work-ing on next. Serena figured telling a bunch of strangers in Seaton Point that she was writing about a family who had mysteriously vanished thirty years ago wasn't the smartest move. She had enough problems already without literally the whole town knowing about her interest in the Dupries. So, she acted coy, told the audience she was working on an idea that was going to thrill her readers but that she couldn't divulge any details just yet. After the talk, a bunch of people wanted her to sign books they'd brought with them or pose for photos. When Serena was finally done, she searched for Hank Macaulay, but he was gone.

After the last fan had departed, Cynthia approached with a million-dollar smile. With her bright yellow halter-neck maxi-dress and jeweled sandals, she could have been walking the red carpet at Cannes instead of hosting a library event. "Well, that was fucking fantastic," she said. "I haven't seen this place so packed in a long time."

"It was fun. I enjoyed it."

Serena realized she meant it. She'd missed interacting with her readers at these kinds of events after her book tour had been so dramatically cut short six months earlier.

"What are you doing tonight?" Cynthia asked.

"Having whatever's in the refrigerator for dinner. Glass of wine. Maybe some writing."

"Uh-uh." Cynthia shook her head, wagged a manicured finger. "You're coming out to dinner with me and Hannah. And we're going to have cocktails. So get dressed up and leave the car at home, because us ladies are getting lit."

Serena couldn't help but smile at the other woman's infectious enthusiasm. "Do I have any say in the matter?"

"Absolutely not."

◆ ◆ ◆

Serena pulled a leather pencil skirt, tight sweater, and sky-high Jimmy Choos from the closet and assessed herself in the mirror. Her dark hair hung loose and shiny around her shoulders, and the expensive concealer did its job and hid the dark circles under her eyes. Not bad, but still nowhere near as glamorous as Cynthia working a library shift. She did as she was instructed and booked an Uber, leaving the Mustang in the driveway. George Evans was on his porch, binoculars raised, scribbling in his notebook. Regular as clockwork.

As the cab navigated the streets of downtown, Serena spotted a round lit-up sign jutting from a nondescript mud-brown building, casting a green glow onto the sidewalk. O'Malley's. She asked the driver to pull over at the curb outside and told him not to wait. She could walk from here to the Shrimp Shack, where she was meeting Cynthia and Hannah.

Serena pushed open the door and stepped into a spit-and-saw-dust dive bar with a pool table in one corner, a dartboard in the other, and a flatscreen TV showing a ball game. The place smelled faintly of warm beer and stale farts. Hank Macaulay was sitting at the bar on his own, with only a tumbler of whisky for company.

Serena fired off a text to Cynthia: *Sorry, running late! Be there shortly.*

O'Malley's was busy, even though it wasn't yet seven p.m., the clientele ninety percent testosterone. To say Serena was overdressed was an understatement. Eyes crawled over her like ants on a sugar cube as she parked herself on the stool next to Macaulay. His shirt and pants hung loose on his skinny frame and had more creases than an origami swan.

"What're you having?" the bartender asked, slinging a grimy dishcloth over his shoulder. He gave her a slow once-over, his expression a mixture of appreciation and confusion, like he couldn't figure out what she was doing in this dive bar but had no complaints about the view.

"Pinot Grigio, please."

He smirked. "We have white wine or red wine. That's it."

"Make it a Bud Light in that case."

He pulled a bottle from the fridge, uncapped it, and set it in front of her. Serena tossed some bills on the counter and turned to Macaulay. He was hunched over his drink and seemed completely oblivious to her presence.

"I saw you at the library today, didn't I?" she said. "Did you enjoy the event?"

He dragged his gaze from the drink and glanced around, as though questioning whether Serena was talking to him. Recognition dawned in his bloodshot eyes. "You're the lady author." He nodded. "I enjoyed listening to your talk."

"Thank you. I appreciate you coming along."

"I borrowed one of your books too. Don't know if I'll read it, though. I'm not what you would call a big reader."

Serena smiled. "But you do spend a lot of time at the library?"

Macaulay cradled the whisky glass. "I guess I like to be around people even if they're strangers and we don't talk to each other. Same reason I come here instead of drinking at home." He lifted his shoulders in a small shrug. "Don't really like being on my own."

Serena felt a stab of sadness at his blatant loneliness. "I was hoping to speak to you at the library, but you'd left already."

"Really?" Macaulay seemed bewildered but delighted. "You wanted to talk to me? Why would a smart, beautiful woman like you want to talk to an old man like me?"

The bartender returned just then to ask if Macaulay wanted a refill. He ordered a double. Serena took a pull of the beer as she waited for the bartender to pour the Johnnie Walker, place the glass in front of Macaulay, and move on to another customer.

Then she said, "I wanted to talk to you about Don Raskin."

Macaulay scrunched up his face, the lines on his forehead deepening into crevices. "The old cop? He's dead."

"I know. That's what I wanted to ask you about. The night he died."

"It wasn't me who killed him. I'll tell you that for nothing."

"Wasn't his death an accident?" Serena asked.

Macaulay snorted. "It was no accident."

"Why do you say that?"

He looked at her with narrowed eyes. "You sure you're an author? Coming in here with your questions . . . Maybe you're an undercover cop. Or FBI or CIA. Trying to get me to talk. How do I know you're really who you say you are?"

"You heard my talk today. You've seen my photo on my book. I've written eleven novels over the last ten years. Believe me when I say there's no way I'd have been able to publish all those books and work undercover for law enforcement at the same time."

Macaulay considered and apparently accepted her point. "So, why the interest in Raskin?"

"I guess I'm the same as you. From what I've heard, I'm not sure it *was* an accident."

This seemed to please him. His rheumy eyes brightened and he sat up straighter. "You reckon there was a cover-up too? That Raskin knew too much, so they had to silence him, right?"

"Uh, right. Did you speak to Don Raskin that night?"

Macaulay gulped down some Scotch. "Sure did. He was sitting right where you are now."

"What did you talk about?" Serena asked.

He leaned in close enough for her to smell the booze on his breath. "He was onto something," he stage-whispered. "Something big. Not JFK or 9/11 big, but it was big enough that they had to shut him up before the truth came out."

Serena was starting to wonder how reliable Hank Macaulay was. If he'd be able to recall a conversation from two years ago when he likely couldn't remember making his way home from the bar last night.

"Who is 'they'?" she asked.

"The person who killed him," Macaulay said, matter-of-fact. "The person Raskin was planning on meeting when he left this place."

Now Serena was interested. "He told you he was meeting someone?"

"Uh-huh. Raskin reckoned he'd seen something. Figured the whole damn town had been fooled but not him. As soon as he had proof, everyone was going to know the truth. That's what he said. Then he got a message on his cell phone. Looked like he'd seen a ghost. Sank a double JD neat in one go. Got off that stool and held up the phone and said, 'It's showtime.' Next day, they fished him out of the water. Try telling me that's a coincidence, because I don't believe in coincidences."

*Looked like he'd seen a ghost.*

Jack Beaumont had said the exact same thing about the last time he'd seen Don Raskin at the station.

"Did you tell the police all of this?" Serena asked. "About the text? About the planned meeting?"

Macaulay shook his head vehemently. "I don't talk to cops."

"But you spoke to Raskin," she pointed out.

"He wasn't a cop no more. In any case, he did all the talking."

"Did he ever mention anything about an old case? I heard he'd been following some kind of lead just before he died. Could it have had something to do with what he told you?"

Macaulay drank and pondered. "Maybe." Then he nodded. "That missing family, I'll bet."

"The Dupries?"

"Yup. That would be big, huh? If he'd found out what happened to them after all them years? After they'd been all over the news. Maybe he tracked down the woman."

Serena's bottle of Bud stilled before it reached her lips. "What woman?"

"The one who was in town asking about the wife back when they lived here."

"Did you know this woman?"

Macaulay shook his head. "Nah, never seen her before. A stranger. Stopped me in the street and asked if I knew where . . . Damn . . . What was her name again?"

"Dani Duprie," Serena offered.

He clicked his fingers. "That's it. This dame, she asked for directions to Dani Duprie's place. I knew the family lived in that big white house up on the cliff, but I didn't tell her nothing. She claimed she was a cousin or something and had lost their address. I wasn't buying it for a second. Figured she was FBI or CIA or an undercover cop."

There was no point asking why Beaumont hadn't mentioned a stranger in town asking about Dani Duprie, because Hank Macaulay had clearly never reported it.

The old man grimaced, exposing small, yellow teeth like sweet-corn. "But I figure someone must have been dumb enough to give out the address. Someone who never admitted what they'd done."

"Why's that?"

Macaulay fixed her with a look that was surprisingly steady considering all the booze he'd sunk. "Because the very next day, that family vanished without a trace. It's like I said, I don't believe in coincidences."

"What do you remember about the woman?" Serena asked.

"Young. Around thirty. Nice-looking. Redhead." He scratched his own head. "Or was she blonde? Might've been a blonde."

Serena suppressed a sigh. "Anything else?"

"Yeah. She was driving an old station wagon. A dark blue Volvo."

# 17

## SERENA

### NOW

"Finally!" Cynthia bellowed. "There's been a Cadillac margarita with your name on it for the last half hour."

It was a warm evening, and Cynthia and Hannah had snagged a table outside on the Shrimp Shack's patio offering a picture-perfect view of the yachts moored in the marina, framed by the twinkling lights strung around the outdoor space. The fresh sea air was a welcome relief after the stink of O'Malley's. On the table were three pale yellow cocktails in classic welled margarita glasses. Cynthia was stunning as always, and Hannah looked pretty too, with her dirty-blonde hair worn down around her narrow shoulders and a pink sleeveless shift dress showing off yoga-toned arms. Serena could see why Jack Beaumont had fallen for her once upon a time.

"Where have you been?" Cynthia demanded. "I was starting to think you'd stood us up."

"Just some work stuff I had to take care of. Sorry for keeping you both waiting." Serena pulled her drink toward her and sucked on the straw. The Cadillac margarita delivered a hell of a kick. "Wow, okay. That'll be me drunk then."

She didn't want to tell the others that she'd been quizzing Hank Macaulay about Don Raskin's death. Didn't want to have to answer their questions. She wasn't even sure what to make of the conversation herself.

By the time she'd made the five-minute journey from O'Malley's to the Shrimp Shack, Serena had realized two things. One: her Jimmy Choo heels were not made for walking even short distances. Two: Macaulay's revelation about the dark blue station wagon might not be as exciting as she'd first thought. Initially, it had seemed significant that the stranger who had been asking about Dani Duprie the day before her family disappeared drove the same make and color of car as the maybe-Dani at the gas station in Nevada. But after thinking about it more, Serena had decided it wasn't a stretch to believe that Don Raskin had told Macaulay about the desert sighting during one of their boozy chats, and Macaulay had either deliberately—or subconsciously—added that detail into his own story about the woman searching for the Dupries.

There were already food menus on the table. The three women browsed for a few moments and a server came out of the restaurant to take their order. When he'd gone back inside, Serena said to Hannah, "You like to eat at the place where you work even when you're not working?"

"Damn straight." Hannah nodded. "It's the best food in the whole of Seaton Point, and I hate the thought of putting cash into a competitor's till."

"You own the restaurant?"

"Sure do. My husband Antonio and I bought the Shack from old Susie a few years back when she retired."

"The best thing about eating here is taking advantage of Hannah's staff discount," Cynthia said with a wink.

Hannah said, "Yeah, but only for the food. Not the fifteen-dollar cocktails."

Now that Serena knew Hannah was Jody's mom, she could see the family resemblance there too. While he'd inherited his father's smile, he had his mother's fair coloring and big blue eyes.

They shared a couple of huge seafood platters and ordered more drinks. Tunes by the Byrds and the Doors and Jefferson Airplane were pumped through speakers hung around the patio. The conversation flowed and Serena found herself relaxing, no doubt helped by the strong cocktails.

"So, what's your story?" she asked Cynthia. "How'd you wind up being a librarian in Seaton Point?"

"I modeled for a while to put myself through college," Cynthia said, dipping a calamari strip into the spicy mayo dip. "Then I worked as an investment banker in Los Angeles. Made a ton of money but completely burned myself out in the process. Working seventy-hour weeks will do that to a gal. So, I decided to retire at forty and live the good life."

"And that's why you moved here?"

"Kind of. I pinned a map to the wall and threw a dart at it. The plan was to relocate to wherever the dart landed."

"You did not!" Serena said.

"I did."

"She's not even kidding," added Hannah.

"My aim isn't the best, so I didn't get too far from LA," Cynthia said. "But there are worse places I could have ended up. I mean, the dart could have landed on Florida."

"Oh, Florida's not so bad," Serena said. "Beautiful beaches."

"Beaches full of old people. Just because I was retiring didn't mean I wanted to spend my days playing pickleball or learning macramé."

"And the library? Were you always a big reader?"

Cynthia laughed. "Hell, no. Don't think I'd picked up a book since high school when I upped sticks and moved here. But something I realized very quickly was that doing nothing gets boring fast. The library had an opening, so I applied for it. I'm overqualified and underpaid, but I like it. I get to talk to people every day and it's zero stress compared to . . ."

Her words trailed off and a shadow passed across her beautiful face. Serena turned to see what had caught her attention and saw Kelly Dunne, from the police station, emerging from the restaurant with a chic older woman.

Kelly's smile disappeared when she spotted them and she seemed suddenly awkward, like she wasn't sure whether to stop at their table or not. She did, and greeted them all with a tentative "Hey, ladies" as she tucked her pink hair nervously behind her ears. Hannah returned a friendly "Hello" and Cynthia nodded curtly.

Kelly turned to Serena. "Everything okay at the house after Chief Beaumont's visit?"

"Yes, thanks. No more issues to report."

"Good. I'm glad to hear it." She smiled mischievously. "Did you enjoy dinner with the chief at Lavente's the other night?" Serena's surprise must have shown because Kelly added, "I made the reservation. He wasn't sure where to take you."

Hannah looked pissed—Serena hoped it was because she'd been dining someplace other than the Shack, rather than because she'd been with Hannah's ex—while Cynthia's eyebrows had hiked up to her hairline at the mention of the dinner date with Beaumont.

Serena said, "It was lovely, thanks. Good choice."

Kelly beamed. "Fantastic. Enjoy the rest of your evening, ladies."

Her gaze lingered on Cynthia, who turned away, then she walked off with the older woman. There was clearly some bad blood there and Serena wondered what the issue was. She knew there would be questions for herself as soon as Kelly was out of earshot. Hannah beat Cynthia to it.

"You've had problems at the Cliff House?" she asked worriedly. "My mom never said anything."

Serena reluctantly told them about the threatening note on her car and the broken porch lights and her belief that an intruder may have been inside the house. The two women appeared genuinely shocked.

"I always did think that place was creepy as fuck." Cynthia shot Serena an apologetic look. "Sorry, not helpful."

"There haven't been any problems for a few days now," Serena said. "So maybe it was just kids pranking the newcomer in town."

She didn't believe that explanation for a second.

Hannah ordered a cab soon after. Two younger kids, aged eight and ten, meant an early cut. She shook her head in dismay. "I dread to think what state the house will be in when I get back. Antonio lets the boys do whatever they want when I'm not there to play the role of mean mommy. They probably had cake and ice cream for dinner."

Once Hannah was gone, Cynthia signaled for more drinks. She nudged Serena and said, "So, you and Jack Beaumont, huh?"

Serena's cheeks flamed. "It wasn't like that. It was a work meeting."

Cynthia grinned. "You keep telling yourself that, sweetheart."

"He's a cop and I write mysteries. That's all there is to it. I've met with a ton of law enforcement for research for my books."

Which was true, but none of them had gotten her pulse pumping the way Jack Beaumont had.

"But you do like him?" Cynthia pressed.

Serena's blush deepened. "I told you, our relationship is strictly professional."

"Hmmm. If you say so. But there's nothing wrong with a little holiday romance. That's all I'm saying."

Serena shook her head emphatically. "Not a good idea."

"Is there someone back in New York? Is that it?"

"There was. Not anymore. My partner, Michael, died six months ago."

"Oh shit, I'm so sorry," Cynthia said. "And here's me shooting my mouth off about you and Jack Beaumont. What happened to Michael? Was he ill?"

*If only.*

"He fell down the stairs at his house and broke his neck. Freak accident."

Cynthia gasped. "Fuck. How awful."

Maybe the booze was loosening her tongue, because Serena kept on talking.

"He'd been cheating on me for months. The night he died, I was out of town on a book tour. His mistress was at his house when it happened. I'd suspected for a while but it was still a shock to have it confirmed. Of course, his death was a far bigger shock."

None of what she'd said was a lie, but it wasn't the whole truth either.

"Jesus." Cynthia leaned over and gave Serena's hand a squeeze. "You poor thing. That's why you came to Seaton Point? To get away from it all?"

Serena nodded grimly. "Yep. Great plan, huh?"

"And now you're having to put up with all this horrible shit happening to you here. That sucks big-time."

Serena wanted to change the subject now. "What about you?" she asked. "Are you seeing anyone? Is there someone special?"

"My last relationship also ended recently, but the breakup wasn't quite as dramatic as yours. Both parties are still very much alive." Cynthia grimaced. "Let's just say I give the police station a wide berth these days. Which, thankfully, isn't hard to do, seeing as I don't make a habit of getting arrested."

"Oh, so Jack Beaumont is your ex?" Serena tried to sound nonchalant. Failed miserably. The blush returned with a vengeance.

Cynthia slapped the table, attracting the attention of other diners. "I knew it! I knew you liked him. But, no, Jack and I were definitely not a thing. He's not exactly my type. You just met my ex."

Realization dawned. "Ah, you and Kelly were together."

"We met on a dating app and hit it off straightaway. I was having fun, but Kelly got serious fast. Thing started moving way too quickly for me. Soon she was talking about us living together. I own the pink house that overlooks Point Beach. You know it?"

Serena had seen the huge super-modern home during her morning beach strolls. It was hard to miss. "Sure, I know it. It's stunning."

"Thank you. I like it. I figured Kelly was angling to move in with me. Assumed the big rush to settle down was because she's turning forty this year. Then she suggested we buy a place together—even had the house picked out despite it not being for sale—and I started to think maybe Kelly was more serious about my money than she was about me. So, we broke up."

Now Serena knew why there had been such a strained atmosphere between the two of them. "I'm guessing you didn't part on the best of terms?"

"Kelly didn't take the breakup well. There were some angry texts and voicemails for a while. Looks like she's moved on now, though. I'm guessing her dinner date was the new girlfriend. Or cash cow, more like. She was what—ten years older than Kelly? More? And that Chanel 2.55 slung over her shoulder was not a fake. Hey, maybe she'll target you next—you've got everything she wants."

There was another round of cocktails and then Ubers were ordered. Serena noticed two missed FaceTime calls from Margot, as well as a new voicemail message.

On the drive home, Serena thought she saw a curtain twitching in the front window of George Evans's house. No doubt watching her with those damn binoculars.

Once inside the Cliff House, she leaned unsteadily against the wall and undid the straps on her shoes. Kicked them off and rubbed her aching feet. Then she padded down the hallway into the living room and settled on the sofa. The voicemail from Margot was short and to the point. "*Call me back when you get this message. It's urgent.*"

It was almost eleven, which meant it was close to two a.m. in New York. Serena would return the call in the morning. She leaned back, sinking into the plush cushions, her eyelids heavy, her head pleasantly fuzzy.

She jolted awake. A loud trilling had startled her. She glanced around for the source of the noise, saw her cell phone vibrating across the coffee table, the screen lit up.

An incoming FaceTime from Margot.

*At this time?*

Serena accepted the call. Margot's face appeared, her expression equal parts furious and relieved.

"So, you *are* still alive?" she yelled. "Why didn't you answer your goddamn phone?"

Serena blinked eyes sticky with sleep and mascara. "Uh, I was out for dinner. Didn't hear my cell phone in my purse. Wait, why are you calling so late and why wouldn't I be alive?"

Margot leaned forward, her features pinched with worry behind the big red glasses. "I'll tell you why. Because someone threatened to kill you, Serena. Someone wants you dead."

# 18

## RUBY

## FALL 1983

Ruby worried that she'd never hear from River again. She feared that she'd been nothing more than a summer fling who would quickly be forgotten, his romance with Pamela Gleeson likely rekindled as soon as she was on the bus back home.

She tortured herself with thoughts of River and "Pammy" at the Evergreen State Fair that was set to roll into town shortly after Ruby left. Imagined them sharing cotton-candy kisses on the Ferris wheel as dusk fell, riding pillion on the Americana carousel, clutching onto each other during the deep dips of the rollercoaster. Maybe River would make love to "Pammy" in a barn too, and whisper sweet nothings in her ear. Maybe he already had . . .

Ruby's fears evaporated when a letter with a Washington postmark and a return address in Monroe arrived a couple of weeks after she returned to Portland. River missed her, he wrote. Life wasn't the same without her. He loved her. He'd told her so several times already but now she had it written down in his big loopy handwriting, to read as many times as she wanted.

He wrote her every week. He had even purchased a cornflower-blue stationery set with matching paper and envelopes instead of using lined paper torn from a notebook. Ruby understood that letter-writing didn't come naturally to him. River was the kind of guy who liked fixing things, pulling apart machines and putting them back together again, wasn't the creative type. She knew it wasn't easy for him to put his thoughts and feelings into words on a page, but he was willing to make the effort for her. It made Ruby love him even more, if that was even possible.

There were phone calls too. Ruby would sneak out of the apartment to the pay phone down the street, squeeze into the booth, and drop coin after coin into the slot. The conversations were infrequent and never long enough, because they were long-distance and costly. She loved hearing River's voice, but she *really* loved receiving his letters. How her belly fluttered when she spotted another blue envelope in the mailbox. The anticipation of tearing it open and discovering what news he had, how he'd been spending his time, how he couldn't wait to see her again. The only tricky part was intercepting the mail every morning so her mom wouldn't find out about her special correspondence. River was her secret, hers alone, and Ruby didn't want their relationship tainted in any way by Coral's jealousy and spite.

By fall, River had been working in an auto repair shop for several weeks, learning new skills and making cash. He still helped at Grandma Pearl's ranch too when he could fit in the odd jobs around his shifts. He'd been saving his wages for gas money to Portland to visit her, but Ruby had shut that plan down fast. She couldn't imagine anything worse than her mom meeting her boyfriend.

Coral was on her own again after Ray had walked out over the summer. Even though it was a relief for Ruby to have him gone, it meant enduring her mom stomping around like a bear with a sore head, the way she always did when she was without a man for any length of time. Ruby figured Coral's bed wouldn't lie empty for too long, though, and there would be another douchebag along soon enough.

It didn't matter. Ruby had already decided she'd save some cash of her own and make a return trip to Monroe—only this time it would be permanent. She had it all figured out. She'd live with Grandma Pearl, help with the chores, pay rent, and never have to be apart from River. Her mom would be pissed, but so what? Coral couldn't stop her. Ruby was an adult now and had every right to live her life the way she wanted. She didn't want to end up like Coral, that was for sure, working long hours at the salon for a pittance, relying on a string of unsuitable men to pay for her nice outfits and fancy jewelry.

Even so, Ruby had agreed to take a job at a salon that belonged to a friend of a friend of her mom's soon after she got back from Washington. The Cutting Edge was anything but; the average age of the clientele was about a hundred. Ruby didn't enjoy the work—spending hours on her feet, washing people's hair, massaging their flaky scalps, sweeping the floor a dozen times a day. But she'd tolerate it for as long as she had to—paint on a smile to earn some extra dollars in tips, until she had enough cash for her ticket out of there.

That had been the plan, anyway. It didn't turn out that way.

Ruby continued to write to River, telling him about the salon and funny stories involving the clients. About the cool bands she'd seen with Tammy and Kim, and their shopping trips to the mall and visits to the movie theater and the ice rink.

It was all lies.

There was no job at the salon. Not anymore. Not since Ruby had gotten fired for being late all the time and throwing up in the tiny staff bathroom and smelling of vomit around the customers. "I know you're young and you want to enjoy yourself," Darla, The Cutting Edge's owner, had told her. "I'm not so old that I don't remember how it is when you're eighteen. But the partying and hangovers are clearly impacting your work, so I got no choice but to let you go."

Partying and hangovers.

If only.

Ruby hadn't seen Tammy or Kim for weeks either. They'd eventually given up asking her to shows and parties and trips to the mall when she kept making excuses not to meet up with them, and then she'd stopped returning their calls altogether.

Her life was over.

It turned out that Ruby Bryant was just like her mother after all.

# 19

## SERENA

### NOW

"You're joking, right?" Serena said to her agent.

"Yeah, I often call people in the middle of the night to crack a few jokes," Margot snapped. "Do I look like Joan Rivers to you?"

Serena squinted at the phone's screen. "Yeah, maybe a little."

"I'm not laughing, Serena."

"Seriously, Margot. I have no idea what you're talking about. No one has threatened to kill me."

Okay, so she had been told to leave town via an anonymous note, but it was hardly a death threat.

"When was the last time you checked your email?" Margot asked.

Serena frowned. "I get alerts on my cell phone, so pretty much whenever I receive a new one."

"I don't mean your regular email. I'm talking about your author account. The one that's on your business cards and website so that fans can reach out to you."

"Uh, I'm not sure. Probably around the time *When Dusk Falls* was published. So, maybe six months ago?"

"You might want to take a look."

Serena flopped clumsily from the couch onto the floor, landing hard on her ass, and opened her laptop on the coffee table. She propped the phone against a decorative bowl filled with seashells, so she still had a view of her agent while logging on to her author email.

"Are you drunk?" Margot's tone was judgmental.

"If a bottle of weak beer and four strong margaritas gets you drunk, then yes, I'm drunk."

Serena felt herself sober up fast when her inbox loaded and she saw a stream of emails from the same sender: *Unknown.* The correspondence had started soon after she'd arrived in Seaton Point, and the most recent email had been sent earlier this evening. They all had the same subject line: *LEAVE.*

She clicked on each one. The first was an echo of the note left under her windshield wiper, indicating the online troll was the same person who'd paid a visit to her rental car on her first day in town. The messages grew increasingly threatening and alarming.

*Leave town now.*

*You're not wanted here.*

*Get out of Seaton Point.*

*I know where you live all alone in that house.*

*Better check your doors are locked.*

*Bad things happen when you're alone at night.*

*Curiosity killed the author.*

*Careful you don't end up dead like your dumb characters.*

*Die you stupid bitch.*

*Leave or die bitch!!!*

"Holy shit," Serena said, wide-eyed.

"Now do you understand why I've been so worried?" Margot said. "Whoever wrote those emails clearly isn't a fan—and I'm not talking about your writing."

Serena closed the laptop with trembling fingers. "It's fine. I'll deal with it."

"Deal with it how? Someone is threatening to kill you!"

"I'll call Jack Beaumont in the morning. I have his cell phone number."

"Who the hell is Jack Beaumont?"

"He's the chief of police in Seaton Point."

"Wait. *What?* Back up a minute. You're on first-name terms with the chief of police? You have his personal number? What the hell has been going on there?"

The volume had increased with each question until Margot was yelling again. Serena heard a muffled voice in the background. Margot turned away from the screen and hollered, "I'm on a call with Serena! Go back to sleep!"

There was more muffled conversation. Margot muttered, "Yeah, yeah. Everyone's a comedian."

"Was that Jonathan?" Serena asked.

Margot's third husband was a VP at one of the big New York publishing houses.

"He said we'd better be discussing a seven-figure deal seeing as his beauty sleep's been interrupted. Someone ought to break the news to him that his youthful looks are down to his twice-yearly fillers, not getting eight hours a night."

"Why were you checking my emails on a Saturday night anyway?"

"I'm dedicated to my authors, that's why," Margot said. "Now stop trying to deflect. Spill."

Serena sighed, then brought her up to speed on recent events. Margot's head was in her hands by the time she was done talking.

"Please tell me you remembered to lock all the doors when you got home loaded up on cocktails?"

"Um, I think so."

"Go check now," Margot ordered.

Serena got up ungracefully from the floor to a disapproving tut and headed to the front of the house. Her designer heels were in a heap by the door. The security chain was in place. The lock was engaged. She didn't recall securing it, but clearly she'd been on autopilot and had done just that. She paused and sniffed the air. Thought she detected a very faint smell. Perfume or cologne maybe. Vaguely familiar, yet out of place here in the house. Had it been there when she got home? She wasn't sure. Serena then checked the kitchen door was locked. It was. The scent was stronger in here.

She went back to the living room and settled back in front of her phone.

"Well?" Margot demanded.

"The doors are all locked. No need to worry."

"So why do *you* look so worried?"

Margot was freaking out as it was, without Serena mentioning the smell. Maybe it was simply the aroma from the foliage outside drifting indoors. She was so used to New York and the waft of garbage trucks and the steam from manholes and exhaust fumes, that nature's perfume was almost foreign to her. "I guess I'm a little spooked by those emails," she said. "Death threats tend to have that effect on a person."

"I'm your agent and it's my job to advise you. So, I'm going to tell you exactly what I think you should do—take that loonball's advice."

Serena raised an eyebrow. "What? 'Die you stupid bitch'?"

"No. 'Leave town now.' Why are you even still there? That's what I don't understand. Anonymous notes, stuff going missing . . . You wouldn't have seen me for dust."

Serena told Margot about the family who'd vanished from this very house thirty years ago and how they were providing the inspiration for the new novel and had cured her of her writer's block.

"I'm glad you've got your writing mojo back," Margot said. "I truly am. Hopefully you'll get your mojo back in other departments soon too. And I love the premise. A whole family disappearing mysteriously in the dead of night? Fantastic. But you have the plot already. There's no need to hang around in that house. So, I'll ask again: why the hell are you still in Seaton Point?"

"I need to know the truth," Serena said. "I need to find out what happened to the Dupries. I think that's what the threats are all about. Someone doesn't want me digging up the past."

"So don't," Margot said firmly. "This isn't an episode of *Murder, She Wrote*. You're not Jessica Fletcher. You don't have to solve mysteries as well as write them. Get yourself on the first available flight to New York. Call this Beaumont guy once you're back in Manhattan and let him deal with it once you've put a few thousand miles between you and the crank who's been stalking you. Because that's what this is: stalking, plain and simple."

Serena shook her head. "I'm not ready to come home. I . . . I just can't face it."

Margot's stony expression softened just a fraction. "Is this about Michael? Listen, I know you've had a rough time of it. His accident was a shock, for sure, and I really did think a change of scenery would do you good. But this is a bad situation, Serena. Please come home."

Fat tears rolled down Serena's cheeks. "Maybe I deserve all this bad shit. Maybe it's my punishment." She laughed bitterly. "Did I really think I could just run away, and everything would be fine? I can't run from myself, can I? I can't hide from the fact that I'm a terrible person."

"What are you talking about? You're making no sense. Jeez. Just how strong *were* those cocktails?"

Serena thought of Mariposa's advice about sharing her burden; how she'd feel better for it. Lighter. Maybe the old hippy was right. Maybe it was finally time to come clean.

"It's my fault Michael died," she blurted out.

"Don't be silly," Margot chided. "It was an accident. You weren't even there."

Serena sniffed, then wiped her eyes and nose with the sleeve of her sweater. "That's where you're wrong. I *was* there. Michael is dead because of me."

# 20

## SERENA

### SIX MONTHS AGO

The Philadelphia night was chilly and dark and damp, mirroring Serena's mood perfectly.

Raindrops peppered the hotel window, obscuring the view of Rittenhouse Square down below, the park's globe lights hazy blobs of amber through the thick glass. Inside, the room was warm, its golden-yellow wallpaper and plush velvet furnishings in jewel tones adding to the lavish coziness. Even so, Serena felt a coldness deep in her bones.

She was now almost sure that Michael was cheating on her.

Michael.

Faithful and dependable.

Or a liar and a cheat?

She glanced at the Saint-Chamant Blanc de Blancs jammed into an ice bucket on the side table by the window, condensation rolling in rivulets down the bottle. A crystal flute stood unused next to it. The champagne was unopened, the cork still firmly in place. It had been a gift from her publisher because Serena should have been celebrating tonight. Her book tour was a huge success so far, with sold-out events in Houston, Scottsdale, St. Louis, and another large, happy crowd at Barnes & Noble this evening. The news that *When Dusk Falls* would be spending a second week on the *New York Times* bestseller list was the cherry on top of the cake.

But Serena didn't feel like celebrating.

She thought, again, of the text she'd received from Michael.

> *Sorry, can't talk. Still at work. Big project to be completed by the weekend.*

It had arrived seconds after he'd sent her call to voicemail. She'd wanted to check in with him, had been excited to tell him the news about her sales. Now, she stared at the Find My app on her phone. The blue dot showed Michael's cell phone was located at his house in New Jersey—not at his office in Lower Manhattan.

Proof that he'd lied to her.

And not for the first time.

Two nights ago, he'd also diverted her call to voicemail while she was in Arizona. He'd claimed to be playing squash with a coworker, a new hobby he'd apparently taken up. Like he was Michael Douglas in *Wall Street*. Michael Douglas in *Fatal Attraction*, more like. The app had placed his cell phone at his home address on that occasion too.

Why lie about where he was unless he was up to no good?

Serena had first suspected something was wrong on New Year's Eve. They'd gone to Times Square as usual for the ball drop, but he'd been distracted, kept glancing at his phone when he thought she wasn't looking. When she'd confronted him about it, he'd told her he was expecting to hear from his daughter—even though Serena knew from previous years that Lucy always waited until the following day to call. She had a young son and didn't participate in the late-night celebrations.

Shortly after midnight, Michael had stepped away from her, into the throng, to take a call. He was on the phone for a few minutes. Mumbled something about Lucy wanting to wish him a happy New Year when he returned. Serena had known instinctively that he was lying. He was antsy as hell. Couldn't look her in the eye. And why would he need privacy to talk to his daughter? Why would Lucy not want to extend the New Year wishes to Serena?

Then Michael had started staying at the office late. Took up squash. Turned up at her apartment freshly showered on more than one occasion. He'd also lost interest in sex—at least with her.

Serena suspected another woman.

If she were the one having an affair, she'd use a burner phone to contact her lover. She assumed Michael would do the same. So, she went through his suit pockets, searched his briefcase, ransacked the drawers and closets at his house, but found nothing. He'd been using his own iPhone at Times Square, and she knew the passcode, so she'd searched the device too and found no suspicious calls or messages. Figured maybe he'd been swapping out the SIM for a secret one that only his mistress had the number for.

Of course, it had also crossed her mind that she'd gotten it all wrong. That there was no affair. That she was allowing her writer's imagination to run wild. But Serena had to know for sure. So, she'd accessed his phone again while he was asleep and had set up family sharing so she could track his location, just as some parents did with their kids.

Then she had waited.

Now, here she was, in a hotel room in Philadelphia with proof of his lies right here in front of her.

Serena opened the Uber app and plugged in the details for a ride to New Jersey. The journey to his house would take around ninety minutes and the fare would be more than $170. She'd need to be back in Philly for a morning flight to Toronto for the next stop on her tour, meaning a return trip and spending the best part of $400.

Still, it was a small price to pay for the truth.

Serena dressed in jeans and sneakers and the hoodie she wore for her morning runs. She rode the elevator down to the lobby and pulled up the hood. Olivia and Penny from the publicity team would likely still be in the bar, and she didn't want them to notice her leaving the hotel and ask awkward questions.

A howling wind buffeted the cab as they raced along I-95. Rain lashed against the windows; the windshield wipers were cranked up to full speed to battle the downpour, squeaking loudly with each irritating swipe. The rain had eased to a drizzle by the time they passed through the toll into New Jersey. She told the driver to drop her at the street next to Michael's. She didn't want the rumble of the car engine or a slamming door to alert him to an unexpected visitor.

Michael's house was situated closest to the entrance of an upscale cul-de-sac comprising ten similar homes with identical manicured lawns and big bay windows and backyard pools. His Lexus was in the driveway. If he was with another woman, her own vehicle wasn't parked outside. A solitary lamp burned in the living room downstairs. Serena didn't know if the bedroom light was on because the window overlooked the backyard.

She walked up to the front door and inserted her key in the lock. Her heart hammered as she stepped inside and closed the door quietly behind her. Straight ahead was the staircase. Faint light from the primary bedroom spilled onto the upstairs landing. She climbed the stairs slowly—needing to know but suddenly not wanting to know—her sneakers silent on the wood.

The bedroom door was open. She heard them before she saw them. Pants and gasps. The creaking of the box spring under the mattress. Serena stepped into the doorway. Michael was lying back on the bed, his eyes closed, his mouth open. A blonde woman was astride him. The slender shape of her back was turned to Serena so she couldn't see his lover's face.

A jumble of emotions crashed through her, one after the other. Shock, horror, revulsion, humiliation, sadness, anger. Mostly anger. If Michael was so unhappy with her, if he wanted to be with someone else so badly, why not just leave her? Why lie to her? Why humiliate her?

Then another question: Why hadn't Serena ended the relationship herself already? Things hadn't been good between them for a long time.

Those were all questions she would ask herself repeatedly in the weeks and months that followed.

Michael's eyes opened and then widened, round as dinner plates. He blinked a couple of times, like he wasn't sure if Serena was really standing there, watching him screwing someone else. She wanted to scream and shout and swear. She wanted to pummel his chest with her fists and scratch out the blonde's eyes with her fingernails. Serena did none of those things. She simply shook her head in disgust.

"What are you doing here?" he gasped.

Serena didn't answer. She backed away toward the staircase on Jell-O legs.

"What is it?" she heard the woman say. "What's wrong, Michael?"

Serena recognized the voice. Nancy Bailey, who lived two houses away. She was married to a bespectacled accountant called Edward. Serena had spoken to her often. Hell, Nancy and Edward Bailey had even attended the neighborhood cookout Serena and Michael had hosted last summer.

"Wait!" Michael roared.

There was a dull thump that she later found out was the sound of Nancy Bailey landing on the floor after being shoved off the bed by Michael as he attempted to chase after Serena.

He didn't get very far.

"Wait!" he yelled again.

Serena was almost at the front door. She whipped around to face him. Michael was at the top of the stairs, trying to descend while pulling on a pair of Tommy Hilfiger boxer shorts at the same time. It was the underwear she had gifted him at Christmas. He lost his footing and seemed to hang in midair, before bouncing once, twice, against the wooden stairs. He landed hard on his neck with a sickening crack at the foot of the staircase.

His neck was bent horribly out of shape. One leg stuck out at an unnatural angle. The boxers were wrapped around an ankle. An arm was trapped under his naked body. His green eyes stared at her but saw nothing.

"Michael?" Nancy called shrilly, her voice laced with panic. "Is everything okay? What's going on? What was that noise?"

Serena tore her horrified gaze away from Michael's broken body to where a shadow fell across the upstairs landing. She turned and left, leaving the door wide open. Then she sprinted from the cul-de-sac and kept on running until she found herself on a street she didn't recognize. Bent over and retched into someone's flower bed until nothing else came up. She wiped her mouth with shaking hands and then dropped her cell phone onto the sidewalk. The screen splintered into a spiderweb of cracks but thankfully still worked. Three shaky attempts were needed to book the Uber. The return journey passed in a daze that she barely remembered.

Serena was back in the hotel room in Philadelphia when she received the news.

# 21

## SERENA

### NOW

"You were the intruder?"

Not much shocked Margot, but Serena's confession had managed to do just that. She took off the big glasses and rubbed her eyes.

"Yes, it was me. Intruding on a private moment between my life partner and his friendly neighbor."

When Nancy Bailey had been interviewed by the police, she'd tearfully informed them that an intruder must have been inside the house. Michael had seen someone outside the bedroom, yelled at them, and then had bravely given chase. He'd presumably gotten tangled in his underwear and fallen down the stairs during the pursuit. Nancy didn't get a look at the intruder. Her focus had been on attending to Michael—even though the broken neck had killed him instantly—and then calling 911. She didn't pursue the person and couldn't provide a description of any kind. All she could say for sure was that they'd left the front door wide open when they'd fled, the winter chill seeping into the house, Nancy shivering and distraught on the floor when the emergency services arrived.

The cops had found no sign of forced entry. No broken windows or jimmied locks. But, Nancy admitted, she couldn't be sure Michael had locked the door behind them, seeing as how their passionate tryst had started the moment they were over the threshold before moving upstairs. The most likely theory was an opportunistic burglar, who had lucked out finding an unlocked door in a nice neighborhood and had believed the occupants were asleep. He had then made his escape when confronted by the homeowner, who had sadly died during the chase.

A freak accident.

"I kept waiting for the police to figure out I'd been there," Serena said. "All they had to do was check my credit card statement and follow up on the Uber rides or ask the hotel how often—and at what times—I'd used my key card to access my room. But why would they be suspicious of my whereabouts? I'd just entertained an audience of a hundred people in a bookstore in another state, I'd personally accepted a gift from my publisher delivered by hotel staff to my room, and I was in that very same hotel room when I was notified that Michael was dead."

"Oh honey, no wonder you've been so upset."

Margot's genuine sympathy was more alarming than comforting, seeing as she wasn't big on expressing her softer emotions.

"Now do you understand?" Serena said. "It's my fault that Michael is dead. If I hadn't made that stupid, crazy trip, trying to catch him in the act, he'd still be alive."

"Now, listen to me," Margot said sternly, the glasses back in place. "None of this is your fault. If Michael had been able to keep it in his pants, he would still be alive. If Nancy Bailey hadn't been in his house—in his *bed*—he would still be alive. If anyone's to blame, it's those two. You did nothing wrong. *You* were the wronged party."

144

Serena shook her head. "I lied to the police. I should have told them the truth from the start."

"You didn't lie to them. You just . . . left out some details. Two totally different things in my book."

"I killed Michael just as surely as if I'd run him over with my car or stuck a knife through his heart." She looked at Margot. "I think I should tell the cops everything."

"Don't you dare!" Margot shrieked. Mindful of her husband overhearing, she lowered her voice to an angry whisper. "What good is the truth going to do now? It's not going to bring Michael back, is it? All you'll succeed in doing is ruining your life."

"His daughter, Lucy, deserves to know the truth."

"She already knows," Margot countered. "Her father was boning his horny neighbor while his trusting and loving partner was out of town earning an honest living. Those are the key facts. No good can come from you spilling your guts six months later. Let the woman move on."

Serena smiled weakly through her tears. "You sure you're not just worried about your fifteen percent?"

Margot looked hurt. "No, I'm worried about my friend. In any case, if they locked you up with nothing to do all day but write, your productivity levels would likely triple. You'd get a ton of free publicity too. Look at Jeffrey Archer—jail time didn't do his career any harm, did it? The difference is you didn't commit a crime. So, keep it zipped, okay? If you need to offload some more, talk to me or a shrink or a priest. Just steer clear of the precinct."

Serena fell silent. She felt conflicted. Would confessing help or hurt the other parties involved? Or would it be a selfish act, only to ease her own conscience? Maybe she was being punished enough, having to spend the rest of her life living with this all-consuming guilt. The final image of Michael's sightless eyes would forever be imprinted on her brain like a bad-decision tattoo.

*Click.*

Serena tensed, sat up straight. "Did you hear that?"

"Hear what?" Margot said. "I didn't hear anything."

"I thought I heard a noise. Like a door clicking shut. It came from the kitchen."

Margot frowned. "All the doors are locked, though. You checked, right?"

"Right."

"Check again."

Serena did as she was told. "Kitchen door is definitely locked," she confirmed when she returned.

Margot nodded, apparently satisfied. "What you need right now is sleep. We both do." She inclined her head in the direction of Jonathan's muffled complaints earlier. "Same as Sleeping Beauty in the next room."

"You're right. My bed is calling me."

Serena was suddenly exhausted. She wasn't sure about feeling any lighter—as Mariposa from Cedarwood Farm had predicted—but she did feel drained of all energy. Like she was running on fumes. Most likely from the tequila in the Cadillac margaritas.

"Wash your face first," Margot advised. "All that crying has left you looking like Alice Cooper."

They ended the call and Serena trudged wearily upstairs to the bedroom, where she undressed and changed into her pajamas. She scrubbed her face clean of the ruined makeup and used the bathroom, before climbing into bed. She quickly felt herself being lulled to sleep by the rhythmic slapping of the waves against the rocks.

*Crunch.*

*Crunch.*

*Crunch.*

Serena sat up. The noise was like footsteps on gravel. She thought again of the soft click she'd heard while on the call with

Margot. She listened in the darkness but, other than the ocean and the wind, there was nothing.

Then she remembered the trail camera.

Serena had opted for a model where the images were stored on an SD card in the camera rather than sent directly to her phone via an app. Otherwise, she'd have spent all her time obsessively checking the app, same as she did with Amazon when her books were in a Kindle deal. If she wanted to find out if the camera had captured any suspicious activity, she would have to go outside and retrieve the SD card. It was not a thought she relished. She could see that nothing but inky blackness lay beyond the French doors.

She had two options: Wait until morning when it was light, but spend the rest of the night listening for weird noises. Or go and investigate now that she was wide awake, and satisfy her curiosity.

The second option won out.

Serena slid her feet into a pair of sneakers and pulled on a windbreaker over her pajamas. She found a flashlight in the utility closet and unlocked the kitchen door. Stepped out onto the patio and flinched as a chill wind bit through the thin fabric of the jacket. She aimed the beam at the thicket of trees, the meager light slicing through the darkness until it landed on the trail camera still attached to the trunk of the tall fir. She made a beeline for the camera, removed the SD card, and darted back inside.

She'd returned the laptop upstairs to the office, following the call with Margot. As soon as Serena switched on the desk lamp, she knew something wasn't right. Her fountain pen wasn't clipped to the cover of the notebook. It wasn't on the desk or inside the drawer or on the floor either. She spun around and surveyed the room. There was no sign of the pen anywhere. The Montblanc Meisterstück LeGrand had been a gift from her father after signing her first book deal. The cancer ravaging his body had taken him before he could see her debut published and displayed in bookstore windows. She knew the gift had been expensive, but it wasn't about the money. The pen was priceless. Its value went way beyond monetary terms. Serena vowed to search for the pen in the morning.

Right now, she had to know what—if anything—was on that trail camera.

She inserted the SD card into the drive that she'd purchased at the same time as the camera. Booted up the laptop, opened the drive icon on the desktop, and saw that there were three new files. She clicked on the first, anticipation prickling her scalp. Then she frowned, deflated. A black blur. The second photo was identical. The third was the charm. A face filled the screen, the eyes shining eerily white in the monochrome night-vision shot.

Even so, it was a face she recognized.

# 22

## SERENA

### NOW

It was just after seven-thirty when Serena woke to bright sunshine pouring in through the balcony doors. She was surprised she'd managed to sleep at all after the trail camera discovery, but sheer exhaustion had won out in the end.

Even though the photo was a game changer, she hadn't felt like it was a 911 situation, or even enough of an emergency to reach out to Jack Beaumont in the middle of the night. Now she pulled up his contact details and tapped the call button. It rang and rang before his message service kicked in.

*Dammit.*

To be fair, it was still early on a Sunday morning. If he wasn't on shift, he could be sleeping late or in the shower or out for a run. She had no idea if he was a morning person or not.

"Um, hi, it's Serena Winters," she said after the voicemail beep. "Could you give me a call when you get this message? I've had some threatening emails and also found something interesting on the trail camera that you might want to take a look at."

She got out of bed and showered, and thought about the prowler and why she was being targeted—and what it meant with regards to the Dupries. Did her stalker have anything to do with their disappearance? By the time she'd toweled off and blow-dried her hair and dressed, Beaumont still hadn't returned her call. There had been no contact at all from him since their dinner at the Italian restaurant several days ago. No follow-up about the house. No request to get together again. So, no romantic interest on his part. Serena's frustration turned to embarrassment. She'd thought there was a spark between them but, apparently, it'd been one-sided. Or her determination to talk shop—focusing on Raskin and the Dupries throughout their meal—had put a dampener on the evening for him.

Serena remembered Beaumont's confession about looking her up online and decided to turn the tables. A search for "Jack Beaumont Seaton Point" returned a bunch of newspaper articles about his promotion to chief of police, and community initiatives he'd been involved in, and appeals for information about very minor crimes. The town did appear to be a safe place to live—except where she was concerned. Beaumont didn't have much of a social media presence, other than the occasional appearance on the official SPPD accounts.

Next, Serena trawled Jody's socials. He had a TikTok account but hadn't posted any videos of his own, apparently content to be a lurker. He was more active on Instagram, his grid filled with photos of him surfing and hanging out with friends and snuggling up to a beachy brunette with a tan to rival his own. There were some posts of family events too that included Jody posing with his dad. A birthday party, Christmas dinner, a summer barbecue. It felt like an intrusion, but she didn't want to look away.

Serena thought about Cynthia's comment about a holiday romance. It had been a long time since she'd felt the weight of a man's body on her own. Under different circumstances—if she didn't have to deal with the grief and guilt over Michael's accident, and the novel's looming deadline, and all the sinister events at the Cliff House—she might have welcomed some fun with Jack Beaumont.

Still no word from him. But still early.

Her thoughts turned to the missing fountain pen. She went into the office and yanked the drawer completely from the desk and emptied its contents onto the floor. Peered under the single bed. Tore off the pillows and the bedsheets. Upended the mattress.

No pen.

Not much dust either. Wanda Stockwell was thorough, that was for sure.

Sweat dampened Serena's brow. The office looked like it had been ransacked by a burglar. She stood with her hands on her hips, breathing hard. Next, she carried out an inspection of her own bedroom, and then the middle-sized room.

By ten a.m., she still hadn't found the Montblanc, and she still hadn't heard from Jack Beaumont. She redialed his number. Again, it rang out.

"Fuck it."

Serena grabbed her car keys. If she wanted to know why she was being targeted by a prowler—and being subjected to a campaign of terror—she'd have to go straight to the source of the threats and demand some answers.

After the biting chill of the night before, the morning sun beat down hard and hot. Serena got behind the wheel of the Mustang, slid on her sunglasses against the glare, and started the engine. Gripped the steering wheel and took a big steadying breath.

"You got this," she said aloud. Then cringed.

When had she started talking to herself so much?

She stamped on the gas, the car spitting gravel as she turned onto Cliffside Drive. After almost a mile, George Evans's olive-green bungalow came into view. As usual, the top half of the Dutch door was open and Evans was on the white chair, gently rocking it. His head turned in her direction when he heard the roar of the Ford's engine. He hauled himself to standing, the binoculars quickly in his hand and brought to his eyes as she drew closer.

Once she'd reached his property, Serena jerked the steering wheel. The car careered off the two-lane and onto the packed dirt that passed as a driveway. She hit the brakes. Hot dust rose around her as she came to a stop next to an old Jeep.

George Evans stood stock-still on his porch. He gaped at her. Then he spluttered, "What the actual fuck?"

Serena tossed the shades onto the passenger seat and retrieved her phone—containing the evidence—from the center console. Got out of the car and stormed up the rickety porch steps that creaked and groaned under her weight.

"We need to talk," she said.

Then she saw the rifle under the rocking chair.

*Oh shit.*

She backed away.

Evans followed her gaze. "Home defense," he said. "A man has a right to protect his property."

Serena said nothing. Her eyes were still on the gun. Why hadn't she waited for Jack Beaumont? Why did she have to be the big hero, steaming in, thinking she was a match for an old man? Well, she was no match for an AR-15. What was it that Margot had said about Seaton Point? *A bad situation.* It was that all right.

Evans noticed she was still staring at the rifle. "I'm going to put the gun in the house, okay? Then we can talk."

Serena just nodded.

He disappeared through the Dutch door and, when he returned, was thankfully minus a deadly weapon. Evans gestured for her to sit on the other rocker. She did so warily. After collecting his notebook from the porch railing, he lowered himself slowly into his own chair. Serena took in George Evans's appearance. Mouse-colored hair slicked back with Brylcreem, like it was still the 1950s. Small eyes that were hooded but bright with intelligence. Neatly pressed pants and a button-down shirt and buffed loafers. A man who paid attention to detail.

"You were outside my house last night," she said.

"I was."

"You're not going to deny it?"

"Not much point, is there? I'm guessing you saw me after hearing me walk across the gravel. I'd forgotten about the gravel on the driveway."

"I didn't see you," Serena said. "But my hidden camera did, which is way better because now I have proof to take to the police."

If he was worried by news of a camera, he didn't show it. "I haven't done anything wrong."

"You were trespassing."

He shrugged. "I guess so. But my intentions were benign."

"Were your intentions benign when you smashed out my porch lights? When you gained entry to the property illegally? When you moved my stuff around? Was that all benign too?"

"I didn't touch your porch lights and I've never set foot inside that house."

"Why should I believe you?" Serena demanded. "You've just admitted to prowling around outside my rental property."

"I wasn't prowling," Evans said calmly. "I was looking for someone."

"Looking for who?"

"Whoever's been making late-night visits to your place since you first got here. I wasn't the only one outside your house last night."

"What do you mean, someone else was there? Who?"

"I don't know. That's what I was trying to find out. I keep a log of every vehicle that drives past my property, going to and from the Cliff House." He opened the thick notebook and handed it to her. "That's the log for your stay so far."

The pages were filled with notes written in a neat hand. He'd recorded the make, model, color, and number plate of her rental car, as well as every occasion she'd passed by his bungalow. The Ubers and Wanda Stockwell's Fiat 500 and Jack Beaumont's cruiser were logged too. There were also entries for an "unknown vehicle." She focused on the dates and times. They were an exact match for all the incidents she'd experienced since her first night in Seaton Point.

"Someone *has* been at the house," Serena said. "I was starting to think I was losing my mind. Why no details, though?"

"I've never gotten a proper look at the car—only ever heard it. The driver always waits until after dark and kills the lights. I know it's been the same car each time because I recognize the sound of the engine. But no visuals so far."

"Why didn't you say anything before? Why not knock on my front door instead of creeping around in the middle of the night?"

Evans looked embarrassed. "At first, I thought maybe you were, uh, entertaining a late-night visitor, and your man friend was trying to be discreet with the car lights out. Figured it might be someone making . . . What is it the young folk call it? A booty call."

Serena laughed. "You thought I was sneaking a lover into the Cliff House?" Then she turned serious again. "What changed? Why'd you show up last night?"

"I saw you head into town in an Uber. Then I heard the car again. Earlier than usual, when I knew for sure you weren't home. I thought something was off. I pondered on it awhile, then decided to investigate. Walked on up there with my rifle. Didn't take my Jeep, so I'd have the element of surprise. Wanted to get a look at the car or the driver."

"And did you?"

"Nah. There was no sign of any other vehicle. Just that Mustang rental of yours in the driveway."

Serena was confused. "So, where did it go? The road dead-ends at the Cliff House."

"It had me stumped too," Evans admitted. "But I think I've figured it out. About halfway between my place and yours, there's a stretch of packed dirt behind a copse of trees. My guess is they've been ditching the car there, hidden from the road, and walking the rest of the way."

Serena nodded. "So I wouldn't hear or see them approach. So they could creep around outside unnoticed." She shuddered. "And possibly inside too."

"You've reported it, right? That's why the cop was at the house?"

"That's right."

"At least they're aware."

He didn't seem particularly reassured.

Serena returned her attention to the notebook and thumbed through the pages to the beginning. There were notes on dozens of vehicles . . . A silver Mercedes SUV, a yellow Ferrari, a red Nissan Kicks, a black Ford Escape, a pair of Harley-Davidson motorbikes, a blue Chevy Malibu . . . All entries presumably relating to previous guests.

"These logs go back three years?" she asked, noting the date of the first entry.

"That's right. To the very first guest once the owners turned the property into a rental after it'd lain empty all those years."

"But why? Why all the interest in the comings and goings at the Cliff House?"

"To stop history from repeating itself." Evans shook his head and sighed heavily. "To make amends for letting that family down thirty years ago."

"The Dupries? How did you let them down?"

"Just like last night, I knew something wasn't right the night they vanished. Their schedule was always regular as clockwork. I knew what time the husband left for work in the morning and when he returned home in the evening. When the mom was doing the school run or the weekly grocery shop. They'd never once had a visitor in the whole time they'd lived in the house. That night they did. I heard an unfamiliar car engine. I knew it was unusual, but I did nothing. Didn't bother getting up from the couch to have a look-see out of the window. Didn't want to go poking my nose in where it wasn't wanted. So, I went to bed. Forgot all about it. That is, until I was woken by a car speeding past just after three a.m. I found out a couple days later that the whole family had disappeared. I told Don Raskin about their visitor but couldn't offer him anything useful. If only I'd taken an interest, been more alert, gotten a look at that damn car, maybe the cops would've had something to go on. Maybe they would have tracked it down. Maybe they'd have found that family too."

"You've made a note of every single vehicle that's visited the Cliff House in the last three years so that you have information to pass on to the cops if anything happens to any of the guests?" Serena asked.

"That's right."

"Very impressive. But why are you so sure something bad is going to happen?" She thumbed through the pages again. "This is a hell of a lot of work 'just in case.'"

"That house has a bad energy. Grady Hargreaves . . . The missing family . . . It's only a matter of time before it bears witness to another tragedy." George Evans fixed her with a worried gaze. "And after what you've told me, I fear you could be its next victim."

# 23

## SERENA

### NOW

The missing fountain pen still bothered her.

It was like losing a wedding ring, or a family heirloom inherited in a will. Irreplaceable. Serena felt sick to her stomach at the thought of never seeing it again. Angry too, because she hadn't lost the pen. There had been no carelessness on her part. After what George Evans had told her about her nocturnal visits, she was certain it hadn't simply been misplaced.

She'd already ruled out a burglar casing the joint and then swiping her possessions to sell. There were more valuable items to be pilfered by a sticky-fingered thief than the pen. Jimmy Choo and Manolo Blahnik shoes. Vintage Balenciaga sunglasses. A Fendi baguette. Her Louis Vuitton luggage. Gold Gucci earrings. Her laptop. The list went on.

Serena figured the Montblanc had disappeared for the same reason the wineglass had switched location and the photo of the Dupries had been taken from the office—to mess with her head. To scare her away from Seaton Point.

The pen was unlikely to end up on eBay or in a pawn shop. The "DBD" inscription—the initials of her debut novel, *Dead Before Dawn*—meant it wasn't much use to anyone but her, unless some random person with those exact initials happened upon it. If it had been moved like the wineglass, hidden somewhere in the Cliff House rather than stolen, she was going to tear the place apart until she found it.

Serena began the search in the kitchen. She pulled spice jars and packets of dried pasta and canned goods from the pantry but found nothing hidden in the far corners. Then she opened the deep cabinet drawers housing pots and pans and colanders. No dice there either. She poured tins containing sugar and instant coffee and tea onto the dining table. Boxes of cereal too, like a kid hoping to find a free toy inside. Emptied the trash can onto the floor and picked through the debris. Wanda Stockwell would have a fit if Serena didn't clear up the mess by her scheduled visit tomorrow morning.

But still no sign of the fountain pen.

Her gaze landed on a decorative jug on the windowsill. It was a pale blue shabby-chic metal thing with a plastic sunflower stuck inside. Not to her taste. She picked it up and shook it, her heart hammering when she heard a rattling. She discarded the sunflower and held the jug upside down. A small item clattered onto the countertop. It wasn't the pen.

It was a key.

Serena picked it up and turned it over in her hand. Once silver and now darkened with rust, it looked different to the others on the keyring she'd been given for the Cliff House. Her scalp prickled with excitement when she realized what it was.

Serena took the key out to the hallway and inserted it into the lock on the basement door.

It fit.

She twisted it, and it turned.

Serena slowly pulled open the door and was hit by a musty smell. Nothing but blackness lay beyond the threshold. Her hand fumbled around for a light switch and brushed against a hanging cord. She tugged on it, and nothing happened, the bulb having likely burned out a long time ago.

Serena retrieved the flashlight she'd used the night before from the utility closet. The beam illuminated a wooden staircase, but the weak light didn't reach the bottom. She gripped the handrail with one hand and the flashlight with the other, and started down the stairs in the half-light. Something feathery tickled her face and she fell back against the stairs in surprise, landing hard on her elbows with a yelp. The flashlight beam arced upward to reveal an ancient cobweb hanging from the ceiling like a Halloween decoration, and Serena laughed in relief. The laughter died in her throat when she heard a scuttling in the shadows down below. She hoped it was only mice. Mice she could deal with.

The air was heavy with the stench of dust and decay. Serena had a sudden flash of terror at what she might discover in the basement. Namely, the skeletal remains of three bodies—two adults and one child . . . She stopped halfway down. Her legs were shaking.

"Get a grip," she said out loud. Surely the cops would have searched the entire house at the time of the disappearances, including the basement.

When she reached the bottom, Serena saw that the space was surprisingly large. Dust sheets covered a bunch of unidentified items and gave them the appearance of bedsheet ghosts, missing only the cut-out holes for eyes. She carefully lifted a corner of one of the sheets so as not to disturb the filth coating it, and peered underneath and saw a stationary workout bike. Another revealed an old stereo system, with a collection of vinyl records by the likes of Simple Minds and the Police and the Beastie Boys stored in the glass-fronted cabinet below the record player and twin cassette deck. There were also free weights and a baseball bat and a portable basketball hoop. Serena figured these were all items that had once belonged to Grady Hargreaves.

Two cardboard boxes stacked in a corner caught her eye. She wiped a layer of grime off the top of one and saw the words "DUPRIE FAMILY" written in faded black marker. Her adrenalin spiked. Both cartons were sealed down the middle, the wide tape yellowed by time. They appeared to have been untouched for decades. While desperate to explore their contents, Serena was feeling increasingly uneasy in the basement. The scuttling and scratching noises courtesy of unseen vermin were still here. There was only one small window, which overlooked the cliffs, meaning no way to enter—or exit—the lower level of the house other than through the door she'd just used. Serena glanced up at the rectangle of light at the top of the stairs and had the sudden skin-crawling fear of the door being slammed shut and barricaded, and her being trapped down here forever with Grady Hargreaves's old record collection.

But she needed to know what was inside those cardboard boxes.

Serena lifted one and was happy to discover it wasn't too heavy. She lugged it up the stairs and dumped it in the hallway and then repeated the exercise with the second box. It was a relief to be out of the dank basement and back in the light of the main house and breathing fresh air again. As she closed the door, Serena again noticed the scratches and scores on the lock, like there had been several attempts to pick it.

Someone had really wanted to access that basement.

After clearing the mess on the dining table into a trash bag, Serena moved the Dupries' cardboard boxes from the hallway to the kitchen. The old Scotch tape came away easily under the sharp blade of a knife from the block on the counter.

This box contained items that had once belonged to Charlotte. There were two Barbie dolls—one dressed in a psychedelic print mini-dress with ankle-length crimped hair, the other wearing a short skirt and palm-tree tee with glitter hair—both unmistakably '90s. A stack of drawings that had likely once been taped to the refrigerator, ranging in skill level from kindergarten handprints to depictions of houses and flowers, and a trio of stick figures that were presumably Bill, Dani, and Charlotte. Beneath the artwork were a flattened first-birthday helium balloon and a candle shaped like the number 1. School reports from three different schools in three different states suggested the family had moved around a lot. There were handmade beaded bracelets, and schoolbooks, and a Goosebumps novel with a plastic cover and a stamp inside for a library in Phoenix where it had never been returned.

The second box contained personal effects for the whole family—clip-on earrings and chunky bangles, cologne bottles, ticket stubs from shows and concerts, wristbands from theme park and zoo visits. Again, these were from different towns and states. A couple of picture frames held a photo from Bill and Dani's wedding day and the same family portrait that had been on the front page of the *Seaton Point Sentinel*. The original was in color and Serena could see that Charlotte's hair was a pretty strawberry-blonde shade and her eyes were hazel, in contrast to her parents' respective dark and fair looks.

At the bottom of the box, she found two leather-bound photo albums. The one on top contained images of Bill and Dani as a young couple before Charlotte came along. Bill was handsome in smart made-to-measure suits and jazzy ties, every inch the successful yuppie. Dani was stylish and glamorous in stretch dresses and jumpsuits and big jewelry. In later photos, Bill was gaunter and paler, his thousand-dollar suits now ill-fitting and hanging loose on his thinner frame. The period when he'd been in the grip of drug addiction, Serena guessed. Dani had been described as a home-maker in the newspaper articles after she'd vanished, but appeared to have had some customer-facing jobs previously, judging by the uniforms she wore in some shots.

The second album was dedicated to the family of three— Charlotte as a chubby baby perched on Dani's lap, walking on unsteady legs as a toddler, ripping open Christmas presents in front of a huge tree decorated with tinsel and gaudy baubles, then a different tree in a different living room a couple of years later. There were school shows and sporting events, and trips to Disneyland, and days out at the beach and fairgrounds, and backyard cookouts for three without any other guests in the frame. The final photos in the album had been taken outside the Cliff House, the remaining plastic-covered pages empty and never to be filled.

Serena closed the book with a sense of sadness that this could have been where the Duprie family story had come to an end; that they might never have had the chance to add to those special memories. But underneath the sadness, something niggled at her. Something didn't feel right about those albums.

Then it came to her. It wasn't the photos, so carefully spaced out on those pages, that had caught her attention.

It was what *wasn't* there.

# 24

## RUBY

### JUNE 1984

Ruby was finally returning to Monroe—and to River. After almost a year apart, she was going to be with her love again.

His feelings for her seemed to be every bit as strong as the day she'd left, judging by his letters. He'd written that he couldn't wait to see her again, would be there waiting at the bus stop in his pickup truck to greet her, just like last summer. He'd even offered to pay for her ticket, but Grandma Pearl had wired her the money. She knew the real story, why Ruby didn't have two dimes to rub together most of the time—where all her cash went.

Ruby was desperate to be reunited with River. She missed him so much it was like a physical ache. But she had no idea whether he'd still be so pleased to see her—whether he would still want her—when she stepped off the bus this time.

When he realized that she wasn't alone.

She had no choice but to be brave—and to be honest. She'd lied to him for long enough. It was time to tell River the truth. Better still, *show* him.

River Henderson was a dad now; Ruby a teenage mom just like her own mom had been. Their daughter, Amber, had been born three months ago. She'd made her appearance in the world a little earlier than planned, had been tinier than expected, but now she was positively thriving. Ruby had decided to continue the gemstone name tradition, and Grandma Pearl had been delighted after getting over the initial shock of the pregnancy. Pearl had never asked about the father, but Ruby suspected she knew it was River. Who else could it be? She trusted that her grandma wouldn't breathe a word to him until Ruby was ready.

When her mom had found out about the baby, she'd looked Ruby up and down with smug satisfaction and said, "Like mother, like daughter, huh?" Then Coral had informed her she'd have to pay for any abortion herself. A termination was never in the cards. Sure, Ruby had been devastated when the pee test was positive, after the longest three minutes of her life, but she'd vowed to make it work somehow.

Coral had marched her straight back to The Cutting Edge to ask for her old job back on the basis that the vomiting had been down to pregnancy rather than partying. Figured Ruby could still work for a good few months yet and bring some cash into the apartment. The owner's gaze had dropped to Ruby's left hand and the lack of a wedding band.

"You're eighteen, right?" Darla had asked.

"Yes."

A frown. "You planning on marrying the dad?"

Before Ruby could answer, her mom had cut in. "He's not on the scene, Darla. Just the way it goes sometimes, right? I didn't even know she had a boyfriend."

Her ex-boss had shaken her head. "No can do, Coral. You know what the coffin dodgers are like in here. They won't approve of a kid with a fat pregnant belly and no ring on her finger. I'm sorry, but it's a no."

Ruby had never told her mom that the dad *was* on the scene, that it was just a complicated situation. Complicated because he had no idea that he had a daughter. She still harbored hopes of a new life in Monroe if River was willing to accept her and Amber as a package deal. If he was prepared to give their little family a real go.

Amber had Ruby's red hair and River's hazel eyes. His button nose too. She hoped her daughter would also inherit his amazing smile, but it was too soon to tell which way that one was going to go. As if on cue, Amber looked up at her from her stroller and giggled and Ruby's heart swelled.

Her mom had been wrong—Ruby was nothing like Coral. She had known instinctively that she would love this baby the first time she felt it move inside her, after that very first kick. That was the moment when two lines in a pregnancy test window had suddenly become a real person. The first time she held Amber in her arms, any lingering doubts and regrets melted away. Ruby had been overwhelmed by the intensity of this new kind of love. Even the depth of feeling that she had for River didn't compare. Surely he would feel the same way when he saw Amber?

Ruby needed to pee before the journey. She felt like she had to empty her bladder a lot more often since being pregnant and then giving birth. The bus for Seattle wasn't due to leave the station for another half hour, so there was plenty of time. She pushed the stroller into the restroom and saw that the bigger, disabled toilet was out of order, leaving only the smaller one in use. The stall was too narrow to squeeze the stroller into. She parked it right outside the stall door next to the washbasin, making sure the brake was on.

Ruby locked the door, pulled down her jeans and underwear and sat, then groaned when she saw there was no toilet paper. Her tissues were in her backpack in the stroller's storage basket, along with the baby bag. She had just started to pee when the exterior door to the restroom opened, and the hustle and bustle of the station outside was briefly louder before quickly becoming muffled again. Ruby remembered the other toilet was out of order.

"I'll just be a moment," she called out. "There's no toilet paper, though, so I hope you have Kleenex!"

There was no answer.

The exterior door opened again—station announcements and passenger chatter and the roar of big engines firing up—then slammed shut.

"Okay, suit yourself," she muttered.

Ruby finished up and fixed her underwear and jeans. Opened the stall door. Looked at the stroller, expecting to see her baby's big smile, drool spilling from her chin onto the brand-new lemon-and-white Gerber sleeper Ruby had purchased for Amber's first time meeting her daddy.

Panic shot through her like a lightning bolt.

The stroller was empty.

# 25

## SERENA

### NOW

Serena looked through both photo albums again. This time, she paid extra attention to each and every glossy shot, making sure she hadn't missed anything. She hadn't. She'd been right the first time.

There were no photos of Dani Duprie during her pregnancy. No switch from the figure-hugging dresses and silk blouses to billowing maternity gowns; no poses by the mom-to-be gently cradling her bump; no images of Bill tenderly touching the belly his unborn first child was growing inside.

And no photos of Charlotte as a newborn either.

The earliest was as a baby, perched on Dani's knees. Serena studied the photo. Charlotte was sitting up, a thick tuft of orange hair standing up like a flame, her eyes bright and alert, a big smile on display for whoever was behind the camera. Serena had no kids of her own and hadn't spent a whole lot of time around other people's babies, but she would guess Charlotte to be around six months old when the moment was captured. There were plenty more photos of Bill and Dani's daughter in the years that followed., but none before this one. Why?

The most logical explanation was that there was a third album, one that was missing just like the family who'd once owned it. An album that slotted in between the ones of Dani and Bill as a young couple and the later family years. Perhaps it had been taken by the Dupries if they'd fled the Cliff House that night, as Don Raskin had always believed. It would make sense, if they did have to leave in a hurry, that they would choose to take with them the photographs that documented the days and weeks when Charlotte first came into their lives.

But still.

Serena turned her attention to the rest of the contents of the cardboard boxes. Inside were greetings cards and birthday pins right up until Charlotte's tenth birthday, but nothing from before the balloon and candle for her first. Of course, it was a big milestone, but what about the day she was born? Didn't parents usually hold on to stuff from that time? Again, Serena was no expert, but she thought new moms and dads often kept locks of hair and tiny booties and those little hospital wristbands from the birth?

Now she picked up the ornate frame that held the family portrait. Bill's brown eyes matched his dark hair, which was still unblemished by any gray. Dani was the quintessential all-American blue-eyed blonde. Then there was Charlotte, who didn't seem to have inherited anything from either parent, with her strawberry-blonde hair and hazel eyes. No likeness to Bill and Dani in terms of features either. No shared jawline or carbon-copy nose or similar smile. Which proved nothing.

But still.

Something gnawed at Serena. A suspicion, a hunch. She hadn't found a copy of Charlotte's birth certificate, but there was no marriage certificate or any other official documents either. Any important paperwork could have been seized by the cops or stored by Bill and Dani in some long-forgotten safe-deposit box for safekeeping. Everything that felt wrong about the Dupries' belongings—or lack thereof—had a perfectly reasonable explanation.

But the thought crystalized in Serena's mind anyway: *What if Charlotte wasn't Bill and Dani's child?*

Okay, so the kid could have been adopted. That would account for the lack of pregnancy and newborn photos, as well as no keepsakes from the first few months of Charlotte's life. It would also explain Dani's apparent overprotectiveness of her daughter. If she and Bill had experienced fertility challenges that had prevented them from conceiving, then it made sense that Dani would be super-protective of the much-wanted and wished-for child that had come to them via the gift of adoption. If Charlotte *had* been adopted, it was likely that no one in Seaton Point ever found out, but so what? It was no one else's business. The Dupries were not obliged to explain to the townsfolk that Dani wasn't Charlotte's birth mom. If it was even true. This was all just speculation on Serena's part.

But why all the secrecy? Why keep everyone at arm's length? Why the reluctance to allow anyone to get close to them? Also notably absent from the albums were photos of Charlotte with other kids at playdates or on outings to the park or at parties. It seemed like the sleepover at Wanda Stockwell's house for Hannah's tenth birthday had been a first—and something Dani had clearly been very uncomfortable with. Even if Dani had wanted to avoid conversations with the other school moms about birthing stories and stretch marks and cravings and so on, why deny her daughter the freedom to make friends?

Dani and Bill's behavior seemed extreme. There was the moving around a lot too. Idaho, Colorado, Arizona. And, of course, the biggest indicator of all that something was off about the

Dupries—their unexplained disappearance on a late summer's night thirty years ago.

Another thought popped into her head just then and Serena tried to shut it down. It was crazy. Impossible, surely . . .

But still.

Serena raced upstairs and unplugged her laptop from where it had been charging in the office and brought it downstairs to the dining table. A quick online search was all it would take to answer the questions flashing in her mind like big red warning signs:

*What if 1994 wasn't the first time Charlotte Duprie had been reported missing?*

*What if she'd vanished the year she was born too?*

Serena typed the search terms into Google and discovered that 1984 was a significant year for missing kids after ten-year-old Kevin Collins vanished from a bus stop in San Francisco. His disappearance had gained national attention when he became one of the first missing children to be featured on milk cartons across the country. He'd also appeared on the cover of *Newsweek* but was never found. As well as Wikipedia's list of people who disappeared that year, Serena trawled their list of kidnappings.

Only one entry stood out.

Three-month-old Amber Bryant was last seen at a bus station in Portland, Oregon, on the morning of June 4, 1984. She was traveling with her teenage mother, who had been planning on visiting her grandmother in Monroe, Washington, so she could meet the baby for the first time. Amber was allegedly abducted from a restroom at the terminal. At the time of her disappearance, she was two feet long and weighed eleven pounds. She had reddish hair and hazel eyes and was wearing a lemon-and-white Gerber sleeper.

Serena checked all the school reports and ticket stubs, but Bill and Dani Duprie appeared to have had no connection to either Portland or Monroe, despite having lived in several states. She paged through the albums again and stopped on a photo of Dani in a work uniform posing outside a Streamline Moderne building that could have been a bus station. The street sign above her indicated she was on "SW Taylor St." Serena gently peeled back the plastic sheet and removed the photo from the sticky page. There was blocky handwriting in ballpoint pen on the back: *First day at work! Nov '83. Beep beep!*

The next photo was of Bill and Dani at a party, both holding cigarettes, half-empty wineglasses on the table in front of them. They were in some kind of function suite, the mahogany wood paneling softened by balloons and banners reading: *Happy Retirement Bruce!* On the back of the photo was the same blocky handwriting: *Bruce Garrett's retirement party. Feb '84.*

Serena googled "Bruce Garrett" and "Portland" and the word "bus" and got a hit—an obituary in a local newspaper from 1999. Bruce had passed peacefully, surrounded by his wife and two sons, after a short battle with cancer. Which was sad but not what interested Serena. The sentence about his beloved career was what got her blood pumping. Bruce Garrett had spent forty years as a bus driver working out of the old Greyhound bus terminal located on SW Taylor between 5th and 6th Avenues. The same bus station Amber Bryant had been abducted from—and where Dani Duprie also appeared to have been an employee.

A baby with reddish hair and hazel eyes.

Who would be forty now, just like Charlotte Duprie.

*Holy shit.*

It was tenuous, to say the least. Circumstantial at best. Wouldn't stand up in a court of law. But just like Hank Macaulay, Serena didn't believe in coincidences. She could feel it in her gut. She was onto something, same as when she hit on a new idea for a novel, or her plot strands came together, or a major twist presented itself to her. She had that same sweaty-palms feeling right now because this was one hell of a plot twist.

Dani Duprie had stolen Ruby Bryant's baby from a bus station forty years ago.

# 26

## DANI

### JUNE 1984

Dani became aware of a dreadful howling noise. A cry filled with pain and anguish.

Her gaze shot over to where the buses moved in and out of the station. Had someone gone under one of the big wheels? Her heart quickened. *Oh God, please don't let it be a child.* Then she realized there was a commotion on the concourse outside the ladies' restroom. Maybe someone had taken ill.

There was a long line of people waiting at her booth, so she dished out tickets and counted out change and confirmed departure times, all the while discreetly craning her neck for a look-see at what was going on. A crowd was gathering now.

Then a woman around Dani's age, dressed in a smart pantsuit and light trench coat and carrying a soft leather briefcase, rushed up to the customer service point, just along from the ticket booths. She was flushed and looked stricken.

"A baby's been stolen," she said breathlessly. "You have to call the police."

"Huh?" said Susan, the customer service advisor, who Dani had always thought was pleasant enough if not the brightest bulb in the pack.

"A baby has been abducted from the restroom!" the business-woman yelled. "Do something! Call 911. The mother is hysterical over there!"

Susan made an announcement over the public address system, summoning the station manager. Pete Friedman took his sweet time making his way over. When he finally appeared and was told what was going on, his face turned as white as his starched shirt.

"Fuck," he said, kind of summing up Dani's own feelings. After reporting the incident to the police, he pulled at the knot of his tie and wiped at a bead of sweat on his forehead and said to no one in particular, "We need to try and find this kid."

Dani placed the "Position Closed" sign in front of her window and ignored the loud complaints of those in line, who were either oblivious to the situation unfolding around them or still prioritiz-ing their journey over the wellbeing of a small child. She'd planned on helping with the search, other staff members and drivers already fanning around the station concourse, looking in trash cans and searching the buses.

Then she noticed a young woman sitting on a bench on her own. Slim, with long reddish hair, pale skin, and a smattering of freckles across cheeks that were wet with tears. She looked numb, in shock, staring into the distance at nothing, her fingers worrying at a red stone pendant around her neck. Next to her was an empty stroller. She didn't look much older than a kid herself and Dani's heart broke for her.

She couldn't begin to imagine what the girl was going through right now. Dani had lost a child too, a miscarriage at eleven weeks, four years ago, but nothing like this. She went over to the vending machine and took some change from her uniform pocket. Made the selection for black coffee, hit the button for extra sugar. Took the drink over to the bench and sat next to the girl and offered her the Styrofoam cup.

"It'll help with the shock," she said, not knowing if it was true.

The girl took the coffee but didn't drink any. She turned to Dani with a glazed look in her eyes. "I only left her for a minute," she said. "Not even a minute. She was right outside the stall door. I could see the stroller's wheels. How could this have happened?"

"What's your name, sweetheart?"

"Ruby."

"And your baby?"

"Amber."

"That's a beautiful name. I'm Dani. Don't worry, Ruby, we're going to find Amber. The police are on their way and everyone's looking for her. I bet this has all been some big misunderstanding and she'll turn up soon."

"She's only three months old." Ruby's lower lip began to tremble, followed by more tears. "Someone has taken my baby. Oh God. She's gone. My baby is gone."

Dani put her arm around Ruby's slim shoulders and pulled her in close. Felt a need to try to help this girl even if all she could offer was crappy coffee and hollow words of comfort. Even if a small part of her was thinking: *Why did you leave your baby on her own?*

"Everything's going to be okay, Ruby," she soothed. "I promise. We'll find her. She can't have gone far."

But they didn't find her. No one had seen the baby with the red hair wearing the lemon-and-yellow sleepsuit. Not with the mom before she entered the restroom and not after with someone else—someone who could have made their escape on a departing bus and be halfway across the country by now.

Dani was still shaken by the events of the day when Bill got home from work. She told him what had happened with the missing

176

baby, and they watched the evening news together. Unsurprisingly, it was the top story. Amber Bryant. Three months old. Abducted from a bus station in downtown Portland. They showed a photo of the baby—red hair, hazel eyes, big toothless smile—and Dani's heart clenched.

Bill noticed her tears. "Oh honey," he said, giving her shoulder a squeeze. "You did your best. You comforted that girl during the worst moment of her life and I'm sure she appreciated it, but there's nothing more you could have done."

"I wish it was me," she said flatly.

"Wish what was you?" he asked, confused.

"I wish I'd stolen that baby."

"You don't mean that."

Dani sniffed. "I do, Bill. What if it never happens for us? The miscarriage, the failed attempts, the bleeding each month, the having to try again and again and again. What if we never have a baby of our own? It's been years, and still nothing." She stared glumly at the image of Amber Bryant on the screen. "Someone else was just as desperate as we are, and now they do have a baby."

Bill didn't say anything. They sat in silence for a while.

Finally, she said, "You think I'm a terrible person, don't you? To even think such a thing. I saw that girl's despair firsthand and all I could think was: *Why do you get to have a baby and I don't? I would never have let that little girl out of my sight for a single second.*"

"I don't think you're a terrible person," he said.

Bill's actions said otherwise. That night, for the first time in months, Dani heard him steal out of the apartment when he thought she was sleeping. Leaving her alone again. She must have drifted off finally, because she awoke to Bill gently rousing her. It was only just starting to get light outside. He was perched on the edge of the bed and still wearing last night's clothes and clearly hadn't slept.

"Bill?" she said, her voice thick with sleep. "What time is it? What's going on?"

Even in the half-light, the expression on his face made her sit up, fully awake now. Dani had never seen him look so serious. She had a sudden flashback to the night of the accident, cops at the front door, saying her husband had crashed his car into a lamppost. No idea if he was hurt or had hurt someone else or if he was even still alive. Thankfully, the only damage had been to the Beamer and Bill's reputation.

But what now? A relapse? Another accident?

"There's something I need to show you," he said. "Just . . . don't freak out, okay?"

"Okay . . ."

"Come with me."

Dani got out of bed, her nerves thrumming, legs weak as she followed him into the hallway.

Bill gestured nervously. "This is what I wanted to show you."

Dani couldn't believe what she was seeing.

"Oh Bill," she said. "What have you done?"

# 27

## RUBY

### JUNE 1984

Amber had been missing for three weeks. Ruby felt a weird kind of detachment from the situation, like it was all happening to someone else.

The first few days had been spent being interviewed—first by the police and then by reporters. She'd made appeals to the public for information, like she was on an episode of *60 Minutes* or in a scene from a movie. None of it felt real. The only aspect that did feel real was being without Amber. It was like a part of her was missing, as though she'd lost an arm or a leg, only much worse. The pain was physical and raw and visceral.

Ruby hadn't heard from River. He'd so far failed to write her or call. She didn't know if the news about missing baby Amber Bryant had reached Monroe, Washington. If River had seen the reports and figured out the truth and wanted nothing more to do with her. Or if he'd been waiting at the bus stop, wondering why she didn't get off the Greyhound she was supposed to be on, or the next one, or the one after that. Had eventually reached the conclusion that she'd rejected him.

It felt like she'd lost the two people she loved most in the world in one fell swoop. River and Amber, both ripped away from her.

Then there was the detective who'd been put in charge of the investigation. Ruby detested the man. Detective Kolinsky was around the same age as her mom's boyfriends. He had greasy hair that Darla at The Cutting Edge couldn't pay Ruby a hundred bucks to touch, and a thick mustache that covered his top lip. He wore creased brown suits and cream shirts and ugly patterned ties, and liked to sit back in his chair with his legs crossed, watching her. Sometimes he appeared to be judging her; other times he had the same wolfish look in his eyes that Ray used to have. Ruby didn't know if Kolinsky was hot for her or disgusted by her—probably both—but he wasn't doing a whole lot to find her baby. Worse, he seemed to think Ruby was behind her own daughter's disappearance. She thought back to her first interview with him.

◆ ◆ ◆

*"A little young to have a kid, huh?" Kolinsky consulted his notes. "Eighteen. Unmarried. I'm assuming it wasn't planned?"*

*"No."*

*"How did you feel when you found out you were knocked up?"*

*"Surprised. Shocked, I guess."*

*"And pissed too, I'll bet. Your life ruined like that."*

*Ruby bristled. "I came around to the idea very quickly. Amber means everything to me."*

*Kolinsky crushed his cigarette butt into an ashtray. Pulled a pack from his breast pocket and sparked up another. His fingers were the color of old library-book pages. "Huh. Okay. And the dad? Do you know who the dad is?"*

She waved his cigarette smoke from her face. "Of course I do."

"Where's he at?" The detective flicked through his notes again. "There's been no mention of him at all."

"He lives out of state."

"Out of state, huh? Convenient." Kolinsky stroked the mustache, fingered the paisley-print tie. "He got a name, this out-of-state guy?"

Ruby didn't answer.

"Could he be involved?" he pressed.

"No."

"Why are you so sure?"

"I just am."

Ruby wasn't going to tell this douchebag that River didn't know about Amber.

There was a long pause. Kolinsky's eyes raked over her body. He stroked the mustache again. Finally, he said, "What really happened at the bus station, Ruby?"

"I already told those other officers."

The uniformed cops who'd responded to the 911 call had been nice. Well, nicer than Detective Kolinsky. Especially the lady cop. She'd brought Ruby hot drinks and offered encouraging words, same as the woman who worked at the bus station. The male cop had taken her statement, though, appeared to be the one in charge.

"I want you to tell me what happened," Kolinsky said.

"I needed to use the bathroom. I was in the stall when the outside door opened, and someone came into the restroom. I called out to them, and they didn't answer. Then the abductor was gone and so was Amber."

"You didn't get a look at this 'abductor'?"

Why was he saying the word "abductor" like that? Like the person didn't exist?

"I already told the police this too," she said, exasperated. "It's in my statement. I didn't see anyone. I was inside the stall. But I'm guessing *it was a woman. It was a women's restroom. A woman with a baby would be less conspicuous."*

Kolinsky stubbed out his cigarette. Didn't light another this time. Instead, he leaned across the table, so his face was inches from her own. He stank of cheap cologne and cigarettes and body odor. "Okay, cards on the table," he said. "Amber was never at the bus station, was she?"

Ruby was shocked. "What? Of course she was."

"We don't have any eyewitnesses who saw you with a baby. Just an empty stroller."

"They probably weren't paying me any attention before . . . it happened. I mean, I wouldn't have been able to tell you anything about the other passengers who were there that day."

"Did you do something to Amber? Take her someplace?"

Ruby was aghast. "No! I love Amber. Why would I hurt her?"

"You said it yourself: you didn't want her."

"No, I said finding out I was pregnant was a shock."

He kept talking like he hadn't heard her.

"And you being on your own and all. Must be hard for a young woman to cope with a baby all by herself. You should be out having fun. You wanted your freedom back. I get it, I really do. Just tell us where she is, Ruby."

"Fuck you. We're done here."

Kolinsky hadn't believed her version of events but at least the media were taking Ruby seriously. Amber's face had been plastered all over the evening news and the front pages of the papers. Maybe a witness would come forward, remember a key detail that cracked the case wide open, force the cops to take her seriously. But Ruby didn't trust Kolinsky to find her daughter, and she couldn't sit around doing nothing, so she'd started searching for Amber herself.

Admittedly, she had made some mistakes. The baby on the blanket on a front lawn, fat legs and arms and a tuft of red hair, just like Amber's. The mom had freaked out when Ruby picked her up, but she'd needed to know for sure it wasn't Amber. And then there was the woman pushing the stroller, its plastic cover speckled with rain, concealing the baby cocooned inside from view. She had stared hard at Ruby and then pushed the stroller faster to get away, and Ruby had pursued her down the street, screaming at her to stop. Turned out the woman had simply recognized Ruby from the news. Her own baby was a dark-haired little boy.

Detective Kolinsky had hauled Ruby back into the station, given her a warning, ordered her to stop harassing innocent people. Told her she'd caused these women and their children great distress. But what about *her* distress? Those moms still had their babies, didn't they? Ruby didn't. She was the victim, but she was being treated like a criminal. Why were people so cruel?

Not all people, though. Not the worker at the bus station, who had put her arm around Ruby and comforted her without judgment.

That's why she was back at the terminal today. Ruby should have come sooner, but had been unable to face it until now. She'd bought a bunch of carnations, hadn't been able to afford anything fancier, all her cash spent printing up flyers and traveling the city in search of Amber. Ruby wanted to thank the woman—Dani, she'd said her name was—for her kindness.

The advisor at the customer service point did a dramatic double take when she spotted Ruby. Surprise was quickly replaced by pity. She clearly remembered her. Her name badge read "Susan."

"Any news, sweetheart?" Susan asked.

"Nothing yet."

"We're all praying for your little girl's safe return."

"Thank you."

"Now what can I do for you?"

"That day . . . one of your coworkers looked after me. She was so kind, and I wanted to thank her, so I bought her these." Ruby held up the flowers. "She told me her name was Dani."

"Oh, how thoughtful. But I'm afraid Dani no longer works here."

Ruby was disappointed. The flowers had been cheap, but still cost more than she could afford to spend. "Oh. I don't suppose you have an address for her?"

Susan hesitated. "We're not really supposed to give out that kind of information about staff members. Although I guess Dani is former staff now." She looked from the flowers to Ruby's drawn face, then lowered her voice. "Ah, heck. What harm can it do? Give me a moment."

Susan returned a few minutes later with a folded piece of paper and discreetly passed it to Ruby like they were two spies sharing information that could bring down a government.

The address was in Goose Hollow, within walking distance of the bus terminal. Dani's apartment was housed within an impressive red-stone building with huge bay windows and ornate trim, nothing like the cramped two-bed matchbox Ruby shared with her mom on the other side of the city. She wondered how someone who sold tickets at a Greyhound station could afford to live in a place this fancy. She pressed the intercom button for Dani's unit and, when there was no answer, tried her neighbor. After a short delay, a buzzer sounded, and the front entrance clicked open.

The door of the apartment facing Dani's was open when Ruby reached the shared landing. A septuagenarian with silver hair and gold jewelry hovered in the doorway. She was all dressed up in tan nylons and a crepe dress and kitten heels even though it was the middle of the day, her red lipstick bleeding into the creases around her mouth.

"If you're here about the apartment, you're too late," she said. "The realtor left a half hour ago. Viewings are over for the day."

"What realtor? I'm sorry, but I don't know what you're talking about."

The woman gestured to the door opposite with a flick of a skinny wrist. "The rental. I assumed you were here for a viewing." She sized Ruby up, taking in her jeans and battered Converse and faded Portland Trail Blazers tee, and said, "No, perhaps not." Then she narrowed her eyes and peered over her glasses. "Do I know you? You look familiar."

"The apartment is empty?" Ruby removed the note Susan had given her from her pocket and showed it to the older woman. "This is the address I was given. I'm looking for Dani."

"You have the right place, but Dani and Bill are gone. Left just over a week ago. All quite sudden. And, no, they didn't leave a forwarding address, before you ask."

Ruby's shoulders slumped. "Well, I guess I've had a wasted journey."

"Friends of yours, were they?"

"No, I didn't know them at all. I was just dropping these off for Dani."

Ruby looked glumly at the flowers, which were starting to wilt now.

"Can't say I'm sorry they're gone," the neighbor continued. "The husband was in and out of that apartment at all hours of the night. Coco, that's my cat, would go crazy when she heard him, start scratching at the front door. At first, I figured he worked nights but, ahh, I'm not so sure. And that baby crying these last few weeks." She shook her head. "Insufferable."

"Dani had a baby?"

That's probably why she'd been so nice to Ruby when Amber was taken, because she was a mom herself.

"No, Bill and Dani didn't have kids. This baby appeared suddenly. Not that I ever saw it, but I heard it plenty, that's for sure. I guess they were babysitting for a couple weeks. In any case, I'm glad of the peace and quiet now. Say, are you sure I don't know you from someplace?"

But Ruby was no longer listening.

She needed to speak to Detective Kolinsky straightaway.

# 28

## SERENA

### NOW

Serena's head was spinning. Could Dani Duprie really have abducted a baby and then passed the kid off as her own for years?

It was like a plot from one of her novels, and that thought gave her pause. Maybe Serena was letting her imagination run away with her. No, her gut was telling her otherwise. Then the internal voice reminded her that she wasn't some grizzled, veteran detective in an old cop show who solved crimes based on a gut feeling. But her gut had told her Michael was cheating on her and she had been right about that.

What was it the ex-reporter Patrick Dolan had said about the Dupries?

*I think they were running from something—or someone. Hiding from their past. And it caught up with them.*

Had they been running from the police? Or Ruby Bryant? Hank Macaulay claimed a young woman had been in Seaton Point asking specifically about Dani Duprie just hours before the family vanished. Could the woman have been Ruby Bryant?

Serena sat back in the chair and pondered what she should do about her discovery. Taking it to Jack Beaumont would be the sensible thing but—she tapped her phone screen—yep, he was still ghosting her. The very idea that he was ignoring her calls because he thought she was looking for excuses to talk to him or was angling for another candlelit meal together filled her with mortification. What would she tell him, anyway? That she had a hunch that Dani Duprie had stolen a baby, with absolutely no facts whatsoever to back up the accusation?

There were still too many unanswered questions. Serena didn't even know for sure if the Portland terminal had still been Dani's place of work when Amber Bryant was kidnapped. Dani was apparently employed there from November 1983 through February 1984, according to the notations on the backs of the photographs, but she could have been long gone by June of that year. After all, Dani and Bill hadn't liked to stay in one place for too long. Or had the moving around only happened after Charlotte came into their lives?

Then there was the Amber Bryant case. Serena needed to know more, but there was a frustrating lack of information online. Websites like The Charley Project and Missing Kids had the basic facts, such as a physical description of the missing person—who'd been a baby in this case—and where they'd last been seen and what they were wearing and so on, but there was nothing about the police investigation or any updates on sightings or leads in the years that had passed since then. Both websites included the same age-progression photo of how Amber might look now, but it was a generic image of a middle-aged woman with long red hair and hazel eyes that could have been anyone.

Serena had to assume the information on those missing person websites was bang up to date, and that, just like the milk carton kid, Amber Bryant had never been found. What she wanted to know was what had happened in the four decades she'd been missing. Did the cops have any eyewitnesses or prime suspects or leads, or any other intel that ruled out Dani Duprie as the abductor? And what had become of teen mom Ruby Bryant?

The kidnapping had happened too long ago for Serena to find original newspaper articles from back then through a general search engine—but what about the twentieth anniversary of her disappearance? The thirtieth? The fortieth, which would have been earlier this year? Surely Ruby Bryant would have renewed her appeals for information in the media on those significant dates? But Serena had found nothing.

Again, her thoughts turned to Jack Beaumont and whether she should be sharing this information with him; whether he'd be able to answer some of those questions through his police contacts. Just then her cell phone started ringing loudly and she almost jumped a foot in the air.

"Jeez," she yelled, clutching a hand to her chest. Serena looked at the screen. The caller ID read *Jack Beaumont.* "Jeez," she said again.

It was like summoning the Candyman by saying his name five times in front of a mirror. She answered the call.

"Hi, Serena?" Beaumont said. "I just listened to the voicemails you left me. I, uh, was on a fishing trip with Jody and had my ringer off. Sorry for taking so long to get back to you."

Why would his phone be on silent all that time? In case he pissed off the fish? Serena had no idea if absolute silence was even a thing when fishing. She could hear voices in the background and the sound of lapping water, like he was outside and possibly on a boat. But surely, even on a weekend, on his day off, the chief of police would be checking his cell phone occasionally in case of any emergencies?

Beaumont went on: "You said you've had some threatening emails? And you wanted to show me something that turned up on the trail camera? Was it an intruder?"

Now she thought he sounded sheepish, like he had deliberately sent her calls to his messaging service and only realized she'd had a legitimate reason for reaching out to him after listening to them.

"It's fine," she said coolly. "The trail camera issue was a misunderstanding."

"A misunderstanding how?"

"It captured an image of my neighbor, George Evans, outside the Cliff House in the middle of the night. I guess I freaked out and assumed he was the person who'd been harassing me. So, I called you. When I didn't hear back, I confronted George myself."

"Wait, George Evans was prowling outside your rental property? Why would he do that? Has he threatened you?"

"No, it's like I said, a misunderstanding." Serena explained about George Evans and his notebooks and how he'd been tracking a car that he'd heard making late-night visits to the house but had thus far been unable to glean any details about the vehicle or the driver. "That's why he was outside the house and inadvertently triggered the trail camera."

"Shit, Serena," Beaumont said. "I'm so sorry I didn't pick up earlier. But you should have waited for me to speak to George about the trespassing, instead of confronting him yourself."

"It's fine. He was only trying to help."

"Yes, George is a good guy, but you didn't know that. You could have been walking into a dangerous situation. Next time— and I'm hoping there isn't a next time—let me handle it, okay?"

"Okay."

"Now, tell me about these emails."

Serena filled him in on what had been written in the emails sent to her public author account and how she believed the same person had been responsible for the threatening note left under her windshield wiper on her first day in town.

Beaumont said, "We're a small operation here in Seaton Point and don't have the kind of technical expertise needed to track down a sender via their IP address, so I'd need to kick that one further up the food chain to the county's tech experts. But you should know that there are no guarantees they'll get anything useful. A lot of these trolls use VPNs to disguise their whereabouts and can be almost impossible to track down."

"That's what I thought," Serena said. "I'm guessing whoever sent those emails is smart enough to cover their tracks both online and in real life. They've managed it well enough so far."

"I'll see what I can do, but I do want to have a look at those emails. Can you drop by the station tomorrow morning with your laptop?"

Serena said that she would.

"I'll follow up with George Evans too," Beaumont added. "Get a statement about this car that's been visiting the Cliff House. We don't have the resources to post a cruiser outside the property twenty-four-seven, but I am going to organize scheduled patrols to keep an eye on things for the time being."

"Okay. Thank you."

Serena hoped she would sleep easier knowing there was a police presence outside the Cliff House. And, with a bit of luck, the sight of a cop car might put the frighteners on whoever was targeting her.

"Was there anything else?" Beaumont asked.

Serena hesitated. She wanted to know more about the Amber Bryant case but—glancing now at the photo albums and books and toys and other knickknacks scattered across the dining table—she realized she couldn't reveal the real reason for her interest. If she told Beaumont about the suspected link between Dani Duprie and the bus station baby, she'd have to admit she'd accessed the

191

basement and gone through the family's personal belongings. This wasn't her house. Serena had no right to poke around in places that were clearly out of bounds for guests. She had complained to the police about someone snooping around the Cliff House and going through her things, so to admit that she'd done something similar would not be a good look.

"I wanted to ask a favor," she said.

"Sure thing. Shoot."

"You know how I'm writing a book about a missing family after finding out about the Dupries? Well, I came across another interesting real-life case about a missing person that I'm thinking about incorporating into the plot. A baby girl by the name of Amber Bryant who was abducted from a bus terminal in Portland, Oregon, back in 1984. I'd really like to know more about the case—if it was ever resolved, what happened to the mom . . . But look, I know you're busy and helping novelists isn't part of your job description, so . . ."

"No, it's fine," Beaumont said quickly, and Serena figured he was still feeling guilty about the ghosting and was keen to make amends. "I can ask Kelly to make some calls. Amber Bryant, Portland, right?"

"Right. That would be great."

"No problem. Remember to stop by the station tomorrow morning with those emails. And call me if you have any more problems before then."

"I will. On both counts."

They ended the call and Serena pulled the laptop toward her. Talking about the emails had reminded her that she hadn't checked the author account since the previous night, when Margot had FaceTimed. She logged on now and her heart dropped to her stomach when she saw there was a new, unread email. It was from the same unknown sender, with the same subject line: *LEAVE*.

Serena opened the email and read it. The room began to spin, and she gripped the edge of the table for support.

*How was this possible?*

She closed her eyes and gulped down several deep breaths. When she opened them, the words on the screen hadn't changed.

*Michael is dead because of you. Leave town now or the cops will know what you did. You were there! Liar!!*

# 29

## RUBY

### SEPTEMBER 1994

Amber had been gone more than ten years now. A whole decade without her daughter. All those "firsts" that Ruby had missed out on—first tooth, first birthday, first word, first step, first day at kindergarten, first day at school . . .

That day at the bus station had changed her life forever. Ruby never heard from River again. Grandma Pearl told her he'd been heartbroken, had waited for hours at the bus stop and concluded that Ruby had dumped him. News of the abduction clearly hadn't made it to Monroe. Pearl had begged her to tell him the truth, but what was she going to say? *I got pregnant and didn't tell you and then I had a beautiful baby daughter and let a stranger steal her?*

She'd heard that River had left Monroe for good not long after her so-called rejection.

Both Grandma Pearl and Coral were dead now, breast cancer taking her mom long before her time.

Ruby had no one.

No, not true. She had a daughter. Her little girl was out there somewhere. Still alive. Ruby could feel it in her bones, even though the cops had given up looking for Amber a long time ago.

Ruby had found out Dani's surname—Duprie—from the bank of mailboxes in the apartment complex's lobby, and had passed on what she'd learned to Kolinsky: a woman who had been at the bus station that day, who had no kids of her own, had left her home in a hurry after a neighbor claimed to have heard a baby crying inside the apartment.

Kolinsky hadn't been interested, had warned her again that she had to stop accusing innocent people of stealing her baby. When she made a scene at the station, he'd threatened to arrest her. So, Ruby had taken her story to the newspapers. They'd printed her claims but left out the key details—Dani's name and place of work—for fear of being sued.

Ruby went back to working in salons. Progressed from floor sweeper to junior stylist to senior stylist. Still, the money wasn't great, and all her spare cash was poured into the search for Amber: missing person posters, following up on potential sightings, and, eventually, hiring a private detective.

Lew Arbuckle was a sleazebag who worked out of a low-rent business park and slept on a filthy cot bed in the back room of his office. But he was all she could afford. Other than River Henderson, it seemed like it was Ruby's lot in life to be surrounded by lecherous creeps, just like her mom had been. She didn't just want Arbuckle to find Amber; she told him to find Dani Duprie too. Figured one would lead to the other. After a couple of months, he said he had a promising lead in California, but he needed more cash to pay his source. Ruby had twenty-four dollars left in her checking account for the remainder of the month. So, she'd pawned the ruby necklace Grandma Pearl had gifted her for her eighteenth birthday. Just eleven years ago, but it felt like a lifetime. Felt like someone else's life now.

Arbuckle had gotten good intel from his source but now he wanted a different kind of payment. Not a cash transaction. At first Ruby had refused. Then she thought again of all those "firsts" she'd missed out on—and the moments she could still share with Amber. Prom night, high school graduation, her wedding day, having children of her own. So, she'd followed Lew Arbuckle through to his back room and lain down on the cot bed and given up the only thing she hadn't lost already: her self-respect.

The PI had tracked down a William Duprie working for a tech firm in San Diego. He went by the less formal "Bill" now and was married with a young daughter. The coworker, who'd spilled the info in exchange for a brown envelope stuffed full of dollar bills, thought the wife might have been called Donna or Dana. He couldn't say for sure because Bill kept to himself and never socialized with the other staff; always turned down offers for after-work drinks and Christmas parties and retirement celebrations. Bill lived by the coast, around an hour's drive from the office, but the coworker didn't know the name of the town.

Ruby gave notice on the apartment, quit the salon, sold all her furniture and possessions, and purchased a one-way Amtrak ticket to Southern California. There, she sourced an old heap-of-junk Volvo station wagon cancered with rust, and stayed in the kind of low-rent motels that even cockroaches would object to. Using a gas station map as her guide, Ruby set out to visit every coastal town and city within an hour's drive of San Diego until she found Dani Duprie.

So far, no dice.

Today, she rolled into Seaton Point.

Fashion boutiques with no price tags on the window displays, sports cars with suspensions low enough to scrape the blacktop, restaurants advertising lobster specials. The place screamed money and privilege. Ruby remembered the opulent building Dani had called home in Portland ten years ago. This seemed like her kind of town. Ruby felt her hopes rise. She parked in the lot of a seafood restaurant and strolled along the marina, searching the face of every passerby for the one that belonged to the Good Samaritan at the bus station. The woman who had stolen her baby.

The day ended in disappointment, but Ruby wasn't ready to give up yet. A feeling in her gut told her she was getting closer. Seaton Point didn't do dive motels so Ruby sacrificed food so that she could afford a room at the Harbor View Inn. It was the best night's sleep she'd had in weeks, the clean sheets and hot shower little luxuries she'd learned to live without. The next day, Ruby decided to be more proactive.

She asked a bunch of folks if they could direct her to Dani Duprie's house—her cover story already worked out—but they were all tourists, in town for the boating and the beaches. Next, she stopped an untidy man who looked out of place among the designer labels in his rumpled slacks, his shirt half-untucked, alcohol on his breath even though it was barely noon.

"Oh, hi!" she said with forced brightness. "I wondered if you could help me?"

The man appeared startled that she'd spoken to him and glanced around, like the question had been directed to someone else. "Help you how?" he asked warily.

"I'm looking for directions to Dani Duprie's place. Do you happen to know where she lives?"

Ruby thought there was a flicker of recognition in his bloodshot eyes at the mention of the name.

"Who wants to know?"

"I'm Dani's cousin. Supposed to be visiting her while I'm in town but I've lost her address. I'm such an idiot! So, can you help?"

He stared at her until it became uncomfortable, then shook his head. "Nah, can't help you. Never heard of her."

Ruby expanded her search area from the marina to downtown, with its fast-food restaurants and retail stores. By late afternoon, she was debating whether she could stretch to a Happy Meal at the McDonald's when a blonde stepped out of a grocery store across the street, two brown paper bags balanced in her arms. Ruby gaped at her.

The woman was mid-forties and effortlessly glamorous, in stonewashed jeans and a tight baby-pink sweater, her hair freshly highlighted and voluminous courtesy of a professional blow-dry. Ruby had only seen Dani Duprie in her drab Greyhound uniform, so couldn't be one hundred percent sure it was the same person— but she thought it might be her. Her pulse raced like the Toyota Supras and Chevy Corvettes zipping around the streets of Seaton Point.

The blonde turned in Ruby's direction, as though feeling the weight of her stare, and they locked eyes for a long moment, but Ruby still couldn't make a positive identification. Then the woman shifted both bags onto one arm, popped the trunk of a Dodge Caravan, and loaded the groceries inside. Quickly climbed into the car.

Then she was gone.

Ruby's Volvo was still parked down by the marina so she couldn't even follow the maybe-Dani.

"Dammit!"

Ruby returned to the marina and decided to stake out the waterfront restaurants now that they were starting to fill up with the early dinner crowd. A group of middle-aged ladies noisily occupied an outside table at one eatery, salads and seafood platters and carafes of rosé wine spread out in front of them, a bright orange umbrella shading them from the sun. One of the group stood up and waved like she was air traffic control and yelled, "Wanda! Over here! What took you so damn long?"

A harried woman, presumably Wanda, rushed across the parking lot in their direction. Ruby guessed her to be similar in age to Dani Duprie. She stepped in front of her, and the woman skidded to a halt.

"I'm so sorry to bother you," Ruby said. "But I was wondering if you could direct me someplace?"

"Oh, sure." Wanda glanced over Ruby's shoulder at her impatiently waiting friends. "Where do you need to be?"

"I'm trying to find Dani Duprie's house. She's my older cousin and I somehow managed to lose her address. How stupid am I, huh? Anyway, I'm supposed to be staying there a few days and have no clue where I'm going now!"

Wanda's attention now turned squarely to Ruby; her brows bunched quizzically. "You're staying with Dani? I didn't know she had any family."

It took every bit of effort Ruby had to maintain a poker face at the confirmation that Dani Duprie did, indeed, reside in Seaton Point. She had found her. Well, almost.

"Oh, we haven't seen each other in ages," she said. "Must be ten years. We're long overdue a catch-up. Can you help me find her place?"

Wanda's gaze drifted to her friends again, who were now even louder, cackling in that way women of a certain age do after a couple of refreshments.

"Sure thing," she said. "Dani and Bill rent the Cliff House. Big white house at the top of Cliffside Drive. You can't miss it."

The sun was starting to set, the sky painted fiery shades of orange, when Ruby pulled up in front of the stunning huge white and glass construction built into the side of a cliff. She shut off the engine and gulped in the ocean air and rolled her shoulders like a boxer preparing for a fight.

*This is it*, she thought.

Ruby Bryant was going to get her baby back, no matter what.

Her hand went to the cold, metal item on the passenger seat beside her.

Lew Arbuckle had taken her dignity and self-respect the night she'd spent on his filthy cot bed. But Ruby had taken something from the private dick as he'd slept afterward, snoring loudly, his dirty lust sated.

His Colt 1911 pistol.

# 30

---

## DANI

---

## SEPTEMBER 1994

A woman was standing on the doorstep. She was pointing a gun at them.

Dani cowered behind Bill, the fabric of his shirt clutched tight in her fists. Her husband had his hands raised.

"Okay, whoa," he said. "What's going on here?"

Dani had seen the redhead at the marina yesterday and at the grocery store earlier today. Her intense gaze across the street had been unsettling enough for Dani to make a detour to the bank and empty their accounts; to convince her husband to flee the home and town that they loved.

But—she realized with a start—this was not the woman she'd spent years fearing would hunt them down, the reason why they'd moved around from state to state.

The woman holding the pistol wasn't Shannon Jacobson.

Even so, there *was* something familiar about her, beyond being seen these last couple of days in Seaton Point. The long red hair, the slim frame, the smattering of freckles across high cheekbones, those sad, haunted eyes. Dani's mind spooled back ten years to the Greyhound bus station in Portland, a job and a city she'd known for less than a year. A blurry memory from the past was fast coming into sharp focus, like a Polaroid photo developing in front of her eyes.

The stolen baby. A distraught mother. The bad vending-machine coffee and words of comfort. Bill and Dani had left Oregon soon after. God, what was the mom's name again? Dani clawed away the layers of time until she had the answer.

"Ruby?" She was surprised by how calm she sounded—and felt—considering there was a gun in her face. This wasn't a random home invasion or an armed burglary. There was something else going on here, something that could be resolved. "What are you doing here?"

"I'm here to take back what's mine."

Ruby was trembling, full body shakes, like she'd been caught in a winter storm. Her voice was tremulous too. Ditto the hand holding the weapon. Not ideal.

Dani stepped out from behind Bill, and he tried to shove her back, tried to continue to shield her. She didn't let him. "I don't know what you mean, but let's talk about it, okay?"

Ruby glanced around wildly like she expected a SWAT team to emerge from the brush. "Good idea. Let's move inside." She waved the gun at them, and Dani had the distinct impression the young woman wasn't used to handling a firearm. She didn't know if that was good or bad news.

Ruby marched them down the hallway. As they passed the staircase, Dani heard music drifting faintly from Charlotte's bedroom. "Dreamlover" by Mariah Carey. She liked to play her CDs while doing her homework. Dani felt the sharp edges of panic break through her calm veneer at the thought of her daughter being in danger. But this woman had lost a child of her own, hadn't she? Surely she wouldn't hurt someone else's.

They went into the kitchen and Ruby noticed the duffel bag filled with bundles of dollar bills. "Going somewhere?" she spat angrily. "Running away again?"

Neither Bill nor Dani answered her. Bill kept throwing confused glances in Dani's direction, asking a question without using words: *Who the fuck is this crazy woman and why is she in our house with a gun?*

Dani wanted to know too. But what Ruby said next made no sense.

"I want my daughter back," she stated.

"I'm sure you do and I'm so sorry about . . ." What was the kid's name again? Amber! That was it. "I'm so sorry about what happened to Amber, but her disappearance has nothing to do with us."

Ruby's eyes were cold and furious. "You stole my baby. You took everything from me. You ruined my life."

Sweat prickled Dani's scalp. This was crazy. She held her hands out, palms up. "Ruby, listen to me. I didn't take Amber. I had nothing to do with her abduction. Please, put the gun down."

The pistol was bobbing up and down as Ruby grew increasingly agitated. "Bullshit! I know it was you."

"Think about it," Dani said. "I was working that day. Selling tickets to passengers. Surrounded by dozens of witnesses and coworkers. How could I possibly have taken Amber? What did I do with her while I was sitting with you waiting for the police to arrive?"

"I don't know. You hid her someplace." Ruby turned the gun on Bill now and he gasped. "Or you had him waiting outside the station to take Amber away. You were both in on it together."

Dani was still mindful of the music playing in the bedroom, a different song now, and she prayed that Charlotte wouldn't come downstairs to investigate the loud voices. "Please, Ruby, you've got it all wrong . . ."

"Oh, shut the fuck up, Dani. I know it was you, okay? I went to your apartment. That crazy old bat next door told me you'd left town in a hurry. She'd heard a baby crying, but you didn't have any kids of your own, did you? It was Amber she heard crying, wasn't it?"

"Oh Jesus," Bill said.

Dani knew the realization of what had happened had just hit him like a sucker punch, same as it had her.

A terrible misunderstanding. That's what this was.

"Where is she?" Ruby demanded.

Dani eyed the knife on the chopping board. Weighed up whether she could reach it in time. Ruby followed her gaze.

"Don't even think about it. I swear I'll put a hole in you before you even get near it." The gun's aim was shifting between Bill and Dani now. "I want to see my daughter. Go get her right now."

The wild look was back in Ruby's eyes.

"No," Dani said.

"Where is she?" Ruby screamed. "Amber! Amber, sweetheart! Where are you?"

The music stopped. Mariah Carey no longer singing about a hero. Fast footsteps bounded down the stairs.

*NO.*

Bill hollered, "Go back to your room, Charlotte! Go back upstairs, honey!"

It was too late. Charlotte walked into the kitchen. "Hey, what's with all the shouting?" She stopped dead when she saw the stranger with the gun. Her eyes bugged out and her mouth dropped open. She was no more than ten feet away from Ruby Bryant. This crazy woman stood between Dani and her daughter. Charlotte's face crumpled. "Mom?"

Dani fought back tears, tried to steady her voice, didn't want to frighten Charlotte any more than she already was. "Go to your room, sweetie. Everything's okay, I promise. It's just grown-up stuff."

Charlotte didn't move. "Who is she, Mom? Why does she have a gun? I'm scared."

Ruby's attention had pivoted to Charlotte. She looked stunned. Overcome with emotion. Dani realized Ruby was sobbing. The hand not holding the gun went to her mouth.

"Oh my God. Amber? It's me. It's Mommy."

Ruby moved toward Charlotte, who backed away.

"Get away from me!" she yelled.

"It's okay. You don't have to be scared. I'm your mom. I'm here to take you home."

Ruby bent down and reached out her free hand to touch the girl's face. Charlotte opened her mouth wide and bared her teeth and clamped her jaws around the woman's wrist. Ruby screamed in agony, tried to yank herself free as Charlotte bit down harder.

Dani locked eyes with Bill, reading his thoughts:

*Ruby is distracted.*

"No, Bill, don't . . ." she started to say. But he had already launched himself across the room, tackling Ruby like a football player. He knocked her to the floor and the gun fell from her hand and skittered across the tiles.

Ruby, white-faced and bleeding, breathed heavily on her back, winded from the impact. Charlotte crabbed backward into a corner, crying loudly, her eyes closed, her hands clamped over her ears. Bill was on top of Ruby. They turned at the same time to look at where the deadly piece of metal lay a couple of feet away.

Ruby reached out and her fingers brushed the pistol's grip, just as Dani darted to the countertop and grabbed hold of the knife.

# 31

## SERENA

### NOW

Someone had found out about Serena's role in Michael's death. But how?

Other than Margot, no one was aware of the truth. The mistress, Nancy Bailey, hadn't seen Serena the night of the accident, the cops had never figured out she'd made a flying visit to New Jersey, and Michael certainly wasn't telling anyone.

Yet someone knew.

Serena trusted Margot with her life as well as her career, so there was only one possible explanation. Her drunken confession to her agent the evening before had been overheard. Someone had been inside the house, listening to every word. Serena remembered the soft click she'd heard while on the call with Margot. It had sounded like a door gently closing. She thought also of the musky scent of perfume or cologne. An intruder had been hiding inside when she'd returned from the Shrimp Shack after dinner with Hannah and Cynthia. They had eavesdropped on her tearful conversation and then left quietly through the kitchen door. But not quietly enough. The click had been the lock engaging behind them.

But why hadn't they triggered the trail camera, like George Evans? There had been three images saved onto the SD card: two strange black blurs, and the clear face of her neighbor. It was as though a cover had been placed over the lens and then later removed. Meaning someone had spotted the camera—or known it was there all along.

Serena considered who else had a key to the Cliff House. Herself and Wanda Stockwell. And, by extension, anyone close enough to the housekeeper to borrow her set or even have a copy made. Which meant Jody, Hannah, Antonio, and Jack Beaumont.

As she lay in bed, staring at the ceiling, a bad feeling began to settle in her belly. Beaumont also knew about the trail camera, had even told her exactly where to place it on the tree. She remembered how good he had smelled at the Italian restaurant, an intoxicating musky smell. And she had first met him at the Shrimp Shack shortly before that note had been placed on her rental car.

But what possible reason would Jack Beaumont have for threatening her and trying to chase her out of town? None that she could think of. His concern had seemed genuine once he'd finally responded to her voicemails. Serena didn't want to believe that he could be behind the campaign of terror.

One thing she did know for sure: there was no way she was making a trip downtown to show him those emails. Not now. Even if she deleted the latest correspondence about Michael's death, it would take an IT expert no more than two minutes to retrieve it. And if Beaumont *wasn't* the intruder, how would she explain the accusations about her partner's death?

◆  ◆  ◆

When her alarm went off, Serena felt like she'd barely slept. She wanted nothing more than to burrow under the sheets for another couple of hours and hide away from the world. But it was Monday, which meant Wanda Stockwell's cleaning day, and she did not relish the prospect of being caught sleeping in two weeks in a row. She forced herself out of bed and went through to the bathroom. Her reflection in the mirror was not a welcome sight. Serena looked like she'd aged five years since her arrival in Seaton Point. Her dark hair had lost its luster, her skin was pasty despite all the sunshine, and the bags under her eyes were now big enough to carry all her woes. So much for getting away from it all by leaving Manhattan.

After clearing up the rest of the mess she'd made in the kitchen, Serena carefully packed the Dupries' belongings into the two cardboard boxes and returned them to the basement. She dropped the key back into its hiding place in the shabby-chic jug and had just made herself a much-needed strong coffee when she heard Wanda Stockwell open the front door.

They exchanged an awkward greeting and Serena escaped to her office to add more words to her manuscript, while Wanda got to work with the cleaning, polishing, dusting, and laundry. When the chores were done, Serena headed back downstairs to intercept Wanda before she left. She wanted to broach the subject of the missing fountain pen without making it sound like she was accusing the woman.

Wanda Stockwell eyed Serena suspiciously as she hovered at the foot of the stairs. "I'm all done here," she said. "Was there anything else?"

"Um, yes. I wondered if you came across a fountain pen while you were cleaning?"

"No, I don't think so."

"It's black and silver with an inscription on it. Very beautiful."

"I didn't see it. Sorry."

"It's just that it's been . . . mislaid somehow, and I'd really like it back."

Wanda's face hardened. "I didn't take your pen."

So much for not sounding like she was accusing the housekeeper.

"Of course not!" Serena said. "That's not what I meant. It's just, it was a gift from my late father and it's very special to me, so I hoped you might have come across it."

Wanda's face softened, ever so slightly. She nodded. "I hope you find it."

Then she smoothed down her apron, picked up her caddy full of cleaning supplies from the console table, and left without another word.

*Great. Well done, Serena. Now the elderly, hardworking housekeeper thinks you're a horrible snob who believes she's a thief.*

The thought was interrupted by her phone ringing in the office. Serena ran upstairs and saw the caller was Jack Beaumont. Her first thought was that the troll had tipped off the cops about Michael. Then she remembered she'd failed to keep her morning appointment at the station about the emails. She let her voicemail service pick up. It was her turn to ghost him.

When he called again a couple of hours later, Serena reluctantly answered. A tiny part of her still wondered if he could be the person making the clandestine trips to the Cliff House in the middle of the night, and moving her wineglass, and stealing her favorite pen. A bigger part of her didn't want the chief of police knowing she had lied to the cops—okay, *withheld some details*—about someone's death. Someone she had loved and been in a relationship with.

"Hey," Beaumont said. "You still going to swing by with those emails?"

"I'm sorry, but I'm not going to make it today. My agent wants to see the first hundred pages of my work-in-progress by the end of the week, so I'm pretty snowed under right now and can't really be without my laptop. I'll try to stop by in the next couple days."

"Okay, but make sure you do. I really don't like the idea of visitors in town feeling unsafe."

Again, Serena thought he sounded genuine. If this was an act, he could give Cillian Murphy, Leonardo DiCaprio, and Brad Pitt a run for their money.

"Did you manage to find out anything about the case I mentioned?" she asked casually. "The missing baby, Amber Bryant."

"Hold on a second." Serena heard rustling, followed by muffled conversation, like Beaumont was holding his cell phone to his chest. Then he was back on the line. "Kelly says it's on her to-do list but she's pretty busy right now so it may take a few days. I'll let you know as soon as we have anything."

"Sure. Great." Serena tried not to sound too disappointed.

She ended the call and then pulled up Cynthia's number.

"Hey, Ms. Bestseller! You up for some more cocktails?"

Serena smiled. "No, I'm looking for information."

"Boring. But go ahead."

Serena said, "You know how you helped me find those old newspaper articles from the *Seaton Point Sentinel*?"

"Uh-huh."

"I don't suppose the library has access to press cuttings from Oregon from the 1980s?"

Cynthia chuckled. "Honey, as much as I'd love to help, I'm not Rupert Murdoch. I can't just magic up newspaper articles from any time and place at the click of a finger."

"Yeah, that's what I thought. Figured it was worth a shot, though."

"Although, I might be able to steer you to the right place. A subscription-based newspaper archive. You'll need a credit card, though."

"I have the plastic if you have the details."

Five minutes and an Amex card later, Serena had access to a whole database of local newspapers, some of them long since defunct, like the *Sentinel*. The search term "Amber Bryant" yielded several hits from a weekly newspaper in Portland. The first couple of results were news reports about the abduction, details she already knew, and appeals to the public for information.

Then a headline piqued her interest: *I KNOW WHO STOLE MY BABY*.

In the article, a clearly emotional Ruby Bryant claimed to have come face to face with her baby's abductor at the bus station minutes after Amber was taken. She said a thirtysomething woman, posing as a concerned citizen, had looked after her while they waited for the police to arrive. Ruby was quoted as saying: "I was panicking, out of my mind with worry. This woman brought me coffee from the vending machine with lots of sugar in it. She said it would help with the shock. She pretended to be concerned about me, but really she was covering her tracks. Trying to come across as a Good Samaritan when she'd already taken Amber and hidden her someplace."

When asked why she suspected the Good Samaritan, Ruby added: "I went to her home a few weeks later to thank her. I'd bought flowers. When I got there, I discovered she'd left town. A neighbor mentioned hearing a baby crying in their apartment before she and her husband moved out. The neighbor said this woman didn't have kids of her own. The crying baby was Amber. I know it in my heart. I know this woman's name, where she used to live and work, but the police won't listen to me. They think I harmed my own baby."

The article concluded with a statement from the police: "We are aware that this is a highly emotional time for Ms. Bryant, who has made allegations against several people. We will continue to investigate all viable leads and, at this stage, are ruling out nothing—and no one—from our inquiries. We remain committed to finding Amber and returning her safe and well to her family."

Poor Ruby, Serena thought. Just eighteen years old, not much more than a kid herself. There was no mention of Amber's father in any of the articles, or Ruby's own parents, just the grandmother she'd been planning on visiting when Amber was taken. Serena hoped the girl had had a support network around her and didn't have to endure such a traumatic experience alone. Especially as it sounded like the cops had chosen to judge Ruby Bryant, rather than believe her. Serena wondered if the Good Samaritan at the bus station had been Dani Duprie.

She then came across a story from June 1994, ten years after Amber's disappearance. The headline read: I'LL NEVER STOP LOOKING FOR MY BABY.

The accompanying photo showed an older, and prematurely aged, Ruby Bryant, solemnly holding up a framed photo of baby Amber. A decade on from the kidnapping, Ruby claimed the police had all but given up on the investigation. She told the reporter she had a private investigator working the case, who had a promising lead in California. Ruby said: "I won't stop looking for Amber. I'll go to the ends of the earth to find her. I'll do whatever it takes to get my daughter back."

There were no more milestone markers from the Portland paper beyond the ten-year anniversary. No more appeals from Amber's mom. Serena changed the search term to "Ruby Bryant" and found out why. This hit was for a Nevada newspaper from December 1995: HUMAN REMAINS FOUND BURIED IN DESERT IDENTIFIED.

As Serena read the story, her hand flew to her mouth in shock and despair. The female remains that had been discovered in the

Mojave a year after the possible sighting of Dani Duprie at a nearby gas station belonged to Ruby Bryant. She'd last been seen in Portland in the early summer of 1994.

According to the newspaper report, local cops were treating her death as murder.

# 32

## DANI

### SEPTEMBER 1994

Ruby's fingers brushed the pistol's grip. Dani couldn't allow her to get hold of it again. She darted over to the countertop and grabbed the knife. When she turned around, she saw Bill was straddling Ruby, his big hands clamped tightly around her slim throat.

Ruby stopped reaching for the gun. She clawed at Bill's hands. Her legs thrashed and thumped against the floor. Her eyes bulged. Her pale face turned dark red. She was making a horrible gasping, wheezing sound, unable to force any air into her lungs.

Ruby Bryant was no match for the man on top of her.

Bill's lips were drawn back, baring his teeth. Beads of sweat rolled down his temples. His eyes were blank, like he was possessed by some kind of savage animal.

Charlotte was still screaming in the corner, eyes closed, hands over her ears. Trying not to witness the horror that was unfolding right in front of her.

Dani stood by the countertop, gripping the knife, frozen to the spot.

*Stop it, Bill! Stop it! You're killing her!*

But the words were only in her head. She couldn't speak. Couldn't move.

After what seemed like forever, the thrashing stopped. The wheezing was silenced. Ruby stilled.

Like being snapped out of a trance by the click of a hypnotist's fingers, Bill blinked and his eyes refocused. He stared down at his hands, still around the dead woman's throat. His face twisted in horror as what he'd done sunk in. He climbed off the body, chest heaving, and scrabbled away. Turned to Dani. He looked sickly; his skin pale and waxy and coated with a sheen of sweat.

"What have I done?" His voice was hoarse, as though it were his own windpipe that had just been crushed. "What the fuck have I done?"

Dani opened her mouth but still no words came out. The knife slipped from her grasp and clattered against the travertine tiles. She became dully aware of silence in the kitchen. Charlotte had stopped screaming. She tore her gaze away from Bill toward her daughter. Charlotte's knees were pulled up to her chin, and her eyes were open, and she was gaping at the body of Ruby Bryant.

Dani sparked into action. Crossed the room briskly and took Charlotte's hands and helped her to her feet. Hugged her tight to her chest. "There, there," she soothed. "I've got you. You're okay now."

The same words she'd whispered the first night Charlotte had come into their lives as a baby.

"That lady . . . Is she . . . is she dead?" Charlotte asked. "What happened?"

"A terrible accident, sweetheart. That's all. No one's fault." Dani took her by the hand. "Let's go to your room. You shouldn't be here." She steered Charlotte into the hallway and glanced over her shoulder to see Bill slumped against the wall. Dazed-looking, sweat dampening his shirt, his hair mussed up. His hands were marred by angry red scratch marks.

Upstairs, Charlotte sat on the edge of her bed, sucking on the hair at the end of her braid, like she did when she was tired or upset. Her round face was filled with worry.

"Why did that lady have a gun?" she said. "Why did she say she was my mommy? She isn't, is she? You're my mom, right?"

Dani kneeled in front of her. "You bet I am. The lady made a mistake, is all. A horrible mistake. That woman isn't your mommy."

"You promise?"

They locked pinkies.

"Pinky promise. Everything is going to be okay, sweetie. Mom and Dad are going to fix this, but we need to have a grown-up talk first, okay?"

Charlotte nodded.

Dani went over to the desk, where a schoolbook was open, the homework exercise only half-completed. She picked up Charlotte's Discman and took it over to the bed.

"Why don't you lie down a while and listen to your CDs?" she said. "Which one do you want to listen to? Mariah?"

Charlotte nodded again. *Music Box* was her current favorite. Dani remembered the disc was in the stereo player. She slid open the tray and removed the CD and inserted it into the Discman. Charlotte lay back on the bed and Dani pulled off her sneakers, then placed the earphones over her head. Picked up a Barbie from the shelf and tucked it under Charlotte's arm.

Then she went downstairs to find Bill. He hadn't moved. He was still against the wall, and he was crying. Big, heaving sobs. The sight was almost as shocking as the woman with a ring of bruises around her neck. Dani had only seen Bill cry once before, after the miscarriage when they'd lost their baby all those years ago. He hadn't cried on their wedding day or when he'd crashed his car or got arrested or been fired from his Silicon Valley job.

She got down next to him and pulled him into an embrace, stroking his hair, until he was all cried out. He eventually pulled away from her and said, "We need to call 911. I killed someone."

Dani shook her head. "She came into our home with a gun. It was self-defense. You have a right to protect your home and your family."

"I didn't need to go that far. I didn't need to kill her. She was unarmed by then."

"She was reaching for the gun, Bill. And she would have used it. You know she would."

"We still need to call the cops. Tell them what I've done."

"You know we can't do that," Dani said. "They'll want to know why she was here; why she was threatening us. It won't take them long to figure out the truth about Charlotte."

"But Dani . . ."

"There are no buts, Bill. You remember what you said the night Charlotte became ours? *We'll do whatever it takes to keep her safe.* That's what you did—you kept her safe from that woman. Now we continue to keep her safe by not getting the police involved."

"So, what do we do?"

Dani looked at Ruby Bryant. She should have felt regret or pity or sadness for everything the woman had endured, all those years searching for her baby only for her miserable life to end like this. But there was only anger. Ruby had ruined their lives now too.

"We get rid of the body," she said.

They sat there together for a long time, coming up with a plan.

First, they agreed it wasn't possible to stay in Seaton Point. They couldn't dispose of a body and then stick around, waiting for law enforcement to make a connection between them and Ruby Bryant. She'd been in town at least two days and someone had told her their address. If she was reported missing—after she'd been asking around about the Dupries—the cops would start looking at them. They'd look even harder when they discovered Dani had emptied their joint accounts. So, they had to leave town, just as they'd planned to do already, only with an extra passenger in the trunk.

They would take nothing other than the bag full of cash. Their cars, luggage, clothing, jewelry, personal effects, even their family photos would all be left behind. Leave the cops with so many questions, their heads would be spinning; no clue where to even begin their investigation. Were the Dupries victims of a crime? Or had they committed one? By the time anyone even realized the family had vanished, they would be long gone. Anything they needed could be purchased once they were on the road.

Where to go? Mexico seemed the obvious choice. They'd be over the border before the alarm was raised and could then lose themselves in the vastness of a foreign country. It felt *too* obvious, though. Plus, blonde Dani, and Charlotte with her strawberry-blonde hair, would stand out too much. Might be spotted by an American tourist.

Instead, Bill and Dani would make it appear like they were heading for the border. Get on the Five and drive south, ditch their bank cards and credit cards and her driver's license by the roadside. They'd hold on to Bill's license for now, in case they were pulled over for a random traffic stop. Then they would double back and head north; dispose of the body on the way to San Francisco. Bill was confident his old dealer would be able to hook him up with a contact who could sort them out with fake passports and papers for the right price. Bill's hacking skills would do the rest when it came to creating brand-new identities for all three of them.

How to explain the move to Charlotte? And a change of name? The story about Bill being promoted to a new job in a different town wasn't going to cut it now. But they'd figure it out.

Dani took a roll of heavy-duty trash bags from the cupboard under the sink and told Bill to go find some duct tape. She searched in Ruby's jeans pockets for her car keys, before wrapping the body. It took a lot of sweat and effort but, between the two of them, Bill and Dani managed to carry the body outside to Ruby's Volvo station wagon. They folded it inside the trunk, next to a small suitcase.

Dani was thankful the Cliff House was so isolated. No neighbors within a mile to witness this horrific act.

Charlotte was asleep on top of her bed, earphones still on, Totally Hair Barbie still in the crook of her arm. Dani returned the doll to the shelf with the others, then opened the closet and found a small backpack. She stuffed a lightweight summer jacket and a spare set of pajamas inside. Added a library book and some CDs and the sneakers lying by the bed. Finally, the Discman that she carefully removed from Charlotte's loose grasp. Dani left all the jeans and sweaters and beautiful dresses hanging on the rail. No one would miss the few items that she'd packed.

She summoned Bill and he lifted the still-sleeping Charlotte and carried her downstairs and laid her carefully on the backseat of the Volvo. It seemed obscene, their beautiful daughter in such close proximity to a dead body. Dani shook off the thought and placed the backpack beside her. She retrieved the duffel bag containing the fifty grand from the dining table, and then they left the Cliff House for the last time.

Lights on, front door unlocked, a mystery waiting to be discovered.

◆ ◆ ◆

A couple of days later, Bill buried Ruby Bryant's body in the Mojave Desert.

Dani was glad to be rid of it, was convinced she could smell the ripe corpse despite filling the car with tree-shaped air fresheners. Bill had purchased a shovel—as well as a rake and shears and potted plants for the sake of appearances—at a garden center the day before.

Dani and Charlotte had waited in the car by the side of the highway, surrounded by dust and Joshua trees and empty road and an endless azure sky, while he worked. A couple of hours after resuming their journey, the gas light came on. Dani had hoped to put a lot more distance between the dump site and any stops they'd have to make, but they were running on fumes. Bill's hands still bore the scratches from the struggle with Ruby, as well as fresh cuts and blisters, and dirt caked under his fingernails, from all the digging.

Dani had already cut and dyed her hair courtesy of a drugstore kit in a grimy motel bathroom in front of a cracked mirror, so she slipped on oversized sunglasses that were a recent purchase and got out at the next gas station and filled up the tank. The store's AC dried the sweat on her body as she picked out potato chips and candy and chilled bottles of water. When she approached the counter to pay for the gas and snacks, Dani noticed a security camera. She kept her head down and hoped the Jackie O shades would provide enough of a disguise.

Back in the car, Bill pulled back onto the highway. Dani became aware of sniffling in the backseat and turned to see that Charlotte was crying. Big, fat tears. Snot running out of her nose. When she'd first awoken in the Volvo, they'd told her they had to leave Seaton Point because of the mistake the lady with the gun had made. They'd find a new house, in a new town, and everything would be just fine. Bill and Dani agreed they'd broach the subject of new identities with her once the fake IDs had been ordered and collected.

Charlotte hadn't spoken much since then. She'd mostly slept or stared out of the window or read her book or listened to music. These were the first tears.

"Are you sad because of what happened to the lady?" Dani asked.

Charlotte shook her head. "No, she tried to hurt you and Dad with a gun and take me away from you. I'm glad that she's dead."

Dani winced.

Bill frowned next to her but said nothing, kept his eyes on the road.

"Why the tears then, sweetie?" she asked.

Charlotte stuck out her bottom lip. "I don't want to leave the house and my bedroom and the beach and my friends at school. It was my favorite house out of all the ones we've lived in. The others were nowhere near as good."

Dani smiled sadly. "We'll find a new place that's even better, huh? And maybe one day, when you're all grown up, you'll be able to go back to the Cliff House."

# 33

## SERENA

## NOW

The writer's block was back with a vengeance.

Nothing to do with lack of inspiration or being unsure of where the plot was going. Everything to do with real life being stranger—and more tragic—than fiction. It was hard to focus on the written word when reality trumped what was on the page.

Serena's attention was drawn away from the blinking cursor by a low rumble in the distance. She cocked her head and listened. A car engine. Getting louder, getting closer. Then the crunch of tires on gravel. It was almost nine p.m. Who the hell was calling at this hour? Serena shot out of the chair and bolted into the middle bedroom that overlooked the front of the house. An SUV police cruiser pulled to a stop in the driveway, and she sighed with relief.

The driver's-side door opened, and a cop dressed in the same forest-green uniform that Beaumont had been wearing got out and hiked up his pants. He was younger than the chief, maybe thirty, and paunchier too. He drained a large takeout coffee, scrunched the cardboard cup between meaty hands, and tossed it into the car. Spotted her at the window and gave her a wave, which she returned. Then he set off at a leisurely amble, hands resting on the gun belt below the paunch, presumably carrying out an inspection of the property. He returned ten minutes later and climbed inside the cruiser but didn't start it up. Looked like he was getting comfortable for a while.

Serena went back to the laptop but, even with a law enforcement officer within screaming distance, she couldn't relax, couldn't concentrate on the manuscript. Her thoughts were consumed by Ruby Bryant and her tragic end after enduring so much pain in her young life. Serena thought about Dani Duprie too. Had she really stolen Ruby's baby? Could she have murdered Ruby ten years later to keep her secret?

Then there was the slightly more pressing matter of who was threatening Serena. How safe was she in a house that an intruder had accessed God knows how many times? Even with a cop parked in the driveway?

She heard the cruiser start up and returned to the middle bedroom window in time to see red taillights getting smaller before disappearing completely as it turned the bend on Cliffside Drive and vanished from view. Her shoulders slumped.

Okay, so now with no cop parked in the driveway.

Beaumont hadn't given Serena a schedule for the patrols, but she hoped another would be back later tonight.

Having given up on adding any pages to the novel, Serena went downstairs and opened a bottle of wine. She took the glass over to the dining table, where she began making a mental inventory of every person she'd spoken to while she'd been in Seaton Point, what motive they might have for wanting her gone, and who would have the means to execute their nasty plan.

Jack Beaumont had to remain on the list. He didn't get a pass just because he was good-looking and had a great smile. He had the means even if she couldn't think of a motive. He'd been older than Charlotte when the Dupries had lived in town, and didn't appear to have had any real connection to them until effectively taking over their cold case when Don Raskin retired. Sure, he might have been pissed at a writer taking an interest in an investigation that the cops had never been able to solve—but enough to resort to all the crazy shit that had been happening? It seemed like a stretch.

Wanda Stockwell had a key, and she had a history with the Duprie family. She'd been friendly with Dani, even if not exactly friends, and still seemed affected by their disappearance thirty years later. But a woman in her seventies visiting the house in the middle of the night, and hiking a half-mile between the property and where her car was concealed behind a copse of trees, felt unlikely.

Hannah had been buddies with Charlotte at school and could have made a copy of her mother's key. She was young enough, and fit enough, to move around unseen in the dead of night. She could have slipped out of the restaurant and tucked the threatening note under Serena's windshield in the Shrimp Shack's lot. Hannah had also left their dinner early on Saturday night to return home to her husband and kids, but could she have detoured to the Cliff House instead? As for motive . . . Perhaps she'd been traumatized by the loss of her childhood friend and thought an author's interest in writing about it was crass and insensitive. Hmmm. Hannah was a maybe.

Patrick Dolan's interest in the Dupries had been entirely professional as far as Serena could tell. A reporter who'd only been after a big story. If anything, a resolution to the mystery might work to his advantage, spur him to finally write that true crime book. For now, he seemed content reading mystery novels on his boat. And there was no possible way—not that Serena could think of—that Dolan would have been able to get into the house.

Ditto Hank Macaulay. A conspiracy theorist who'd likely crossed paths with Ruby Bryant all those years ago but, these days, couldn't walk from the bar stool to the bathroom in a straight line. Far more likely to be poured into a cab at the end of an evening than carry out a well-orchestrated stealth mission.

Serena took a long sip of wine. Who else? Mariposa at Cedarwood Farm. She figured the hippy's only beef would be with anyone who threatened their peace-and-love philosophy, and Serena was no threat to them—unless the Dupries really *had* been hiding out in one of the commune's cabins all this time.

Then there was Kelly Dunne. The station's office manager had told Serena about the cult after her dad witnessed Bill Duprie making several visits to Cedarwood Farm, including once with Charlotte. Facts that had been confirmed by Mariposa even if the place wasn't really a cult. But Kelly didn't have any other connection to the Dupries. She'd told Serena she was two years younger than Charlotte, which would make her around thirty-eight, so . . .

Wait.

Serena put down the wineglass and frowned. That wasn't right. Or was she remembering wrongly? She closed her eyes and replayed the conversation at the police station. Kelly had asked Serena to sign her copy of *Murder After Midnight*, then she'd brought up the Dupries, said she'd heard Serena was writing a book about them. Kelly had then told Serena she was a couple of years younger than Charlotte, which is why they hadn't been friends, and she didn't know much about the family, only the theories she'd heard about them since then.

That was how their chat had played out. Serena was sure of it.

She pulled up her recent call list and redialed Cynthia's number. It was late, after ten now, but the librarian picked up.

"Don't tell me," she said, by way of introduction. "You urgently need a side column from the *Long Island Herald* published in 1958 and you think I'm your gal?"

Serena didn't laugh this time. "I have a question."

"Okay . . ."

"Your ex, Kelly. You said she turned forty this year?"

"That's right."

"Are you sure? Definitely forty? You're not mistaken?"

"No mistake, believe me," Cynthia said. "We broke up the night of her birthday. We were out for dinner at her favorite Italian restaurant—the one she booked for you and Jack Beaumont—and we had a massive blowout about buying that house together. I accused her of being a gold digger and she stormed out. So yeah, a fortieth to remember."

"She told me she was thirty-eight," Serena said.

Cynthia snorted a laugh. "What'd I tell you? She's got her eye on you. Knocked a couple of years off her age to present herself as a younger, more attractive prospect."

*Buying that house together . . .*

Serena said, "You told me Kelly had a particular property in mind that she wanted you to purchase together, even though you own that amazing pink house on Point Beach already. What house did she have her eye on?"

Serena was pretty sure she already knew the answer.

"Uh, the one you're staying in right now," Cynthia confirmed.

"Why? What's so special about the Cliff House?"

"Kelly stayed there a few years ago when it first became a rental property. Fell in love with the house and with the town. That's why she moved here when she got the job with the SPPD. She was obsessed with the Cliff House, said she had a real connection to it, but had nowhere near the funds to own it by herself. Cue her interest in me and my pension plan."

Serena thought of George Evans's notebook filled with descriptions of vehicles belonging to previous guests. There had been a black Ford Escape on the list. Serena had seen that car herself. It had been outside the police station in the otherwise-empty cruiser bay. Kelly Dunne's car. Then she realized what Cynthia had just said.

"Wait—what do you mean, *moved here*? Don't you mean when she moved *back* to Seaton Point? Kelly grew up in the town, right?"

Now Cynthia sounded confused. "No, Kelly is an out-of-towner, same as me. She officially relocated to Seaton Point a couple years ago, around a year after I did. What's this all about, Serena?"

Serena didn't answer. Another thought occurred to her just then. Something she should have figured out already. Who else would have a key to the rental property? A former tenant with a set who'd had copies made so they could access the house whenever they wanted. That's who.

Someone like Kelly Dunne.

A forty-year-old woman with a special connection to the Cliff House who had lied about her age and her background to Serena.

"Serena?" Cynthia said. "Are you still there?"

"I've got to go."

Serena killed the call. She had to phone Jack Beaumont. *No.* She pushed back the chair and stood up. What Serena needed to do was go see him. Get out of the house. It wasn't safe here. She tucked the cell phone into her jeans pocket and picked up the car keys from the console table in the hallway and opened the front door.

A woman was standing on the doorstep.

She was pointing a gun at her.

# 34

## SERENA

### NOW

With the Glock, as well as the pink hair and ultra-blue eyes and the tight leather pants, Kelly could have been a cool character in a Tarantino movie.

But this was real life, and a very bad situation. Her hands were sheathed in latex gloves.

"What's going on, Kelly?" Serena asked, even though she had a pretty good idea.

Kelly Dunne was Charlotte Duprie, and she'd had her sights set on a return to the Cliff House until Serena had come along and ruined her plans by taking an interest in the disappearance of her family.

Kelly ignored the question. "Inside, now," she said, gesturing with the gun.

Serena wasn't going to argue with Kelly or the Glock. She turned and started walking down the hallway toward the kitchen and living area. Heard the front door close behind her.

Kelly's voice at her back said, "Upstairs. We're going to your office. You've got some writing to do."

*Huh?*

Serena felt the barrel of the gun pressing against the small of her back as she climbed the stairs slowly on shaky legs. She gripped the banister for support. There was no need to ask how Kelly knew about her workspace or where it was located. Kelly had been inside the Cliff House several times already, when she'd removed the photo of the Dupries—which included herself as a child—and moved the wineglass and stolen the fountain pen. When she'd smashed the porch lights and slammed doors and generally made Serena believe she was losing her mind.

Then Kelly had overheard Serena revealing the truth to Margot about Michael's death.

*Shit.*

"Sit," Kelly ordered, once they were both inside the office.

Serena pulled out the chair from the desk and lowered herself into it. She faced Kelly, who continued to stand, still pointing the weapon at her. The gun hand was steady, not even a hint of a tremor. Unlike Serena. Fear pumped through her veins.

"You know this is crazy, right?" Serena said.

"No, *you're* the one who's supposed to think she's crazy. A house with a dark past; weird shit happening in the dead of night. Anyone else would have been long gone by now. But not you. You had to keep digging, didn't you? Couldn't just let it go. This could all have been avoided if you'd just packed your stuff into your fancy Louis Vuitton luggage and left again that first day you got here."

"I know you left the threatening note on my rental car outside the Shrimp Shack. But how did you even know I was in town and interested in the Duprie case? I'd only just arrived."

"Chief Beaumont texted me from the restaurant," Kelly said. "He was excited to discover that a famous author was in Seaton

Point. I was excited too. Here's the ironic part—I genuinely am a fan of your books. Then Beaumont told me you'd been asking questions about my family, and that wasn't quite so fun to hear."

Serena nodded. "So, you tried to scare me off. When the note didn't work, you used the key you'd copied after renting the Cliff House yourself, to start messing with my head. I'm guessing you accessed the house via the kitchen as the chain was always secured on the front door. But why tell me about the cult? Which isn't even a cult, by the way. As far as I can tell all they do is paint landscapes and listen to George Harrison and drink passionflower tea. Their leader Mariposa is hardly Charles Manson."

"I know. I met her, remember?" Kelly snapped. "I wanted to test you, see how seriously you were taking your little investigation, how far you'd go. When you were prepared to visit a so-called cult for answers, I knew you weren't going to give up easily. And there was another complication by then."

"What complication?"

"Chief Beaumont's schoolboy crush on you. He'd asked me to make a reservation at a nice restaurant, wanted to impress you, said he was helping with research for your new novel. He even asked my advice about what cologne to wear. I knew what book he was talking about so you can imagine my frustration. Then, the day after your cozy dinner, he confided in me that he thought there was a real spark there. I couldn't allow you two to get together—I'd never have gotten rid of you if that happened. Good thing the chief trusts me completely, pretty much tells me everything. Which is why he listened when I warned him about getting too close to an author with a bunch of wild accusations but no witnesses or hard evidence. I may even have hinted that you were behind it all yourself, so you'd have a great story to recount in interviews when promoting your novel: *My terror in the cursed house of tragedy.* I told the chief that he should be wary of being made to look like a fool."

So that's why Beaumont had suddenly become distant and ghosted Serena. Another thought occurred to her. The musky scent she'd noticed lingering in the air on Saturday night had been the same cologne Beaumont had worn on their date. Kelly had spritzed it when she'd snuck into the house. As well as pouring poison in Beaumont's ear about Serena, she'd had Serena suspecting Beaumont of being the intruder. Very smart.

"Beaumont told you about the trail camera too, didn't he?" she asked. "Exactly where it was located, on the tree facing the side door. You covered the lens on Saturday night so the camera wouldn't capture any images of you breaking into the house."

"I type up all his notes, so yeah, I knew where to find it," Kelly confirmed. "And I'm glad I was able to get inside unseen, because I wouldn't have wanted to miss that show you put on after all those cocktails at the Shack. That tearful confession about poor Michael's death? Boy, that really was an unexpected bonus. Which brings us to why we're here in your office."

Kelly stuck a latex-covered hand into the back pocket of her leather pants and produced Serena's fountain pen. Held it up for her to see. "This pen is about to write what will become Serena Winters's most famous piece of work."

"Which is what?"

"Your suicide note."

A chill rippled through Serena's body. She barked a laugh that had no humor. "You're kidding, right? You've lost your mind. Why would I write a suicide note?"

"Because you're going to die, Serena. There's no other way for this to be resolved. Not now. It's gone too far. When the chief asked me to make some calls about a baby stolen from a bus station in Portland, I knew you knew too much. You were going to destroy me and my family by revealing the truth about Ruby Bryant, and I can't let that happen. Here, catch!"

She threw the pen suddenly at Serena, who failed to catch it. It fell to the floor, and she snatched it up, grateful to have it returned to her even if it was in these batshit circumstances.

Kelly gripped the gun with both hands now. She said, "You're the writer, so I'll let you decide the exact wording, but the gist of the note is going to be that you caused your partner's death, and you can't live with yourself any longer. The grief has driven you mad to the point of seeing and hearing things that don't exist in the place that was supposed to offer you an escape from your guilt."

Serena shook her head. "That's not going to happen. I'm not going to write the note and you're not going to kill me. I don't know what happened between Ruby Bryant and your parents, how that poor woman ended up dead, but I do know that you're not a killer."

Kelly smiled coldly. "Oh yeah? Tell that to Don Raskin."

# 35

## SERENA

## NOW

Kelly Dunne had killed Don Raskin.

Hank Macaulay was right. The former chief of police's drowning had been no accident. Serena had doubted the official verdict too, but she would never have guessed that Kelly Dunne was behind his death.

Now the fear cranked up several notches.

Breaking into the house, writing threatening notes and emails, moving stuff around—those acts were small-time compared to taking a life. Even with the gun and the latex gloves, Serena hadn't really believed Kelly would kill her. She'd thought—hoped—the woman wanted to give her the fright of her life, do enough to make sure Serena would get out of Dodge this time. Serena would readily agree to return to Manhattan and never breathe a word to another soul about what she'd discovered in Seaton Point.

But now Kelly had confessed to the murder of Don Raskin and everything had changed.

Serena needed to keep her talking, try to buy herself some time. Maybe Cynthia would realize something was wrong after she'd suddenly ended their phone call. Or Beaumont would pay a surprise visit. Or—the most likely to happen—the paunchy cop would return to carry out another check. But how to alert him to the fact that she was in danger? How would she get a signal to him?

"Why kill Raskin?" she asked.

"He figured out who I am, so he had to go," Kelly said simply. "I always knew it was a risk moving back to Seaton Point. That even with the dyed hair and colored contact lenses and losing the puppy fat, I'd be recognized. I thought Wanda Stockwell—or her daughter Hannah—would be most likely to make the connection between Kelly and Charlotte. But Wanda didn't even give me a second glance when she handed over the keys to this place. Same with Hannah the first time I dined at the Shrimp Shack. I was so nervous that she'd look at my face and the years would fall away, and she'd know who I was. She hadn't changed much at all since our schooldays but, in my case, the chubby, plain little girl with the strawberry-blonde hair and jeans and sneakers was long gone. I started to relax, decided to make my return to Seaton Point a permanent one, figured my secret was safe. I was wrong."

"You came face to face with Raskin and he recognized you?"

Kelly nodded. "I'd been working at the station for about a month, didn't know about Beaumont and Raskin's donut-and-coffee sessions. Then he walked through the front door with a Krispy Kreme six-pack and three big coffees. Apparently, Raskin had always included the previous office manager in his donut order before she'd followed him into retirement. He came up to the desk and handed over the takeout cup and started making small talk, asking how I was enjoying the job. Suddenly, he stopped talking and stared at me hard and all the color drained from his face. I thought he was going to have a heart attack where he stood. It's a shame he didn't, as it would have saved me a job.

The guy might have been pickled in eighty-proof JD half the time, but he'd seen what no one else had. He'd worked it out."

"But he didn't tell anyone?" Serena asked. "Didn't make any accusations?"

Kelly shook her head. "He'd been a cop for decades. Probably wanted to search for evidence, try to prove his theory before revealing the truth. I had to stop that from happening. I had planned on destroying the original police file and any evidence from my family's disappearance. The opening at the SPPD had been a godsend, meant I'd be aware of any unexpected developments in the Duprie case. I knew it was still gathering dust in the archives, no one giving it much thought after all these years. But after Raskin's visit, I discovered the file was gone. Guessed he'd taken it when he'd retired and was still trying to work the case on the downlow."

"So, you lured him to the marina, and you murdered him in cold blood," Serena said.

"I found his cell phone number in the files. Sent a text saying: *I'll tell you everything.* Told him to meet me down by the harbor at midnight. Figured he'd be good and loaded by then, an easy target. Especially with a Glock held to his head. I told him to hand over his phone and house keys, then get in the water. Raskin refused. Confessed he wasn't a strong swimmer even though he'd lived his whole life in a beach town, didn't even like sailing in boats. He was kind of missing the point that he wasn't supposed to be getting back out of the water. So, I pistol-whipped him, he hit the deck, and I pushed him in. When he bobbed back up to the surface, I held him under. Then I trashed the cell phone, used his house keys to retrieve the file, and trashed that too."

"You knew he'd fallen into the water once before. The incident had been hushed up, but you'd found out because you type up the police reports. You knew Beaumont would assume the drowning was another accident after a night spent drinking in O'Malley's;

that he would have no reason to suspect the death was suspicious. But was it necessary, Kelly? Killing an innocent man just because he'd worked out your real identity? Because you might have had to answer some difficult questions about the night you and your family vanished? It all seems a bit . . . extreme."

Kelly shook her head. "An ice-cold case that suddenly becomes hot again. Old leads being revisited. Loose threads being followed up. No. I couldn't risk the cops making the connection between my parents and Ruby Bryant. After all, you did." Kelly looked at Serena with narrowed eyes. "How did you do it?"

"I found your family's old photo albums in the basement. Realized there were no photographs of Dani Duprie while pregnant or you as a newborn. I found out about Amber Bryant's abduction and realized Dani had worked at the same bus station she'd disappeared from. Concluded that you were Ruby's missing baby."

The cold smile was back. "I've been trying for years to get into that damn basement and see what's down there. But your theory is wrong. Ruby Bryant wasn't my mother. She was just a crazy woman who thought she was and tried to abduct me at gunpoint. My parents had no choice but to stop her. My *parents*. Dani was, still is, and always will be, my mom."

"No," Serena said sadly. "I don't think she is. I think your real mom was dumped in an unmarked grave in the Mojave Desert thirty years ago."

Kelly looked pissed now. "My mom looked me straight in the eye and swore that Ruby Bryant wasn't my mother. I believe her. She's never lied to me. She never hid the fact that a woman died on our kitchen floor and my father buried the body. They did it to protect me and I'll do whatever it takes to protect my mother."

"I'm confused," Serena said. "A woman died in this house—was *murdered*—so why were you so desperate to come back to Seaton

Point and the Cliff House? Surely this place is filled with nothing but bad memories for you?"

Kelly shook her head impatiently. "You don't understand—those years in Seaton Point were the happiest I'd ever been. I'd never seen the ocean before we moved here. I loved the beach and the cool house and my pretty bedroom. I had friends and even got to go to Hannah Stockwell's birthday sleepover. Everything was good. Then that crazy woman turned up and ruined it all. Stole the life I should have had from me. Do you realize what it was like growing up afterwards? Being given a new name, never staying in one town or city long enough to get to know anyone? I knew if I returned to Seaton Point one day—returned to the Cliff House—I could be happy again. I could finally have the life that I deserved."

While Kelly talked, Serena strained to listen for the sounds of a car outside, tires on the gravel driveway. Maybe she wouldn't have to signal to the cop. Maybe he'd realize she wasn't okay if she didn't wave at the window. All the lights were on so he wouldn't think she'd gone to bed already. Kelly had shut the front door, but Serena didn't think she'd locked it.

As if reading her thoughts, Kelly said, "Officer Bush isn't scheduled to return until midnight. He'll be stuffing his face at McDonald's right about now. We have plenty of time despite your stalling tactics. Bush isn't going to save you. When I leave and he arrives, he'll notice the front door ajar, he'll enter the house to investigate, and he'll find your note and then your body." Kelly covered the short distance between them and pressed the barrel of the gun to Serena's forehead. "Now write the fucking note."

Serena opened the yellow Leuchtturm1917 notebook to a fresh page, uncapped the pen, and wrote the note. The handwriting was messy on account of her trembling hand, didn't look entirely like her usual script, but the cops would simply assume she'd been overcome with emotion at the time of writing. They'd be right.

Kelly nodded her approval. "Good. Leave the note on the desk and get up. Primary bedroom next."

Serena stood, feeling like her legs might give way beneath her. She moved unsteadily through to the bedroom, Kelly's breath hot on the back of her neck, in contrast to the cold metal that was once again shoved into the small of her back. Kelly marched her over to the balcony doors and threw them wide open.

"Outside," she said.

Serena realized now how Kelly planned on ending the story. Her body—battered and broken—on the rocks fifty feet below, just like Grady Hargreaves. Her suicide note would rule out any suggestion of foul play or an accident. When Serena didn't move, Kelly pushed her roughly with the gun and she stumbled out onto the balcony.

The sky was fully dark now. No stars or even a sliver of moon. The waves crashed loudly against the rocks. The wind whipped at Serena's hair. She shivered in the cold.

"Do it now," Kelly urged. "Jump!"

"No." Serena took a step back from the glass railing. "You're insane. I'm not going to jump."

"If you don't, I'll put a bullet in your head," Kelly said from behind her. She sounded like she was on the threshold between bedroom and balcony.

"You'll have to shoot me then. If nothing else, it'll ruin your suicide plan. People will ask questions."

"I'll figure it out," Kelly said. "I always do."

Then the sound of gunfire rang out.

# 36

## BEAUMONT

## ONE MONTH LATER

Jack Beaumont stood in front of the unmarked grave.

He tossed a single pink rose onto the fresh soil and wiped his tears with the back of his hand. He hadn't known her for long, but they'd hit it off straightaway and he'd liked her a lot. He would miss her despite the things that she'd done; even though she had caused a death and had blood on her hands.

It was too soon for a headstone to be erected. Beaumont wondered what name would be on the inscription.

Kelly Dunne?

Charlotte Duprie?

Amber Bryant?

Beaumont hadn't known Charlotte Duprie before her family vanished from the Cliff House thirty years ago. He'd been older, had never met her as a kid. Then, when he'd been appointed chief of police, there had been no real reason to do a deep dive into the family's disappearance. No reason to suspect that his new office manager was the girl who'd gone missing with her parents all those years ago. Not like Don Raskin, who'd worked the case, obsessed over it, lived and breathed it for decades, and still hadn't given up hope of finding answers even after his retirement.

Beaumont could be forgiven for not making the connection between Kelly Dunne and Charlotte Duprie. But he'd never forgive himself for his failure to investigate Raskin's death properly. To be duped so easily. A cop with all his years of experience and he'd been played like a fiddle. The red flags had been there—the abrasion on Raskin's face that he'd put down to a fall on the deck, the missing phone and keys that were never recovered—but Beaumont had rushed to a conclusion and had got it badly wrong.

He had let down his old boss.

And he had let down Serena Winters too.

Beaumont had been attracted to her that first day at the Shrimp Shack, then bewitched by her on their dinner date at the Italian restaurant. He'd felt like a teenager with a crush. Thought she'd felt the same way even though she was clearly still grieving the loss of her partner. Beaumont hadn't been in a relationship for a while, hadn't met anyone who set his pulse racing, who he could see himself sharing a life with, but he'd dared to hope that was about to change after meeting Serena Winters. Then Kelly had shared her concerns that the bestselling author was using him, that Serena had orchestrated the incidents at the Cliff House to garner media attention once her novel was published, that he was being played for a fool.

He'd believed Kelly, had trusted her, and had backed off where Serena was concerned. Big mistake. Beaumont hadn't been there for her when she'd needed him most—when she was at the mercy of a woman with a gun trying to force her to jump to her death.

It was George Evans who had come to the rescue.

He'd heard Kelly's car again, driving to the Cliff House, not long after a cruiser had passed by in the other direction heading back into town. Evans had grabbed his rifle and set off on foot to hike the mile from his property to Serena's rental. Hadn't wanted the sound of his old Jeep to betray his approach. He'd found the black Ford Escape concealed behind the copse of trees, then saw the rag taped over the lens of the trail camera. Figured there was a bad situation going down. Grady Hargreaves, the Dupries . . . George Evans didn't want Serena Winters's name to be added to the list. He'd tried the side door and found it locked. Moved around to the front of the house and found that door unlocked.

Evans had hesitated briefly, he told Beaumont later in his statement. What if the author was fine, sitting in her living room with a glass of wine, and would be furious and frightened by his intrusion? But what if she was in trouble? He'd thought again of the hidden car and the doctored trail camera and then stepped into the house. If he was wrong, he'd deal with the consequences. If the Cliff House claimed another victim, that would be a whole lot harder to live with.

The house did claim another victim—but it wasn't Serena Winters.

When Evans had witnessed what was unfolding on the balcony—the pink-haired woman holding a gun and telling Serena to jump or be shot—he didn't hesitate a second time. He put two rounds into Kelly Dunne's back. She didn't survive her wounds.

A search of the deceased's apartment and cell phone led the SPPD to track down Dani Duprie to St. Petersburg in Florida. She had remarried, following the death of Bill, and was living under the alias of Lori Benson née Dunne. She collapsed when informed of her daughter's death. Said she'd known a return to Seaton Point was a bad idea, but Kelly had been determined to call the Cliff House her home again. Her daughter wouldn't listen to reason.

Dani was in her seventies now. She'd spent half her life running and looking over her shoulder. She was tired. It was time to stop running. Dani Duprie confessed to being an accessory to the murder of Ruby Bryant, who had been strangled to death by Bill Duprie. Despite admitting to her role in Ruby's death, Dani denied kidnapping her baby from a bus station in Portland four decades ago.

Fast-tracked DNA results confirmed there was no genetic link between Kelly and Dani. Bill had been cremated so there was no way to know for sure if he'd been Kelly's biological father or not. Beaumont was still tangled up in a whole reel of red tape trying to convince the cops in Nevada to exhume Ruby Bryant's remains to obtain the DNA sample that wasn't taken at the time of her death. The Nevada cops had their confession, their cold case was closed as far as they were concerned, but everything pointed to Kelly being Ruby Bryant's child.

Serena had returned to Manhattan after giving a statement that included everything she'd discovered about the Dupries. Turned out she wasn't just great at writing mysteries; she was pretty good at solving them too.

A light rain was starting to fall, the sky turning an ominous gray. Beaumont turned away from Kelly Dunne's grave and walked briskly through the cemetery to his car. Smiled when he saw that he had a new text from Serena: *Deadline smashed! Now I need ALL the wine . . .* He switched from the message app to the web browser and searched for flights to New York.

A second date was long overdue.

# 37

## DANI

## JUNE 1984

"There's something I need to show you," Bill said. "Just . . . don't freak out, okay?"

"Okay," Dani said.

But she *was* freaking out.

"Come with me . . ."

She followed Bill into the hallway, and he gestured nervously. "This is what I wanted to show you."

A sleeping baby was snuggled inside a garishly patterned car seat sitting on the floor. She looked a lot like the kid whose photo had been all over the news last night. The soft, wispy red hair was lighter in real life, more strawberry-blonde, but maybe it had just appeared darker on the TV screen. Ruby Bryant's missing child.

No, not missing.

Stolen.

"Oh Bill," Dani said. "What have you done?"

He pushed his hair agitatedly off his face. "I did it for you. For us. It's what we always wanted. A child of our own."

"But this isn't our child. You can't steal someone else's baby! That little girl's mom is frantic. I was there, I saw how upset she was. How did this even happen?"

Bill's eyebrows knitted together in confusion behind his glasses. "I didn't steal anyone's baby." Then realization dawned. "Oh honey, no. This isn't that abducted kid from the bus station. That would be crazy!"

"Then who is she?" Dani demanded. "Where did this baby come from?" She lowered her voice to a sharp whisper, aware that the old crone with the black cat next door was likely listening to every word. "This is one hell of a coincidence, Bill."

"The baby on the TV was called Amber, right? Three months old? This little girl is older. By a month, I think."

"You're gonna have to give me more than that."

Bill dropped his eyes to his feet and Dani knew she wasn't going to like what he was about to say. She was right.

"It's Shannon Jacobson's daughter."

"Wait, *what*? The junkie? The woman you swore you'd never see again?" Dani's voice was getting louder again but she didn't care. "What the hell is her kid doing in our apartment? What the actual fuck, Bill?"

"Shannon is struggling big-time with her sobriety. Doesn't think she can stay clean much longer. Says she can't look after her daughter properly. So . . . I guess she's our daughter now."

The realization of what Bill had done hit Dani like a punch in the face.

"Oh no. Please tell me you didn't." She threw herself at him, pummeling his chest with her fists. "You got someone else pregnant. You lied to me. You fucking piece of shit. You've been screwing someone else this whole time. Someone who's not much older than a *kid*."

Dani had followed him once. Saw the woman—no, *girl*—he was meeting just before she climbed into his car. Rake-thin, DIY peroxide dye job, bad skin, dressed in ratty old sweats that were too big for her. Nineteen, maybe twenty. The bottle blonde should never have been a threat to Dani—but Bill had clearly been weak. The strain of trying for a baby all these years had taken a toll, had sucked all the enjoyment and spontaneity out of their sex life, and he'd gone elsewhere to satisfy his needs.

Bill gently grabbed her wrists. "Look at me, Dani," he said firmly. "You've got this all wrong. I'm not the father. How could you even think such a thing? Shannon was already pregnant when we met, when she showed up at that first NA meeting. She's not sure who the dad is. Figures her pimp or maybe one of her clients."

"You never told me she was pregnant," Dani said, relieved but still hurt.

Bill looked pained. "How could I? After everything we've been through. Especially the miscarriage . . . But you're right, I *did* lie to you. I didn't stop seeing Shannon. I'd meet her while you were at work, during my lunch breaks, after I'd clocked out for the evening. She told me she was planning on giving up her daughter. The baby would have gone into the care system unless there was a good adoption prospect, and that could take months, years even."

"So how did her baby wind up here?"

"Remember what you said earlier? About being so desperate for a child that you wished you'd taken the bus station baby? Well, I kind of offered to solve Shannon's problem—and ours too. I paid her five thousand dollars."

Dani stared at him in disbelief. "You *bought* a baby? For God's sake, Bill. Have you completely lost your mind?"

"I thought you'd be pleased," he mumbled.

"There's a stolen baby all over the news right now! What are people going to think?"

Just then, the little girl stirred in the car seat. Her face scrunched up and turned bright red. She opened her eyes—a beautiful hazel color—and glanced around. Then she unleashed an earsplitting wail.

Bill stared in horror. No idea what to do, how to deal with the fit of temper.

Dani acted quickly. She dropped to her knees and unclipped the harness and lifted the baby into her arms. Stood up and held her to her chest, rocked her gently, rubbed her back. The cries eventually abated, and the little girl snuggled into the nook of Dani's neck.

"There, there," she soothed, inhaling the unique baby scent. "I've got you. You're okay now."

Bill watched in awe, a goofy smile on his face. "You're a natural, Dani," he whispered.

Dani kissed the baby's head, the hair impossibly soft against her lips. She'd waited her whole adult life for this moment. She knew there was no way she could give up this precious little girl. Couldn't allow her to return to a junkie or an uncaring care system.

"What's her name?" she asked.

"Tiffany."

Dani shook her head. "No, that's all wrong." She thought for a moment. "Charlotte. We'll call her Charlotte."

"It's perfect." Bill grinned. "Does that mean . . . ?"

"Yes." Dani said. "But Shannon could change her mind at any time or keep coming back for more money, try to blackmail us. We need to leave this city and make sure she never finds us. Move someplace where no one knows us; where they don't know that Charlotte isn't ours. We keep to ourselves, so folks don't ask too many questions, and if we think Shannon has tracked us down, we move again. Deal?"

Bill nodded his agreement. "Charlotte's ours now," he said. "And we'll do whatever it takes to keep her safe."

# EPILOGUE

## ONE YEAR LATER

The bookstore was packed. Every ticket sold; every seat filled.

Outside the big picture window, sirens wailed, horns honked, folks yelled, and the lights of Manhattan glittered. Serena finally felt like New York was home again.

She spoke for two hours, which included a reading and a Q&A with an engaged audience. There were a lot of questions about the night she'd almost died, a gun pointed at her, the choice between a bullet or plunging off a cliff.

Her agent, Margot, stood off to the side, beaming. No wonder. *Dead of Night* was Serena's fastest-selling book. An instant *New York Times* bestseller, charting at number one after half a week of sales.

Following her return from Seaton Point, and discovering the truth about the Dupries, Serena had scrapped the witness protection plot and written about a desperate couple and a stolen baby instead. The novel was still a work of fiction, still a Layne Farraday mystery, only very loosely based on the Dupries and Ruby Bryant and Kelly Dunne, but the media frenzy that followed the events at the Cliff House had been a sales driver all the same.

The signing line lasted forty minutes. Halfway through, Margot leaned over and whispered in her ear, "Catch you at the restaurant soon, okay? I'm heading there now to meet Emma." Serena's editor, Emma Rivera, had reserved a table for the whole publishing team to enjoy a late dinner to celebrate. Lots of champagne on ice. Then Margot added, "We might need an extra space at the table. You have a visitor."

Serena looked up from the book she was signing and saw Jack Beaumont standing at the back of the room. Dark jeans, dark shirt, arms folded across his broad chest, still impossibly handsome. He noticed her looking and lifted his hand in a little wave. She grinned. The night had just gotten even better.

The last person in the line was a striking woman of about forty, with long red hair and pale skin and hazel eyes. She held out her hardcover for Serena's signature. "What an amazing talk," the fan enthused. "I'm so glad you survived all that craziness in California. You're my all-time favorite author and I'd have been absolutely devastated if there were no more Layne Farraday mysteries."

Serena laughed. "I'm kind of glad I survived too."

The woman wore a delicate gold chain around her neck, its yellow-colored pendant sparkling under the store's lights.

"What a beautiful necklace," Serena commented.

The redhead's hand went to her throat, and she flushed in delight at the compliment. "Thank you. It was a gift for my eighteenth birthday."

Serena turned to the title page and asked what dedication she should write.

"If you could dedicate it to Amber, that would be amazing."

The Montblanc fountain pen stilled over the page for a beat at the mention of the name, then Serena gave herself a mental shake and did the honors. Closed the book and handed it over. "I hope you enjoy it."

"I'm sure I will!"

Serena watched the redhead make her way to the exit, her copy of *Dead of Night* clutched to her chest. Then Jack approached and kissed Serena deeply and the woman was quickly forgotten.

"Surprise," he said.

"I thought you weren't going to make it?"

Beaumont had used up all his vacation days already on trips to New York over the last twelve months.

"I pulled some strings. Wouldn't miss it for the world." Then his expression turned serious. "Plus, I kind of have a work reason for being here."

"Oh?" Serena frowned.

"We finally got access to Ruby Bryant's DNA sample. Plot twist—Kelly wasn't her daughter after all."

The redhead entered her East Village apartment quietly, so as not to wake her two sons, who should both be in bed by now. She found her father in the kitchen, cradling a mug of coffee.

"They're fast asleep," he said.

She gave him a quick hug. "Thanks for babysitting, Dad."

"Always a pleasure. How was your book event?"

"Oh, it was fantastic! So interesting. I can't believe all the stuff that happened to the author in Seaton Point. Talk about truth being stranger than fiction!"

Amber placed the hardcover on the counter. The jacket showed a beautiful but ominous-looking house perched on a clifftop. She'd already read the opening chapter on the subway ride home and had been so engrossed in Layne Farraday's investigation she'd almost missed her stop. Her dad picked up the book and turned it over and read the text on the back.

"I might borrow this when you're done," he said. "Sounds intriguing."

"Really?" she asked—surprised, but pleased. Her dad wasn't much of a reader. "Sure thing! The Layne Farraday series is so good. You never know, Serena Winters may just convert you from your movies to books."

◆ ◆ ◆

River Henderson picked up his daughter's copy of *Dead of Night*. "I might borrow this when you're done," he said. "Sounds intriguing."

He'd read interviews given by the author where she'd stressed that the novel was a work of fiction and only loosely based on real events. The missing family at the center of *Dead of Night* were not the Dupries. But the background to the writing of the book was so insane that he reckoned some of it must have transferred to the pages.

He wondered if any of it had been inspired by Ruby.

Ruby Bryant had been the love of his life. He'd had a huge crush on her when they were kids that he'd thought he'd grown out of. Then, when he saw her step off the Greyhound coach, a feisty girl transformed into a beautiful young woman, all those old feelings rushed back tenfold. River had fallen hard and fast for Ruby that summer in Monroe back in '83. Really believed they'd had a future together.

Then she'd lied to him.

Failed to tell him he had a daughter.

His own flesh and blood.

He'd decided to surprise Ruby by saving up gas money from the auto repair shop and driving to Portland to visit her. He missed her like crazy, couldn't stop thinking about her, even had dreams about her. River thought he'd find her at her salon job but, when he asked after her at The Cutting Edge, a salty woman by the name of Darla looked him up and down and told him Ruby Bryant had been fired months ago.

"Big pregnant belly and no ring on her finger," she said pointedly. "Not a good look."

Then she gave him another hard stare and started up the hairdryer in her hand.

River was stunned. Ruby, pregnant? This Darla woman must have gotten it wrong. So, he staked out Ruby's apartment. Spotted her walking down the street toward her building, pushing a stroller, a huge pack of diapers in the storage basket. She looked exhausted. The kid appeared to be a couple of months old. Math had never been River's strong suit, but it didn't take a lot of brains to work it out—the baby in the stroller was his and he'd had no idea he was a dad. Why had Ruby kept it secret? Why lie to him? Was she ever going to tell him the truth?

River Henderson returned to Monroe with his heart shattered into tiny pieces. He reread every single letter Ruby had written him, then ripped them to shreds. While he'd been baring his soul with every word in his own letters, she'd been feeding him lie after lie. Eventually, he told his mom everything.

Tonya Henderson was furious.

"I always knew that girl was trouble," she said, her frosted pink lips pursed into a thin angry line. "Shoulda stuck with Pammy Gleeson."

"Not helpful, Mom," he replied, failing to hold back his tears.

Her face softened then and she took him in her arms, enveloping him in her familiar scent of menthol cigarettes and Chanel No.5 perfume. She wiped his tears and consoled him like she'd done when he was a kid and he'd fallen over and scraped his knees.

Then she said, "Listen to me, River. You have a beautiful baby girl and you've already missed out on so many precious

251

moments with her because Ruby Bryant kept the truth from you. That's not right. But if she didn't name you as the father on the birth certificate—and I'm betting she didn't—it's going to be tough as hell to stake any kind of claim. To prove you're the dad."

"So, what do I do?" River asked miserably.

His mom considered this for a long moment. "I have an idea. It's high-risk and we'd need to work out the details, but I think we can pull it off. It's time to take back what's rightfully yours, River Henderson."

# ACKNOWLEDGEMENTS

The main character in this book is a bestselling author who is undoubtedly more successful, and richer, than I'll ever be. But what Serena Winters and I do have in common is a shared love of a good mystery, packed full of twists. Writing *Dead of Night* was a lot of fun (and thankfully less dramatic than Serena's own experience as a novelist) and I hope you enjoyed reading it as much as I enjoyed working on it. If you're a previous reader of my books, thank you for your loyalty. If you're a new-to-me reader, I hope you'll stick around for more!

It's my name on the cover, but it takes lots of people to make a book happen.

A huge thank you to my fabulous editor, Victoria Haslam, for all your support and enthusiasm. I am lucky to have such a fantastic publisher, and working with the team at Thomas & Mercer is a truly joyful experience. A special shout-out to developmental editor Ian Pindar for your positive feedback and brilliant suggestions.

Thanks also to my agent, Phil Patterson. You took a chance on me and changed my life and for that I will always be grateful. And to everyone else at Marjacq—thank you for everything that you do for me.

To my friends—Lorraine and Darren Reis, Danny Stewart, Susi Holliday, and Steph Broadribb—thank you for the cheerleading, advice, and support. It's always appreciated. And to the bloggers, reviewers, and social media influencers who shout about my books—thank you!

As ever, the biggest thanks go to my family. Mum, Scott, Alison, Ben, Sam, and Cody—you believe in me when I don't always believe in myself. I love you more than words can say. And to my dad—I miss you every single day.

# ABOUT THE AUTHOR

*Author photograph © Bob McDevitt 2022*

Lisa Gray is an Amazon #1, *Washington Post*, and *Wall Street Journal* bestselling author and has sold over one million books. She has been longlisted for the McIlvanney Prize and is an ITW Thriller Awards finalist. Lisa previously worked as the chief Scottish soccer writer at the Press Association and the books columnist at the *Daily Record* Saturday Magazine. She is also the author of the bestselling Jessica Shaw series and standalone thrillers *The Dark Room*, *To Die For*, and *The Final Act*. Lisa lives in Glasgow and writes full-time. Learn more at www.lisagraywriter.com and connect with Lisa on social media @lisagraywriter.

# Follow the Author on Amazon

If you enjoyed this book, follow Lisa Gray on Amazon to be notified when the author releases a new book!
To do this, please follow these instructions:

## Desktop:

1) Search for the author's name on Amazon or in the Amazon App.
2) Click on the author's name to arrive on their Amazon page.
3) Click the "Follow" button.

## Mobile and Tablet:

1) Search for the author's name on Amazon or in the Amazon App.
2) Click on one of the author's books.
3) Click on the author's name to arrive on their Amazon page.
4) Click the "Follow" button.

## Kindle eReader and Kindle App:

If you enjoyed this book on a Kindle eReader or in the Kindle App, you will find the author "Follow" button after the last page.